THE

I threw back the covers of the bed and let the sunlight fall across my body. Charlotte's eyes were all over me, on my large round breasts, on the red-brown nipples already erect and waiting expectantly, on the dense bush of copper-toned hair at the mouth of my sex.

I walked across the room towards her, enjoying the look of adoration in her eyes.

'Kiss me,' I said breathlessly . . .

The Finishing School

Catherine Duval

Delta

First published in 1994
by HEADLINE BOOK PUBLISHING

A HEADLINE DELTA paperback

10 9 8 7 6 5 4 3

ISBN 0 7472 4400 6

Printed and bound in Great Britain by
Mackays of Chatham plc, Chatham, Kent

HEADLINE BOOK PUBLISHING
A division of Hodder Headline PLC
338 Euston Road
London NW1 3Bh

www.headline.co.uk
www.hodderheadline.co.uk

The Finishing School

1

My decision to leave England for Switzerland had been sudden and unexpected, as much a surprise to myself as to those around me. But given the circumstances there was nothing else for me to do. There had been no time for reflection, no time for second thoughts to cloud my mind. Looking back, now that it is all in the past, it was better that way. If I had hesitated, if I had allowed logic to intrude in the affairs of the heart, then I would never have gone and I would have missed out on the most idyllic year of my life.

In memory we mark things out clearly, setting up border posts around the events of our lives, secret frontiers where none existed in reality. For me it all began at the airport, at that very moment when I was going to leave my home for ever. I remember it so clearly, as if it were yesterday, exactly as it happened.

I was standing by the ticket desk, the hustle and bustle of the airport passing me by. I looked at the pretty young woman behind the ticket desk with cold anger in my eyes. The smile on her face was fixed, a pleasant enough mask for her to hide behind.

'I'm sorry, Miss Taylor,' she said evenly, 'but there

has been some sort of mix-up. I'm afraid there are no places left on the Zurich flight. The next available flight is late tomorrow afternoon. If you wish, I can book you on that.'

She wasn't sorry, despite what she said. I was seething, I had to get on that plane, simply had to. 'But don't you have computers?' I spluttered. 'How could this possibly happen? When I booked I was told there would be no problem.'

'I'm sorry, Miss Taylor,' she said again, her voice cool and calm, and all the more annoying for it. 'I have explained the situation, there are no places left, not even in Business Class. We can't upgrade your ticket.'

'Where am I going to sleep tonight? I've got nowhere to go,' I said, voicing the thought uppermost in my mind. It was true, I had nowhere to go. It was a horrible feeling, it suddenly hit me that I had burned my bridges and that there was no turning back.

The girl behind the counter allowed her real smile to shine through, her eyes seemed to light up. 'Perhaps I can help you,' she suggested. 'It's not company policy,' she whispered, leaning across the counter so that her perfume mingled with my own, 'but I can put you up at my place for the night.'

I relaxed a little. She had long dark hair that contrasted with the delicate pale tone of her skin. Her eyes were dark, intense, inviting. I couldn't tell how tall she was, but her crisp blue and white uniform revealed enough of her for me to guess that her breasts were small and round, not as large as my own but just as I liked them. She looked to be about twenty years old, just a few years younger than myself. It was a tempting offer, I suddenly wanted to have her under me, licking my nipples, her hands running over my body while I sucked the breath from her lips. The thought of it drained the anger from me completely and brought a smile to my face.

'Perhaps I can help,' a man said, stepping forward just as I was going to accept the girl's offer.

I turned round quickly, annoyed by this unwelcome intrusion, but the irritation was smoothed by the charming smile on the face of my would-be Samaritan. He was tall, with dark silver-streaked hair, clear blue eyes and the kind of smile that would melt any girl's heart.

'Yes, sir,' the girl behind the counter said, looking at me mournfully, realising that I had already slipped from her fingers.

'I'm booked on this flight with another colleague,' he explained calmly, 'but he's had to drop out at the last minute. Perhaps this young lady would like the seat?'

'Yes. Yes, please,' I said. I felt myself blushing, my cheeks tinged with pink for the first time since my school days. He really was the most sexy-looking man I had seen for a long time.

'Good,' he said forcefully. 'The seat is booked in the name of Carr, Michael Carr. Can you arrange for the transfer,' he asked the girl, reserving a special smile for me.

'I'll pay of course,' I said, suddenly remembering myself.

'It's Business Class,' the girl told me sourly, angrily

3

tapping away at her console.

'No, I won't hear of it,' the man said, handing over a gold-rimmed credit card.

'No, I must insist . . .' I began to say, though perhaps not very insistently.

'Your ticket, miss,' the girl said as it rattled off the computer printer. Her smile was gone, replaced by a cold mask of efficient politeness.

'Good. I'm glad that's settled,' the man said. 'I'll see you on board then.'

'No!' I said, a little too loudly. 'At least let me buy you a drink,' I suggested.

'I don't see why not,' he agreed.

We checked our luggage in and then made our way to the Business Lounge. We hardly spoke, exchanging pleasantries until we entered the lounge. Once inside I relaxed a little, glad to be away from the bustle of the check-in desk. We sat down in a quiet corner, the soft lighting heightening the soothing atmosphere.

'Really,' I said, 'I must insist that you let me pay for the ticket. I mean, we haven't even introduced ourselves properly.'

'Russell Cross,' he said, holding out a hand.

'Melissa Taylor, Mel to my friends.' We shook hands, his strong fingers wrapped around my own for a second too long. Our eyes met and lingered.

'Does this mean I can call you Mel?'

'Of course. I'm ever so grateful, I was in a real fix.'

'It's nothing. To be honest, if it's a choice between sitting next to a dull old lawyer or a pretty young lady

4

then I know which I'd rather have.'

I ordered a brandy and it soon started to have effect, at least I think it was the brandy. He had the most heavenly eyes, blue and tinged with a darkness that added depth and intelligence. I felt a warmth passing through me, making me feel relaxed and very sexy. The lounge was almost deserted and soon my mind was weighing up the possibilities.

I was wearing a long black skirt and when I let the split fall open I saw his eyes light up. My elegantly long thighs were framed by the silky blackness of the skirt, making them stand out even more. Every time I moved, every time I shifted as he made me laugh, the skirt fell open a little more.

'I do like these long skirts,' he said at one point, looking down at my thighs greedily.

'They can be so effective,' I agreed. My knees were together, legs angled so that he could see as much as possible.

'Beautifully effective,' he whispered, placing a hand on my knee.

I leaned forward and he took my chin in his hand and pulled me across. We kissed once, long and hard, and then his hand was smoothing along my thigh. My pussy was already wet but the feel of his fingers snaking towards it made me sigh with pleasure.

He took my hand and pressed it against his trousers. His prick was long and hard, throbbing as I rubbed it up and down.

'I wanted to make love to you the moment I laid eyes

on you,' he whispered, his breath hot against my neck.

'We can't do it here,' I mumbled, suddenly aware that the stewardess at the bar was staring at us open-mouthed.

Russell rubbed his fingers against the dampness of my knickers then pulled away reluctantly. His prick felt like heaven under my fingers but I forced myself to stop. I sat back and covered my thighs again, smoothing my skirt back to respectability. My eyes were fixed on the hardness pressing against the grey trousers of his smart Italian suit. If looks could kill then Russell had already done that to the stewardess, still staring down her nose at us.

I have always found airports to be sexy places. Perhaps it's the thought of all these strangers passing through, knowing they can let themselves go and never have to worry about it again. Perhaps it's the pretty young stewards and stewardesses, the pilots and navigators, the fashionable women passengers. Now, sitting opposite Russell, all the thoughts and fantasies came back to me. My nipples were hard, aching to be sucked by his strong masculine lips.

We fell silent, frustrated in our desires. I kept wishing the lounge would empty completely, but the reverse happened. As the departure time approached it began to fill up, loud groups of business men were assembling, their voices shattering the silent mood that had enveloped us.

'Look,' Russell said finally, a note of exasperation colouring his voice, 'I have to get some things. If you don't mind I'll see you on the plane.'

'That's a good idea,' I said, remembering that I hadn't

bought a present for Aunt Amelia. 'I need to buy some things too.'

Russell hesitated for a moment then smiled. We walked out haughtily, breezing past the stewardess, who still wore the faintly disapproving look that had stopped us earlier. The duty-free shops were crawling with Japanese tourists, buying up everything with a Union Jack on it as if it were going out of fashion.

'I'm seeing an important client,' Russell explained on the way. 'The man's had one heart attack but he's addicted to Havana cigars and fine cognac. I know I shouldn't, but I also know he'll be disappointed if I turn up empty-handed.'

We split up near the concourse of duty-free shops. I watched him disappear into a shop stacked full of alcohol and tobacco and then I made a bee-line for the perfumery. Thanks to Russell's extreme generosity, I had saved the price of an air ticket to Zurich and I wasn't going to let the money go to waste! In the space of fifteen minutes I had a lovely little collection of expensive bottles, each satisfyingly opulent, clicking together in a chintzy little bag.

Next stop was the hosier. Bare legs were fine with a long skirt, I knew that the sight of a bare leg carelessly exposed in the loose folds of material would set any man's heart racing. But sometimes nothing can beat the feel of sheer silk stockings. I soon found exactly what I was looking for, a lacy black suspender set with matching seamed stockings. The assistant, a pretty young thing with glossy red lips, watched as I put them on, carefully removing my damp knickers before putting my skirt back on.

'Have fun,' she said softly as I paid.

'I will,' I promised.

I went looking for Russell straight away. I was feeling hot and sexy again, my wet pussy naked under the loose skirt, the black suspenders contrasting strongly with my white skin.

'Finished?' Russell said, coming up behind me.

'Yes, and so are you by the looks of it,' I said, pointing to the plastic bags full of bottles and square boxes of cigars.

His reply was drowned out by the metallic words of the airport announcer. We both groaned, our flight had been delayed for one hour. He swore under his breath, his face suddenly set in an expression of pure anger.

'I couldn't face that snooty stewardess in the Business Lounge,' I complained.

'We won't have to,' Russell said, smiling darkly.

'What do you mean?' I asked, intrigued by the look on his face and the fiery expression in his eyes. I had never seen that look before but it was enough to get me going, my heart was pounding and I could feel the excitement growing in the pit of my belly.

He took me by the hand and led me back past the shops, past the hosier where the young girl waved to me, a knowing look on her lovely face. We came to a door marked 'Staff Only' and he pushed through. I tried to protest but my heart wasn't in it.

The door led to a long thin corridor with other doors

leading off it. It was dark, a single shuddering strip light casting the only illumination. Russell tried the first door but it was locked, the second gave way at once. We bundled into a tight little room, laughing like children in a game of hide and seek. It was a tiny little office, with barely enough room for a desk and chair. Russell flicked on the light switch and we looked around carefully, certain that the coast was clear but wanting to avoid any unwelcome surprises.

'It's empty,' I said, turning to face Russell. He grabbed me at once and pulled me close to him. We were joined at the mouth, our lips sealed tight. His hands were all over me, cupping my breasts, running down my back, holding my mouth. I was on fire, my sex aching with desire. This time I wasn't going to be denied, I was going to have that hard prick deep inside me. We separated suddenly and I was on my knees, helping him undress, rubbing my face against the smooth darkness of his cock. He was naked in a moment, his body taut and well defined, the hairs on his chest patterned with silver. I took his lovely long cock and cradled it in my hands.

'Take it in your mouth,' he said, his breathing deep but uneven.

I needed no prompting, the tip of his prick was already being smothered in my lips. I wanted to explore every inch of his lovely organ. A wet tear was weeping into my mouth and I swallowed the drop of fluid with delight. He was leaning back against a wall, his hands running wildly through my long auburn hair.

His prick was like heaven in my mouth, I was driving

up and down the entire length, kissing, sucking, nipping playfully. He was whispering wordlessly, pressing his cock harder and harder into my mouth, filling it with his delicate masculine fragrance.

'Now I want it in my pussy,' I said, slipping a hand under my skirt to feel the heat in my sex. My pussy lips were already puffy, oozing with little drops of sex cream. He pulled me up and our mouths were joined once more. He pulled my blouse open and cupped my breasts, flicking his thumbs back and forth over the ripened nipples. It was ecstasy, waves of pleasure passed through me, making me sigh softly.

He bent down and hungrily took a nipple into his mouth. His hot tongue passed over the sensitive points of flesh, making me shudder with pleasure. I cried out, unable to hold myself back. I climaxed with his mouth clamped over my breast and my soaking fingers pressed inside my cunt.

His hand moved down, parting my skirt for the first time. He froze. 'You've got stockings on,' he exclaimed.

I stepped back and unclipped my skirt, letting it fall in an untidy bundle around my feet. 'Well,' I asked, posing provocatively, 'what do you think?'

'Lovely,' he said, shaking his head in quiet disbelief as his eyes feasted on the sight of me in pure black stockings, lacy black suspenders and the pinkness of my sex peeking through the mat of reddish-brown hair.

He stepped forward and took me in his strong powerful arms, his hard prick pressed against my thigh. He was like a man possessed, his hands and mouth were all over me. The train of sensations was too much, the pleasure too great. I climaxed again, arching my back and uttering strangled cries. He lifted me in his arms, held me up and eased his beautiful rod deep into my well of desire. He was so hard, so strong, he filled my sex completely, making me cry out with the pleasure of penetration.

I held onto him, moving myself with his rhythm as he fucked me urgently. The pleasure was intense for him too, his eyes were closed, his face wearing an expression of unbridled ecstasy. He went in and out with a hard, almost brutal rhythm that had me crying out for more. He put me down and made me face the wall, I arched my back and offered him my behind. He held me by the waist and then pressed his prick, dripping with my juices, into my sex from the rear. I was twisting and stretching like a cat on heat, wanting him to go hard and deep until I could take no more.

We climaxed together. He cried out once, his body went rigid, moulded onto mine. I felt his prick pumping inside me, his thick cream washing into my own pussy juices. He rolled off me and I turned to him and we kissed on the lips.

'What are you doing here?' A voice demanded, cold and harsh, shattering the blissful silence that held us together.

It was a security guard, a short but aggressive-looking man in a blue uniform and peaked cap. His face was cold and impassive, his eyes hidden by the cap so that we couldn't read his expression.

'We can explain,' Russell said quietly, reaching down to pick up our clothes.

'No you can't,' the guard said. 'I'll have to call the airport police.'

'You don't need to do that,' Russell insisted. 'You can see what we were doing here.'

'You could be spies or smugglers or anything,' the guard said, stepping closer. I realised that he was looking at me, at my open blouse and naked sex.

'Like this?' Russell laughed. 'Spies are supposed to blend in with the background, not have sex where they might get caught.'

'Please,' I said, not bothering to cover myself, 'we are very sorry.'

'Sorry isn't good enough. I've got to call the police. If your story checks out, you should be out of the cells by tomorrow.'

'Tomorrow?' Russell said loudly, brushing a hand through his hair. 'But I've got meetings to go to. Isn't there any way we can sort this out quickly?'

Russell was genuinely upset and I could understand why. A night in the cells was the last thing either of us wanted. I smiled, hoping that the guard wasn't as icy as he tried to appear. 'Yes,' I said, purring seductively, 'isn't there some other way?'

'What sort of other way?' the guard asked, suggesting that imagination was not one of his strong suits.

'Why don't you loosen up?' I suggested, stepping up close to him, letting my perfume dance around him.

He tipped his peaked cap back and I saw that his eyes

were all over me, he could hardly believe what was going on. I put my hand on his chest and smiled, my lips parted, pursed lightly waiting for him to react.

'Okay, just this once . . .' he said, letting the words trail to nothing as I reached up and kissed him on the lips. His arms were around me, pressing me tighter, pressing me up against the hardness between his thighs. Our lips were together for a moment and then he let go of me. I watched as he undid his trousers and freed his raging cock.

I absolutely love the feel of a prick in my mouth and I just couldn't help myself. I was on my hands and knees sucking his lovely stiff tool in an instant. I cupped his balls and squeezed gently as I sucked, making him moan loudly with pleasure.

Russell watched for a moment, I could see him from the corner of my eye, watching us intently. He had started to get dressed but changed his mind. I changed position, taking the guard's member deep in my throat, and saw that Russell's prick was swollen, rising majestically as I mouthed the other man's cock.

'I want her mouth,' the guard managed to say. His words were broken as I flicked my tongue under his bulbous glans. I understood, arching my back and offering my rear to Russell.

I couldn't quite see what Russell was doing but I soon felt his hot breath on the underside of my thighs. His tongue was flicking between my pussy lips, making me squirm with excitement. I opened myself, parting my pussy lips with my fingers. His tongue found the target and he was licking my cherry bud with delirious abandon. I could feel my juices running into his mouth as I shook with pleasure.

The guard was pumping hard, fucking me in the mouth with long slow strokes. The taste of his prick was on my tongue and in my throat, I could feel it throbbing, aching for release.

Russell flicked his tongue over my rear hole and then he took me by the waist and speared me with his prick. It seemed to take forever to slide into the wet folds of my sex. And then I was being fucked deliciously in the sex and in the mouth, enjoying the feel of two lovely hard pricks going in and out of me. They were moving faster and faster, pumping waves of ecstatic pleasure through me.

My body was convulsed, I climaxed again and again, driven by the feel of the two cocks and by the feel of the guard's fingers on my nipples. The guard climaxed too, flooding my mouth with thick wads of juicy come. I swallowed it with relish, sucking every last drop of his essence. A moment later, Russell filled my sex with come for the second time, his prick throbbing and twitching as it emptied into me.

We dressed hurriedly, the guard now eager to get rid of us in case he got into trouble.

Russell and I were the last people to board the plane and I wonder, even now as I look back, whether any of the other passengers ever guessed the reason for our flushed faces as we hurried to our seats.

* * *

14

After all that, it was hardly a surprise that I was half asleep minutes after take-off. My body was still tingling and the gentle rocking of the plane soon lulled me into sleep. Did I dream? I can't remember, but I do know that as I drifted between sleep and wakefulness I couldn't help but be apprehensive about my future. I was leaving everything behind and heading for a new life certain only in its uncertainty.

It had been nearly ten years since I had seen my Aunt Amelia and my memories of her were the happy memories of childhood. I could remember her warm smile and sparkling eyes, the golden curls of her hair, the subtle scent of her perfume. I could remember the sound of her laughter, a soft bubbling of sound that was infectious. Those hazy memories, part fantasy and part reality, were all I had. Yet when I needed her she had answered at once and her offer to go out and work with her had been impossible to refuse.

In England, the very idea of a finishing school sounded so archaic that it was easy to see why Amelia had moved to Switzerland. There she looked after the daughters of the rich and famous, of the nobility and aristocracy of Europe. The young women, between the ages of sixteen and twenty, studied for the baccalaureate, prepared for life at court, learnt half a dozen languages and all the things a rich young woman would possibly need to know. What did I know about life at court? The thought had plagued me for days after Aunt Amelia's offer, but then I really had no other choices open to me.

Perhaps I did dream. I remember turning over at one

point and finding that I had been carefully wrapped in a thick blanket. It was dark, the only sound the muted roar of the jet engines. The lights were out and all the passengers around us were asleep. If I had been dreaming then I knew what it had to be. My nipples were pressing hard against my white blouse and my pussy was moist. I think I had been rubbing my thighs together, I could feel the wet heat trickling down the crack between my buttocks.

Russell leaned across and kissed me on the cheek.

'What's that for?' I asked, surprised by this unexpectedly affectionate gesture.

'For being so good when the guard caught us,' he whispered, looking into my eyes as if reading my soul.

'It got us out of a jam, didn't it?' I said, turning round to snuggle up to him. In the heavy darkness, it was possible to imagine staying with Russell, sticking with him as he did his business in Zurich and then flying on with him to wherever he was going next.

'Actually,' he said, sounding almost apologetic, 'there is one other fix you could help me get out of.'

'What's that?' I asked eagerly. After everything that he had done for me there was nothing I would not have done for him.

'I'm afraid I was a bit too enthusiastic with the duty free,' he said, sounding very tense all of a sudden. 'I've got too many Havana cigars with me. I'm not sure that the customs will be as understanding as the guard.'

'Cigars?' I laughed. 'I thought you meant a real fix. I'll take the cigars. Is that all there is? I mean, do you want me to take some of the drink through customs too?'

'No, I exercised more caution there. I'm only over the limit on the cigars. You don't mind then?'

'Don't be silly. I'll take them,' I said, failing to understand why he was so uptight about something so trivial.

Russell seemed to relax. 'I just wish that guard hadn't been so possessive,' he smiled, lifting his arm so that I could cuddle up to him.

'What do you mean,' I murmured, closing my eyes and resting on his chest.

'I wanted your luscious lips . . .' he whispered, kissing me chastely on the head.

'We've still got time,' I said, reaching under the blanket. Sure enough his prick was already hard, flexing powerfully when I stroked it over his trousers.

He shifted quickly, undoing his trousers deftly and letting out his hard pole. I stroked it gently then brought my fingers to my mouth. I could smell myself, still scenting his prick. I licked my fingers clean and watched the excitement in his eyes. He kissed me then, reigniting the fire in my pussy.

'I want you to come inside my mouth,' I told him, 'I want to taste your cream, to swallow it all.'

I ducked under the blanket, my hand on his prick already. I took him in the mouth and, for a second, all I could taste was the sweetness of my sex on him but then I sucked that away and tasted his prick once more. I played with him, licking his cock with long slow strokes, closing my lips over the glans, sucking at it to draw out the golden drops of fluid. I gave him the works, deep-throating him, taking his full length in my mouth and throat. I could feel him trying to hold back, wanting to prolong the pleasure for as long as possible. But I was greedy, I wanted him to fill my mouth with his delicious spunk.

My pussy was aching and my fingers were soon working inside of me, sliding in and out of my wetness. My clit was throbbing, pulsing like mad. It felt so good that I could hardly control myself. Even though I had Russell's gorgeous prick in my mouth I was still making enough noise to wake half the plane up.

Russell moved round, his arm snaking down my back and between my bottom cheeks. I lifted myself higher, taking another half inch of prick into my mouth, so that he could tickle me between my arse cheeks. He was gasping for breath, moving his pelvis up and down, pumping his lovely organ into my mouth. His fingers were playing between my pussy lips, slipping into me with the same rhythm as my own fingers.

He came suddenly, jerking his cock deep into the back of my throat. I didn't swallow straight away, I wanted to savour his come in my mouth. I felt his prick pumping, throbbing, spurting warm sticky come onto my tongue. I waited, let it linger on my tongue, then swallowed just as I climaxed on his fingers.

I sat up, my face flushed, and found his fingers waiting for me. They were coated with thick honey, perfumed by my pussy. I licked them clean, sucking every last dewdrop into my mouth. I felt so happy, my mouth was filled with the taste of us and my body tingled blissfully all over.

I was still licking his fingers when the pilot announced that we were coming in to land. In a second, the lights were on and the stewardesses were checking our safety belts. Russell reached under this seat and pulled out a box of cigars from one of his bags. I glanced at it cursorily, then stuffed it into my bag without a thought, nestling it beside my collection of expensive fragrances.

Even the bumpy landing couldn't jolt my good mood. Russell had dispelled all my doubts and hesitations. I was sure that everything was going to turn out for the best.

In my mind that was the beginning, a beautiful, fantastic start to my Swiss adventures. Even today, when I can look back comfortably with hindsight, I can think of no better beginning to my story.

2

After the delay to the flight, a delay in the baggage collection was inevitable. Russell asked one of the porters the reason but he just shrugged and suggested it was because the baggage was being given an extra security check. The further delay did nothing to dampen my excitement. I couldn't wait to start my new life, the optimism I felt was almost tangible. It was as if I had cast one life aside and was now intent that this one would start off on the right footing.

When the bags started to emerge there was a ripple of applause from our exasperated fellow passengers. I could see that Russell was growing ever more tense. His ready smile had gone and I noticed that he kept looking apprehensively at the security guards. My bags were among the first to arrive and Russell helped me load them onto a trolley.

'I think I'm going to be last in the queue,' he explained sullenly, brushing a hand through his hair.

'It's OK, I don't mind waiting,' I said brightly, hoping that his bad mood would wear off quickly. I hoped that I would see him again afterwards.

'No, I've got a feeling I'm in for a long wait,' he said

and his tone suggested that he wasn't just saying that for effect.

'What shall I do then?'

He looked suspiciously at the security guards milling about, their faces chiselled into icy expressions of disdain. 'Why don't we meet outside? There should be a driver out there to meet me. If you get bored waiting you can let him have the cigars. I think that's best, don't you?'

'If you say so,' I agreed reluctantly.

'If you leave an address with him we can meet up again in a few days,' he added, recognising the disappointment I felt.

'In a few days then,' I mumbled. He was brushing me off, the signs were clear enough.

'Yes, a few days. And don't forget the cigars, give them to my driver.'

We didn't even kiss, I turned and left not bothering to look back. I didn't feel bad about it, we'd had some fun and I had been hoping that we could carry on where we had left off but I wasn't going to let anything spoil my good mood. As I passed the rows of customs men I couldn't help wondering why Russell had been making such a big deal about a few smelly cigars. But even that tiny shadow of doubt was swept away when I finally passed into the arrivals lobby.

There was a crush of people waiting, a row of chauffeurs in uniform holding up little placards, and a crush of families and friends waiting to greet their loved ones. It was bewildering to be confronted by so many different faces. I scanned the cards looking for my name, expecting

that Aunt Amelia had sent a driver from the school to
pick me up.

'Hello, Melissa, don't you recognise your aunt?'

I turned suddenly and there she was, my darling Aunt
Amelia. She looked stunning, with long blonde hair and
golden ringlets cascading over her shoulders. Her eyes
were blue and grey and every shade in between, her lips
full and red and parted in a loving smile. She looked as if
she had just stepped from a Parisian style magazine.

'Auntie . . .' I said and kissed her on the cheek the way
I had done as a child. In memory she had been a vivid
image, in real life she was just as perfect. She wore a
smart red jacket with matching skirt and high-heeled
shoes, the skirt short enough to reveal long lithe thighs.

'Don't look so surprised, Melissa,' she laughed,
making me laugh too. It seemed that she hadn't changed
at all, she looked as beautiful as she had done ten years
earlier, her face unmarked by the passing years.

'I thought you'd send somebody down to pick me up,'
I explained.

'My favourite niece? Never,' she smiled. 'Let Rudi
take your cases,' she said, waving over a tall young man
who nodded to me then took my bags.

'I'm so glad you invited me. I don't know what I was
going to do . . .'

'We've got plenty of time for that,' she said softly,
stopping me in mid-flow. 'We've got a long ride back to
the school, why don't we just relax for now?'

'Yes, that's a good idea,' I agreed. Suddenly I
remembered the cigars. 'I've just got a favour to do for

23

someone,' I explained, diving back into the rapidly thinning crowd.

I searched all over for Russell but there was no sign of him, nor any sign of his driver. I asked several of the chauffeurs but they shook their heads when I mentioned his name. I could see Auntie growing impatient so I gave up. Besides, I reasoned, what was a box of cigars worth?

'What was all that about?' she asked as we emerged into the cold night air.

'I promised a friend I'd bring in some cigars for him, he'd bought too many.'

A sleek black car pulled up, the lights blazing in the darkness, and Rudi jumped out to open the door for us. I slipped into the inviting warmth of the back seat and Amelia followed.

'A good friend?' she asked as Rudi steered the car away from the airport.

'Sort of,' I smiled evasively. Would Aunt Amelia approve of my goings on? In many ways she was still a perfect stranger and I had no idea what sort of person she was.

'How long have you known him?'

'Not long,' I mumbled, staring out into the darkness as the car sped along.

Amelia laughed. 'He must have been very handsome then,' she smiled, her eyebrows raised just a fraction.

'Very,' I agreed, laughing with her.

'And these cigars, where are they?'

I was still holding my bag of goodies, unwilling to entrust my expensive bottles to Rudi. I handed her the

box of Havanas, still sealed with wax, the box stamped
with all sorts of recommendations.

Amelia looked over the box quickly then handed it
back to me. 'I'm sure your friend won't mind losing
them. I would guess they are a small price to pay . . .' She
let her words trail into a smile, making me blush a little.

We drove through beautiful mountain passes,
illuminated by the silver light of a full moon. The scenery
was breathtaking, the mountains capped with sharp cones
of ice and snow, the lower slopes thickly wooded. We
crossed mountain streams that rushed and roared in the
night. It was enough to make one forget everything. The
car rocked very gently and the comforting warmth soon
had me dozing off. I remember looking down at Aunt
Amelia's long thighs and smiling dreamily.

I was woken by the feel of a woman's lips on my own. I
floated dreamily, enjoying the flood of pleasurable
sensation before sitting up suddenly.

'Where am I?' I asked, looking wide-eyed around the
room in an effort to regain my bearings.

'In your new room,' Aunt Amelia explained, sitting
on the edge of the bed. I recognised her perfume, could
still feel it in my lungs, my lips still tingling from the
taste of her.

The room was large and airy, the sun streaming in
through two large windows, the wooden shutters open to
the day. The view was delightful, the Alps framed by a
brilliant blue sky, waters cascading down a mountain
stream that edged its way through a thick Alpine forest.

'How did I get here?' I asked, racking my brains to remember what had happened. All I could remember was thinking about Amelia's long legs as I drifted to sleep.

'I had Rudi bring you up,' she explained, as if it were the most normal thing in the world to be carried up to bed by a strapping young Swiss.

I peeked under the thick quilt that kept me a cosy and warm. 'Who undressed me?' I whispered.

'Rudi, of course,' Amelia laughed again. 'With a little help from your aunt.'

I just lay back in bed and closed my eyes, revelling in the feeling of my naked body wrapped in the thick warmth of the quilt. Already my mind was full of images of Rudi staring greedily at my breasts, at my nipples puckering from the cold, at my freshly fucked pussy.

'Well,' Amelia said, nudging me gently out of my day dream, 'are you fit and ready to make a go of things.'

'Of course, auntie,' I said, sitting up eagerly. I lifted the coverlet, hiding the fullness of my breasts, knowing that Aunt Amelia had already seen me naked but still clinging to a modicum of modesty.

'That's got to go,' she said, shaking her head. 'I can't have you going around calling me auntie all the time. That's so . . . so . . .'

'Old-fashioned?' I suggested tentatively.

'So petit-bourgeois,' she corrected. 'My girls all call me Miss Amelia. You can address me as Amelia. Except,' she leaned across the bed and touched her lips on mine, 'that you can call me auntie during our most intimate moments.'

26

I shivered with a desire so hot that I felt my sex moisten instantly. Aunt Amelia, I realised, was in love with the pleasures of Eros as I was. I breathed deeply, hoping that she would pull the coverlet away and make love to me there and then.

'Yes, auntie,' I whispered, the breath escaping like a sigh from my parted lips.

'Now, up you get,' she said brightly, ignoring the disappointment on my face.

'Setting me to work already,' I complained, not really wanting to emerge from the warmth of my bed. I would much rather Amelia slipped under the coverlet to join me.

'There's lots to do,' she said. She went over to the window, her golden hair shining in the bright sunlight, a golden halo that lit up her eyes and face. 'I've assigned a young lady to look after you. She'll clean your room, look after your wardrobe, run errands for you and so on. Miss Charlotte Dupuy will be your little helper for the next few weeks or so, unless she's not to your liking. She's a lovely girl, the daughter of an ambassador, possibly the prettiest girl in the school and with a sweet nature to match.'

I was puzzled, why set the daughter of an ambassador to be my maid? My surprise must have been clear to see because Amelia turned to me and said, 'It's very important that we do this. These young women come from some of the most privileged backgrounds in the world. All their lives they have been surrounded with nannies and fawning servants. Now they have to learn what it is to do things for themselves and for others. It's important for building character, it adds something to their make-up, something that would be sorely lacking otherwise.'

'I see,' I commented. 'That makes perfect sense. But don't some of the parents, not to say the girls, object?'

Amelia laughed. 'The girls that object the loudest are the ones that end up enjoying it the most. But don't worry, Charlotte was very happy to be selected, I'm certain that she'll be devoted to you.'

There was a knock on the door, so soft I wasn't sure that I had heard correctly.

'Enter,' Amelia said.

The door opened and an elegant young woman came in. She was dressed in a short blue skirt and white cotton top, the sheer simplicity of her clothes matching the angelic purity of her looks. She had beautiful dark skin, a soft chocolate colour that was flawless, and her lips were full and red, pursed naturally in an alluring pout that was all the more seductive because it was not posed. Her breasts were pear-shaped and firm, her nipples dark round disks beneath the white cotton. Her large round eyes looked at me for a second then she turned away, blushing lightly.

'*Bonjour, Madame Amelia, bonjour, Madame Melissa*,' she whispered, her soft voice alive with the music of the French Caribbean.

'Good morning, Charlotte,' Amelia replied, putting her arm on my shoulder and squeezing gently. She had seen how taken I was with Charlotte. My eyes were feasting on her and my belly was alive with butterflies of desire.

'Good morning,' I added. At that point I distinctly remember wondering why I hadn't come to Aunt Amelia's years earlier. In the bright sunny morning I felt that I had entered paradise.

'Be so good as to prepare a bath for Miss Melissa,' Amelia instructed.

'*Oui, madame,*' Charlotte said, curtsying. She turned and walked across to the adjoining bathroom, watched by two pairs of eager eyes.

'She's lovely,' I said to Amelia after Charlotte had disappeared into the bathroom. I could hear the rushing sound of water in the bath and with it a soft lullaby of a French song.

'Yes, she's an utterly delightful girl. I like to change my helpers every few weeks but it was a terribly hard decision to turn her over to you,' Amelia said wistfully. 'But I want your stay here to be a happy one and I'm certain that none could make you happier than Charlotte. When you've been bathed, I'd like you to join me for breakfast and then we can talk properly about what you're going to be doing.'

Amelia stood to leave. At that moment I was filled with intense gratitude. I took her hand and kissed her fingers. 'Thank you,' I said and I meant it more than anything else in the world.

'See you later,' Amelia said, kissing my fingers in return before leaving.

'The bath is ready, madame,' Charlotte said, standing in the doorway of the bathroom.

I threw back the covers of the bed and let the sunlight

fall across my body. As expected, Charlotte's oval eyes were all over me, on my large round breasts, on the red-brown nipples already erect and waiting expectantly, on the dense bush of copper-toned hair at the mouth of my sex. I walked across the room, enjoying the look of adoration in her eyes.

I took her hand and stepped into the bath, ostensibly holding onto her for support, though all I wanted was the feel of her fingers in my own. She really was the most adorable creature, her long frizzy hair was tied in a loose bundle and that ribbon was an in invitation to pull it away, to let her hair fall freely over her delicate brown shoulders.

The water was just right and scented with aromatic oils that filled my nostrils with enticing fragrance. Charlotte began to pour water down my back and down my chest, letting the warmth radiate all over my body. The drops of water caught the light as they rippled down my smooth flawless skin, dripping down between my breasts and cascading like raindrops from my nipples. Her fingers were all over my skin, the contrast of her dark skin on mine adding an extra touch of sensuality. I pressed my chest forward and she took my breasts in her hands, cupping them lovingly, playing gently with the erect nipples until I was aching for her mouth.

'Kiss me,' I said breathlessly and her lips were on mine. She was soft, her mouth warm and inviting. She kissed my mouth and throat, my shoulders and caressed the glistening wet valley between my breasts with her lips. I cried out when she took a nipple in her mouth, crushing it in her lips, while her hand kneaded my other breast. I was on fire, the heat from my nipples sending spasms of pleasure right through to my cunny.

I took her hand and put it between my legs, spreading my thighs so that she could feel me there. A finger rubbed enticingly up and down, opening my pussy lips very gently, letting the warm water mingle with my own pent-up heat. She pressed a finger into me tentatively and explored.

Charlotte was proving to be the most exciting female lover I had ever had. She seemed to know how to excite me beyond measure. I orgasmed when a second finger entered my pussy, gently grazing my engorged clitty. Then I was on my hands and knees, arching my back while the water poured from my wet body.

'Suck me, suck me . . .' I pleaded urgently.

She put her hands on my backside and parted my bottom cheeks. I turned and saw the look of eager anticipation on her face and in her eyes. She kissed me very gently, almost reverently between the thighs. Her tongue sought my rear hole and she licked me there before opening my pussy lips. Her tongue floated into me, lapping up the hot cream that was pouring from my red-hot sex. I could feel her sucking it, drawing out every last bead of honey as if it were the most precious thing in the world.

I climaxed again and again under her tongue, crying out louder and louder every time until I was sure the entire Alps were reverberating with my cries of orgasmic pleasure.

* * *

Breakfast was a little later than anticipated, but my aunt was discreetly silent about the reason, preferring to comment on how radiant I looked after my bath.

'Right, I'm raring to go,' I said, having finished the last of my rich and buttery croissants. We were breakfasting in a large, well-lit dining room, the windows framing postcard views of the distant mountains.

'Good, that's what I like to hear,' Amelia replied. 'First I ought to tell you a little about our school, then we can talk about your new duties.'

'Couldn't I start by explaining why I'm here?' I suggested, wanting to get my confession off my chest. I had worked out everything I was going to say and wanted to get it over with.

'At dinner,' Amelia decided. 'We have all the time in the world for that. First some background.'

'As you wish,' I agreed.

Amelia signalled to Rudi and he stepped forward with more piping-hot coffee, refilling our cups before retreating smartly to the corner.

'There are many,' Amelia began, 'who view the very concept of a finishing school as anachronistic, a throwback to an era long past. It conjures up images of rich young women dying of boredom, learning the finer arts of needle-point and flower-arranging. Nothing could be further from the truth.'

'Thank God,' I muttered.

'Today a young woman needs to have her wits about her. She needs to be versed in economics, politics and commerce – and also in the erotic arts. Where better to learn than in the company of other young women, tutored by elegant ladies with experience in all of these matters? Here, our young ladies learn how to play the stock market and how to give and receive sensual pleasure. It is this that has made our school the most exclusive institution of its kind in Europe. We are perhaps unique in that we only accept the best, we turn away many more than we accept. The more exclusive we become, the more parents beg us to take their daughters. What you will see here is the elite, Europe's finest young women. And every single one of them is intelligent, mature, sensual and attractive.'

'If Charlotte is anything to go by then I'd say you've done a fine job,' I remarked.

'Charlotte is one of only fifty young women. To take more would be to dilute our standards, and that is unthinkable. Our location has much to do with our success. We are relatively isolated and so free to act as we wish, yet we are close enough to Zurich to attend to our other needs. The building is a converted hotel and in the grounds there are a number of chalets where the girls stay. It is all self-contained and, as I said, it leaves us with the freedom to do things our own special way.'

'That's all very well,' I interrupted, 'but I can't help wondering where I fit into all this. What do I know about commerce and the stock market?'

Amelia laughed. 'I trust you have other experiences to draw upon, darling. As I'm sure that Charlotte has already discovered.'

I laughed too. 'I dare say there are some things I can

teach your young ladies,' I agreed.

'Good. Not all our girls are as mature as Charlotte. Many of the new arrivals are still innocent with regard to the pleasures of the flesh. And of course we have high standards to maintain. The parents would be furious if their innocent daughters were suddenly thrust into the hands of eager young men with more strength than finesse. For initiation into the carnal pleasures, there is nothing to beat the hands of another woman.'

'So, Amelia,' I said, 'is this the task you have chosen for me? To look after the new girls . . .'

'Precisely, my dear,' she agreed. 'I wanted someone that I could trust, someone in whom I could have the utmost confidence.'

'But, auntie,' I said, 'how could you be certain that I was interested in . . . in making love with other women?'

She sounded quite hurt. 'Don't you remember what happened the last time we met?'

'Of course I do,' I assured her.

It had been my sixteenth birthday and up until then it had been the most exciting day of my life. Later that evening my aunt made sure that it also became the most memorable night of my life. It was something I was certain never to forget, my first step on that rocky path to carnal pleasure.

Amelia smiled and continued, 'We also ensure that we have a supply of virile young men on hand. I prefer to keep a tight rein on this, unwelcome accidents would do our reputation the utmost harm. But if a girl is good, if she progresses well, then she is allowed a special prize.'

I grinned. A special prize, it was an almost poetic description of the feel of a stiff cock inside a wet pussy. 'But how do you make sure the prize is special?' I asked, my mind filled with visions of the girls sneaking out into the forest with these virile young men. It was what I, or any other healthy young woman, would do in that situation.

'Because my boys are devoted to me and I love them all. They would do nothing to endanger that affection,' she snapped her fingers and Rudi was at her feet in an instant.

She had said 'boys', plural not singular. 'How many are there?' I wanted to know.

'Eight, every one of them a prince. And I have six female staff in addition to the cooks and the house staff. So you see, with these numbers every girl is almost guaranteed individual attention.'

'You've thought of everything,' I complemented her. It had taken her a long time but it was obvious that she had achieved everything that she had set out to do.

'Rudi, go and fetch Erich please,' Amelia waved her hand and Rudi was gone.

'When do I start?' I asked eagerly.

'I think you can spend a few days just getting to know people. There is no real rush and our pace is always very leisurely here. We have a new girl, Isabella Bertolusci, starting on Monday, by then you should be settled in enough to begin your duties officially.'

'"Duties", it sounds more like a pleasure to me,' I exclaimed happily.

'Here, every duty is a pleasure,' Amelia replied, her voice tinged with laughter.

The door opened and Rudi entered, followed by another man. Erich was as tall and as powerfully built as Rudi, but whereas the latter was blonde and blue-eyed Erich had tanned skin and fierce dark eyes. They stood together in front of Amelia, ignoring me completely. They were looking at her hungrily, a look of supplication in their eyes. They were wearing tight jogging pants which were moulded to their strong thighs and, as I moved closer, I saw that they were both hard, their long pricks etched in black between their thighs.

'Breakfast,' Amelia explained, not even turning to look at me. She was stroking Rudi's thick prick with the tip of her long painted fingernails. 'I want to look at you both,' she told them.

Obediently the men untied the cord and opened their jogging pants to reveal hard pricks. Amelia stroked them, taking one in each hand and touching them lovingly with the tips of her fingers.

'I can see why you look so young and fit,' I commented, realising that Amelia had eight young men to chose from, night and day.

'Which would you like?' Amelia turned to ask me, smiling sweet innocence as she stroked the two gorgeous pricks.

'Erich,' I snapped back, preferring his dark good looks to Rudi, and jumping at the chance to have his hardness buried in my mouth.

Amelia nodded and Erich came over to me, his muscles

rippling as he walked. I kissed the glans of his rod, drawing circles with the tip of my tongue. He tasted divine and soon I was going down on him, my mouth filled with his bulging hardness. Both he and Rudi were generously endowed and there was no doubt in my mind that all of Aunt Amelia's young men were similarly blessed. I was going to learn to love each and every one of them, that was for certain. The possibilities opening up before me were endless – both male and female, stiff pricks and juicy pussies, it made my head swim just to think of it.

As I sucked Erich, I kept my eyes on Amelia and Rudi. She was feasting on his prick as if there were no tomorrow. Her eyes were closed, her face a picture of contented bliss as she moved up and down, drawing her mouth tightly over his glistening hardness. His prick was smeared with red lipstick, making it seem all the more attractive. I watched Amelia sucking Rudi and did the same, savouring the taste and feel of prick between my lips.

Erich fucked my mouth expertly, pressing deeper without causing me any discomfort. He was so big that he filled my mouth completely. His balls were cool to my touch and I knew that when he climaxed he was going to fill me with juice. He put a hand on my head and supported me, allowing me to rise and fall swiftly, letting my lips envelop the tip before swooping down to the thick hard base.

His silence, which was a little unnerving, soon gave way to a hiss and a sigh as he drew breath and let it escape from his lips. I swirled my tongue all over his cock, making him moan and cry involuntarily. The flexing of his prick told me he was nearly there and the raging heat between my thighs meant the same for me. My head was glued to him but I managed to look over to Amelia, who was sucking Rudi's glans between her glossy red lips while wanking his shaft with her elegantly painted fingers.

Rudi exhaled loudly and I watched as his cream was squirted into Amelia's waiting tongue. I was fascinated as he pumped out wave after wave of spunk. Amelia squeezing his prick and balls until he had shed it all. She held it on her tongue for a moment then swallowed, closing her eyes to savour the taste. It was the most erotic thing I had ever seen.

Erich cried out and I drew back, eager to copy my aunt, who had now been revealed to me as an expert fellatrice. It felt so good to take his come on my tongue and on my lips as it jetted in bursts from his swollen prick. I held it there, careful not to waste a drop until he was done. My eyes were closed but I felt Erich withdrawing, stepping back silently.

I opened my eyes and Amelia was beside me. We kissed and shared Erich's juice. Her breath was hot, scented with the taste of Rudi. We kissed and kissed until we had swallowed Erich's load, the taste sweetened by another woman's lips. I climaxed at the same time, my cries swallowed by my adoring aunt.

Amelia drew away and dabbed at a trickle of come on her lip with a white serviette. The two men had already gone and we were alone in the dining room. I could feel that my panties were soaked and decided to remove them. It seemed silly to wear panties when I knew I was going to be wet and on heat most of the day.

'Welcome to my finishing school,' Amelia said, smiling.

'I'm ever so grateful,' I said earnestly, taking my aunt's hand and squeezing her fingers tightly.

'There's no need to be, I'm sure that you are going to be a real asset in our work. I'm certain of it.'

I wasn't so sure but I vowed to do my best to live up to her high expectations.

3

After breakfast, I joined my aunt for a grand tour of the school. My early morning experiences with the delectable Charlotte and Erich had been so powerful and erotic that my mind was filled with a dozen sexy images. I imagined that the finishing school was one long orgy, a feast of bodies making love day and night under the icy vista of the wintry Alps. What I wasn't prepared for was the industrious atmosphere and the evidence of hard work all around me.

I saw small groups of young women huddled around computer terminals deep in discussion about their work, enjoying every moment of the intellectual challenges before them. Another group were involved in a heated discussion about politics, their earnest faces pink with excitement. I met some of the other staff, attractive young women full of good humour and keenly aware of the responsibilities they each had.

'I see what you mean about high standards,' I commented at one point, realising that all my expectations had been totally surpassed. Aunt Amelia's finishing school took its tasks very seriously, there was certainly much more to it than pure sex and sensuality.

'I'll take that as a compliment,' Amelia said.

The chalets were very spacious and kitted out in fine Alpine fashion, combining comfort and style in equal measure. Every girl had her own room and each chalet also housed one or more members of staff. From what I saw, relations between the girls and the staff were excellent, it was very friendly with just the right hint of formality that could be called on if required. The girls were very respectful towards Amelia, some of them curtsying and all of them addressing her as 'Miss Amelia'.

We lunched in the main house, with Rudi at our beck and call. I tried to tell Amelia of my reasons for leaving England but again she stopped me, putting her finger to my lips and suggesting I leave it till the evening.

After lunch I went up to my room, eager for a chance to settle in. I thought about all that I had seen and felt the same excitement that I had on the flight over, the same certain feeling that everything was going to turn out for the best. The sky was clear and the sun bounced from the mountain peaks, the air was pure and fresh and I felt on top of the world and nothing was going to change that.

Charlotte woke me just as the sun disappeared into the thick green forest on the horizon. I had fallen asleep, the crisp air and change of scene making me feel more relaxed than I had been for ages. The feel of her lips on my fingers was enough to have my whole body tingling. I sat up and brushed the dark waves of hair from her face. She had such lovely eyes, so dark and sensual, yet also a little sad. I kissed her on the mouth, parting her lips with my tongue so that I could suck the breath from her.

I passed my hand under her skirt and smoothed my palm up and down her long silky thighs, it was a feeling I had always loved, the sensation of touching another woman's thighs. I stroked her for a full minute, just holding her there so that I could enjoy the feel of her smooth skin under my fingers.

'Are you wet?' I asked her, whispering into her ear, knowing that my hot breath was as likely to excite her as the touch of my fingers near her pussy.

'*Oui, madame*, very wet and very hot,' she closed her eyes, her lips were quivering.

I kissed her again and pressed my fingers into her panties. She fell into my arms, her hands clutching my shoulder as if she were about to fall into space. I held her and pressed my fingers harder, pressing the thin filmy panties deeper and deeper into her sex, making her wetter and wetter. I liked the feel of her in my arms, the feel of her cunny juices soaking through to my fingers.

She moaned, her breath like a whisper, but she held back, afraid to let the cry of pleasure escape her. I played with her, toying with the panties pressed between the puffy lips of her sex. I leant over and kissed her neck, biting gently the pure soft skin of her throat. Her perfume was sweet and erotic, it filled me with a desire so hot that I wanted to sit over her tongue and ride her mouth to orgasm.

'Please ... please ...' she whispered, hiding her face from me, her eyes closed so that I couldn't see the waves of desire pulsing through her. I pressed harder, forcing the thin strip of material deep into her backside and hard into her sex. I was driving her hard, making her twist and turn on my eager fingers. At last she cried out, throwing her thighs apart so that I was deep inside her. She held onto me and then collapsed, falling away like a leaf from a tree.

I pulled her up, sat her on the bed and kissed her all over, on the mouth and throat and eyes and nose. I had made her climax so ecstatically that her soft brown skin was tinged with a delicate shade of pink.

'You're beautiful,' I told her, kissing her again, unable to keep my lips from her.

'No, madame, it is you that is beautiful,' she replied, fixing me with her oval eyes. 'You even make love beautifully,' she said, sounding a little embarrassed.

I parted my thighs and lifted my skirt a fraction. She understood at once and fell to her knees before me. She looked up at me with a sweet smile of pleasure and gratitude. I closed my eyes and let her move forward. She kissed me softly at the top of the thighs and then she kissed me at the mouth of my aching sex. Her tongue lapped at my juices, pulling the dewdrops of love juice into the hungry warmth of her mouth. I put out a hand, stopping her from going deeper. The feeling was so sensual, so delicious, her tongue lapping at me as if were the finest meal she could have. I lay back and enjoyed it, the waves of bliss making me wetter and wetter while she tried to suck it all away.

Her tongue never really entered me, her lips merely brushed against my sex, her tongue dabbing into the heat

44

of my desire, but it was enough. I climaxed, filled with an overwhelming pleasure that made me cry out with joy. At that moment, with darling Charlotte on her knees kissing my swollen clit, I knew that I had found my true vocation in life.

Charlotte dressed me, passing her fingers all over my body while she did so, obviously enjoying every second of being with me. I had selected a simple black dress, very short and low cut to reveal my breasts, but not overdone for my first evening meal at the finishing school. Amelia and I were to be joined by Suzanne, Amelia's deputy, who had been in Zurich on business for the last few days. I wanted to make a good impression on her, aware that my sudden arrival might not have been to her liking.

Charlotte kissed me on the lips before I went down, her eyes filled with longing once more. 'Will you be here this evening?' I asked, pointing to the empty bed.

'If you wish, madame,' she said excitedly, her eyes lighting up at the prospect.

'Yes, I wish,' I said patting her gently on her soft round bottom.

Amelia and Suzanne were waiting for me in the dining room. Suzanne was dressed in a smart mustard outfit, short tight skirt, jacket and matching high heels. She could have stepped from the pages of a magazine in her stylish Italian clothes and the way she walked had all the grace and elegance of the top fashion model she had once been.

'Welcome to our finishing school,' she said, kissing

me lightly on the cheek. Her voice was low and sultry, accentless in a mid-European kind of way.

'Thank you, I'm very happy to be here,' I said, noting that she had used the proprietorial 'our' when talking about the finishing school.

We took our places around the table, the lights were dimmed and the flickering orange glow of the candlelight cast a soft sheen over everything. Suzanne seemed to be in her early thirties, a few years younger than my aunt and a little older than myself. Her dark hair was in contrast to steely blue eyes that glittered in the candlelight.

'As you know,' Amelia said, interrupting my searching gaze into Suzanne's eyes, a gaze that was returned with equal vigour. 'Swiss cuisine is renowned the world over . . .'

'. . . which is why we brought over a chef from Paris!' Suzanne added, her face breaking into a laugh that softened her, made her seem more approachable.

'You mean I'm not going to learn to love the fondue?' I asked, relieved that I had been spared that particular misery.

One of the girls poured the wine and I couldn't help noticing the way Suzanne stroked the girl's thigh as she did so. The food was served by one of the young men. The atmosphere was so cosy and sensual that it made me feel dreamy, what better life could there be than this?

We spoke casually – small talk about the school and Switzerland, about the girls and their parents, but all the time I was waiting for my chance to tell all. I knew that Amelia didn't mind about what had happened, that she would have taken me in no matter what, but I simply had to tell. I had left England under a cloud and it still hurt.

'Now then, Melissa,' Amelia finally said, as the meal drew to a close, 'you've been dying to tell me what's behind your departure from England. I'm sure that nothing you did was wrong. I have never doubted that for one moment.'

'It's true,' Suzanne added, taking my hand in hers and looking at me directly, 'we are just glad to have you here.'

'Thank you, both of you,' I said, touched by their obvious sincerity, 'but I've not had a chance to put my side of the story yet, not to anyone. I want you to know, because I know you'll not judge me harshly for what happened.'

'As you wish, darling,' Amelia agreed softly.

I sat back, took a sip of the fine cognac that had been served and began my story.

'After graduation and training, I was lucky enough to be offered a position at a very old and prestigious sixth-form college near the City of London. I remember entering the building for the first time and being awed by the atmosphere, sanctified and steeped in history. What I failed to appreciate was that this once-great institution was suffocating under the weight of tradition. The place was dying, its past only serving to hide the moribund state of its present. It was a place that failed to excite any enthusiasm either in its students or its teachers.

'But I wasn't to know any of this until much later. At the time I was flattered to be asked along for an interview, still convinced that I was entering the gates of one of our most distinguished educational establishments. I was ushered into a small room and told to wait for a moment. I remembered looking around at the portraits staring down at me from the walls, stony faces sneering at me for daring to imagine that I could have a place amongst them. A few moments later, the Principal appeared, and I have to say I was very pleasantly surprised. I had imagined him to be an elderly disciplinarian, a grizzled old man who had lost the ability to smile. Instead he was youthful, his dark brown hair was streaked with grey at the temples and he beamed me a welcoming smile that relaxed me at once.

"'I wasn't sure you were going to turn up," he said brightly, as if he were surprised to see me there.

"'Why ever not?" I asked, puzzled by his question.

'He then proceeded to tell me the truth about the state of his college. The number of students was falling, the building cost a fortune to maintain and the few benefactors to the school were becoming increasingly restless about the steady decline. He had been brought in to try to reverse the trend and recapture past glories. It was proving to be a difficult job, far more difficult than it should have been.

'He had been eager to recruit a new team who were young and enthusiastic, eager to shake things up a bit and to displace the old dinosaurs who still stalked the lecture halls. He had not counted on so much opposition, however, particularly not from the board of governors.

"'But why not?" I asked. "Surely they would prefer to

save the college rather than see it disappear completely?"

'He laughed. "I'm afraid that's not the case," he explained. "They would prefer we slide into failure rather than risk changing one iota. For them, tradition is everything and anything that is new must be wrong on principle."

"'Why me?" I asked suddenly, wondering why he had sought me out. I hadn't applied for a job, the offer had come out of the blue.

"'Your tutor from university singled you out for special praise, he told me that you are certain to make a name for yourself."

'I was flattered by this but he was right, I did make a name for myself, though not in the way he had meant.

'The interview itself was awful. I sat before a team of five individuals: Alan, the Principal, two other members of staff and two members of the board of governors. It was like the third degree, I was questioned on everything and anything. It soon became clear that there was indeed a battle going on, between Alan and the staff on one side and the members of the board on the other, one of whom seemed particularly to resent my presence. Her name was Lady Agatha Morton and she had the same sneer on her face as I had seen on the haughty portraits hanging from the walls.

'I did the best I could but I have to admit that I was worn down by the relentless hostility of her remarks. I left for home fully expecting never to have to return. So it was with some surprise that I received a letter a few days later offering me a permanent post.

'It was a challenge and I accepted right away. I called Alan on the phone and he told me that in the end he had to threaten resignation before the governors would give their approval. I was touched, he hardly knew me but had been willing to lay his job on the line for me. I promised him that I would do everything in my power to show Lady Morton that she was wrong.

'He then gave me one word of warning. Lady Morton, in a final desperate attempt to dissuade them, had suggested that a pretty young woman like myself would have a bad effect on the young male students. She had painted a picture of me as some kind of seductress that would have the young men in a state of permanent heat. She had told them that the academic achievements of the college would suffer drastically and that it was not a good idea to employ young women in a school full of young men.

'"She would prefer ugly old harridans like herself," I said, laughing.

'"True enough," Alan agreed, "but be careful, she's going to be watching you like a hawk. Any mistakes you make will be reported directly to the full board of governors."

'It was warning I took very seriously, I had no doubt that she had her spies among the older members of staff who resented my presence as much as she did. I worked very hard, harder than I've ever worked before. And the results were there for all to see. I can't take all the credit, I was part of the nucleus of a young team that Alan was putting into place. We added life and sparkle to the old college, the corridors even echoed to the sound of laughter for the first time in decades. The number of students started to increase, the academic results remained as consistently high as they had always been and money even started to trickle in for the restoration of the more decrepit parts of the buildings.

'This success was not to the liking of Lady Morton, she seemed to turn red in the face every time she saw me. And I admit I played up to this, once my position was secure I took great delight in calling her "Aggie", finding the resulting explosion of rage the funniest thing around. She was also starting to lose allies on the board of governors. Some of her older male colleagues were really rather sweet and they liked nothing better than to see me turn up at a board meeting in a tight skirt, the shorter the better.

'Once I was settled in, I suggested to Alan that we really needed a few more female members of staff. Young women added something special to the atmosphere. He agreed at once and we set about looking for a suitable candidate.

'It wasn't all work and no play. Alan was absolutely dishy, good-looking, intelligent and very sexy. But he was always so busy and, in his way, so serious that I avoided him for a while. I think he took Lady Morton's warning personally, as if she were hinting that he would go weak at the knees when I was close to him.

'Another of the young team was the head of the sports department, Chris. He had challenged me to a game of tennis one evening, a few weeks after I had started. We laughed and joked as we played, he was good and he had me running back and forth just to keep up. At the end of it, I collapsed on the floor exhausted, bathed in sweat. My white cotton top was sticking to me, my nipples pressing darkly against the simple white material. My tennis skirt was short enough and I had seen the way his eyes had been eating up my long thighs and tight round bottom.

"'What now?" I asked, lying sprawled out on the floor, too tired to move.

"'Shower time." he announced, as if the strenuous game had been nothing for him.

"'I'm too tired," I complained.

"'Then I'll have to do it for you," he said brightly. Before I had time to protest he had scooped me up off the floor in his arms and carried me back to the staff changing-room. I was still protesting when he pushed me, fully clothed, under the showers. The steaming jets of water soaked me through to the skin, my top becoming a wet transparent skin, my nipples puckering provocatively. It felt so refreshing, so erotic, that all my exhaustion was washed away by that lovely rush of water.

'He stripped off quickly and joined me, the water making his naked body glisten seductively. My pussy was soaking, my hot sex cream mingling with the rivulets of water coursing down over me. It was an odd feeling, to be soaked to the skin like that and yet to feel so incredibly sexy. His hands were all over me, pinching my erect nipples, sliding under my wet skirt and over my pants.

"'I suppose you're too tired to make love," he laughed

wickedly, rubbing his fingers up and down my panties.

"'I'm never too tired for that," I purred, pressing myself against him, eager to feel his long hard prick sliding into me. I knelt down in front of him, letting the water spill over my face. His cock was in front of me, big and wet and terribly inviting. I kissed it, a soft peck of the lips on the tip so that he murmured appreciatively.

'He moved around me, wrapping one leg over my shoulder so that I was pinned under him, his prick pressed urgently against my face. I opened wide and took him in, eager to feel it deep in my mouth. My hands were all over him, over his thick strong thighs, caressing his tight masculine backside, cradling his balls. It made him wild, soon he was bucking his hips, fucking me urgently in the mouth. I sucked him lovingly, wanting to swallow every drop of fluid that seeped from his glans. I licked from the very tip down to the wiry hair at the base, exploring every inch of his gorgeous tool.

'He pulled me up and round, making me face the wall and thrust my backside out. My skirt was stuck to me so he pulled it off roughly, ripping my panties at the same time. His passion was growing by the second, I could feel him gasping for breath as I pressed my backside up against his abdomen.

'The feel of his stiffness pressing into me was electric. I cried out, my moans lost in the swirl of water from the shower head. The water poured over my glistening body, down over my breasts and down my thighs. I was aching for him and when he speared me with his prick I pressed back, wanting to take him to the hilt. He moved in and out urgently, his knuckles white against my skin. His mouth was on my shoulder, on my throat, kissing and biting, his hands pulling deliciously at my burning nipples still covered by my wet shirt.

'I couldn't help myself, I swivelled and turned, opening myself to the thrill of his cock. I climaxed in a white frenzy of pleasure but still he fucked me, harder and harder. The feel of his fingers on my nipples added to the pleasure. He was so strong, so virile, making me come again and again until he gripped my waist and pulled me down on to his prick. The thick come burst inside me, a hot lava filling me with delightful waves of blissful energy.

'We fell apart, sat down on the tiled floor of the shower and let the warm water wash over us, just as our passion had done. His prick still looked delicious and I licked off the mixture of his come and my pussy cream that was smeared over its length.

'From that day on, we fucked whenever we could. He couldn't get enough of me and, in turn, I loved the feel of his hardness buried deep inside me. But we were always careful, we gave no hint of what we were doing to anyone. We both knew that Aggie would have been down on us like a ton of bricks.

'The fact that we were so discreet indirectly contributed to our undoing. Alan hadn't an inkling of my liaison with Chris and so, when he finally decided to notice me as a woman, I was taken by surprise. We had been working late in his office, sifting through potential female candidates for the college. We were looking at a CV of one candidate, a student-lecturer called Samantha. She had included a photograph of herself winning a medal for swimming, she had a pert backside, long thighs and pair of small round breasts.

'"Lovely legs," I commented matter-of-factly, passing the picture to Alan.

'He studied it for a second then looked up shyly. "Yes," he agreed, "but not as good as yours."

'I was surprised, I was certain that he had never really looked at me in that way. Our eyes met and something just clicked. I had fancied him from the start but Lady Morton's strictures had kept my feelings at bay. He leaned across the desk and kissed me on the lips, very shyly, as if he expected me to slap his face or something.

'"What would Aggie say?" I asked, returning his kiss softly.

'"Forget the old dragon," he whispered, reaching out and pulling me close to him. We kissed again and I knew that I was wet between the thighs already. I stood up and went round to him, sitting myself on the edge of the desk. We kissed again, more passionately and this time he slid his hand up my thigh, the flat of his hand smooth against the glassy feel of my thighs.

'"You're wet," he said and that made me wetter. I stood up and began to strip off slowly, letting him feast his eyes on my full breasts, on my black stockings and suspenders, on the bulge of my pussy.

'He took my breasts in his hands and kissed each one reverently, flicking his tongue over each nipple in turn. Soon he was naked too and I stroked his prick with my fingers, making him sigh with pleasure.

'"Over the desk," I told him, bending down and laying myself flat against the coolness of the oak desk. My legs were parted, straight, my bottom sticking up and out. He knelt down and began to kiss me, behind the knee and then working up slowly. His hands parted my arse cheeks and I heard him whispering to himself, "Beautiful, beautiful". His mouth was down under my sex, his fingers pulling my pussy lips apart. The feel of his breath on the soft folds of my sex made me ache with want. I straightened my legs still more, impatient now. He flicked his tongue into my wetness and I cried out softly.

'He sucked me expertly, his tongue caressing my clitty so that I had to beg him to stop. I wanted his prick, wanted his hardness to fill my aching sex. But he knew how to drive me wild. He used his mouth and fingers on me until I had climaxed, bucking deliriously under his snaking tongue and expert fingers. And then he stood up and pressed his raging cock into my cunt. My naked breasts were flat against the oak top of the desk, my nipples grazing the polished surface sending dizzying spasms of sensation to my prick-filled pussy. I couldn't contain myself, my cries were echoing down the hallowed corridors of academe as he pumped his thick juicy spunk into me.

'Things became very difficult after that. I didn't want to end it with Chris and nor did I want to stop making love with Alan. It was surprising how many people told me I looked radiant at the time, and they had no idea why I looked so good. Believe me, I was getting the best tonic a girl could possibly have: lots of hard fucking!

'Samantha, the new student lecturer, started soon after that. Aggie, the redoubtable Lady Morton, was absolutely livid but I had canvassed enough of the old boys on the board to get Samantha taken on immediately. She had nowhere to stay at first so I suggested she live with me for a bit. She was such a friendly, open girl that I soon told her all about my problem with Alan and Chris.

'"If you're going to have a problem it might as well be that one," she said cheerfully. We had been up watching a film and had drunk a bit of wine so that we were both feeling very relaxed.

'"I've never thought of it like that," I replied. Suddenly she leaned across and kissed me full on the lips. I looked at her strangely, not at all certain how to react.

'"Don't you like girls?" she asked, crestfallen.

'I didn't know what to say. My life had been so focused on men that I didn't really give women a thought. But my most vivid memory had been of my sixteenth birthday . . .

'She kissed me again and this time I returned her caress. Her gown fell open and I touched her breasts tentatively, wanting to feel her nipples under my fingers. We made love all night, in every conceivable position. I sucked her pussy, her breasts, even the tight little button between her bottom cheeks. And she did the same to me, making me scream with ecstasy when I climaxed.

'Now my life was even more complicated. I had two men and a woman to contend with and I loved all three. It was okay with the two men because they didn't know about the others, but Samantha had a possessive streak and it made her very jealous. I would return to the flat bright and cheerful from Alan or Chris and find her waiting for me, ready to tear off my clothes and make love to me, angry that I had been with someone else.

'It couldn't go on, of course. But when the end came it took me completely by surprise. I had received a message from Alan early in the day to see him in his office when college was finished. I knew what that meant and I spent all day looking forward to our love-making. I adored being spread across the desk with him screwing me urgently. It felt so wicked to be doing it in his office, under the disapproving portraits of his illustrious predecessors.

'When I was finally free I rushed to his office. As was usual on these occasions his secretary had already gone home. I knocked on the door and went straight in. He had poured me a drink and soon we were in each other's arms, undressing, kissing, caressing.

'"Over the desk again," I begged him, eager to have him mount me from behind.

'I was naked in an instant and he was licking my pussy as if it were the food of the Gods. Then delirious moans and sighs of pleasure were suddenly interrupted by a knock at the door. I tried to get up quickly but Alan pressed me down with his hands. The door opened and Chris walked in, completely to my surprise!

'I tried to make some excuse but I was robbed of breath by Alan's silky tongue, his lips sucking in the hard bud of my clitty. I needn't have bothered, however, for

Chris was naked in an instant and standing before me, holding his raging hardness in his hand. I fell on it hungrily, sucking it into my mouth. It felt like heaven. Alan had pressed his prick into the smooth wet pocket between my thighs and Chris was fucking me in the mouth.

'I guessed then that Samantha had betrayed my trust. She had told them what was going on but her plan had failed. Rather than fight over me, they had decided to give me twice the pleasure. My cries of delight were muffled by the huge prick in my mouth, pressing deep into the back of my throat. And Alan was still fucking me beautifully, his long slow strokes building up into an indescribable crescendo of pleasure.

'Chris was unable to contain himself, I could tell that the excitement of our three-way session was making him lose control. He was whispering wordlessly and I felt his cock throbbing and pulsing. I sucked harder, my fingers stroking his prick at the same time. The warm spurts of come filled my mouth and I swallowed every drop, wanting his essence inside me.

'A moment later Alan cried out loudly and then fell over my body, covering me while his prick pumped into my pussy. I felt ecstatic, my body floating on a cloud of unbridled pleasure.

'"So this is what goes on!" a stentorian voice declared, pulling me down to earth with a wicked bump. I was still dazed but I looked up to see Lady Morton before me, her face fit to explode. She stepped aside and I saw that several members of the board were with her, staring at our three naked bodies with a mixture of fascination and disgust.

'There was nothing we could do, Samantha had betrayed us all. If it got out, the scandal would be too much for the college to bear and Lady Morton was threatening to reveal all. It would have meant the end of everything. I felt trapped and isolated. Alan tendered his resignation immediately but it was refused – he was simply too valuable to the college. Besides, it was I who had rubbed Lady Morton up the wrong way. If there was to be a sacrifice it had to be me.

'Lady Morton had friends in high places and I soon found that the story had been whispered from one place to the next. Not only was I going to be sacked, she was also ensuring that I could not get any other job. All my hard work, all my plans and ambitions looked set to be denied. It was then that I decided that there was no future left for me and that I had to leave England and make my way somewhere else.'

4

I fell silent, chastened by the memories that my story had brought to the surface. I didn't feel anger or even bitterness, I just felt sad that Samantha had betrayed me.

'But it has all been to the good,' Amelia said softly. I looked up at her, a ready smile on her sweet lips.

'Don't be angry about it,' Suzanne said comfortingly. She moved closer to me, her blue eyes gazing into mine, making my heart beat faster. Her lips were full and generous, rouged pink and inviting, glossy where she had licked her lips seductively.

'I'm not angry, Suzanne,' I told her mournfully, 'just saddened that something so good should end so sordidly.'

She leaned forward and kissed me, her perfumed lips caressing mine, making my mouth tingle with anticipation. I kissed her back, opening my mouth to her probing tongue. Her hand was under the table, sliding softly up and down my long thighs.

'My poor child . . .' she whispered hotly, pulling away for a moment. She looked at Amelia and I saw my aunt nod her head and smile.

'I'm ashamed to say it, Mel,' Amelia said, getting up from her place at the table, 'but your story has quite exhausted me. I have a busy day tomorrow. If you'll excuse me, I shall retire to bed.'

She kissed Suzanne passionately on the mouth then turned to me. At that moment I feel a deep and passionate longing for my aunt, I wanted her, wanted to make love to her to show her just how much I adored her. She kissed me softly, a lingering kiss that had my pussy soaking. I put my arm around her and pulled her closer, her hands caressed my nipples, poking against the tight blackness of my dress.

'Good night, darling,' she said, her eyes glittering excitedly.

I watched her go, followed by two eager young men, knowing that the three of them would spend the night locked in each other's arms.

'Your aunt loves you dearly,' Suzanne said, stroking my face with her long elegant fingers. I turned to her, found her mouth close to mine.

'And I love her also, Suzanne, more than she can ever imagine.'

We kissed again, soft fluttering kisses that only a woman can give to a woman. Her mouth escaped from my lips and she kissed me on the neck and on the valley between my ample breasts. I sighed, parted my thighs slightly, pulling the dress higher so that my sex was partially exposed. Suzanne's hands stroked my thighs, her warm fingers pressing firmly up and down, rushing pulses of sensation through my body.

I moaned, Suzanne's finger was playing between the lips of my sex, playing in the sticky warmth. 'This is heaven,' she whispered, bringing her finger to our mouths where we shared the taste of my sex.

I turned, leaned back in my seat and lifted my leg, resting it on the empty chair beside me. Suzanne smoothed her hand down the length of my thigh, from my knee down to tickle my cunny lips. She was biting my neck, sucking at my flesh so that I squealed softly. I looked up and saw that one of the young men was watching, his eyes fixed on me.

'I forgot . . .' I whispered, suddenly embarrassed that we were not alone.

Suzanne laughed. 'Haven't you met Alex?' she asked, cupping my breasts and squeezing, moulding her hands over the generous swell of my chest.

'No, not yet,' I said, glancing at the tall dark young man standing silently in the corner. He was dark-skinned, with a head of tight curly hair that made him look like a Mediterranean god.

'Then he should join us,' Suzanne said, laughing merrily. She called to him and I saw his face break into a greedy smile. He took my hand and kissed it, his full lips warm against my skin.

'Taste her, Alex,' Suzanne cried, kissing me fervently once more. 'Isn't Miss Melissa lovely?'

He ran his lips down my thigh, kissing and sucking at me feverishly and then he was at the apex, his hot breath on the delicate flesh of my open pussy. 'Oh, suck me, Alex,' I breathed, eager to have his tongue on my swollen clitty.

Suzanne pulled the straps of my dress down slowly,

first one arm and then the next, pulling it down so that my breasts were free. Her fingers were soon playing with my nipples, pinching them, soothing them. I squealed, and she laughed gaily, twisting my head round to kiss me once more.

Alex used his fingers to spread my pussy lips. I watched his eyes grow wide with delight and then he breathed on my exposed sex, making me shiver in anticipation. He swooped down, lapping furiously at the waves of sex juice that filled my quim. His tongue explored me, going deep into me while I opened my thighs as far as I could. His hands were under my thighs and I shifted to sit on his hands so that he could steer me to his mouth as he desired. I closed my eyes, giving myself to the sensations playing all over my body. Suzanne's hot lips were clamped tight on my left nipple, her tongue flaying the bud of flesh which seemed to grow in her mouth.

I cried out suddenly, arched my back and forced my hard pussy-bud into Alex's mouth. My climax filled his mouth with cream and he lapped up every drop. He sat up and Suzanne saw that his lips were still sticky with my juice. She looked at him greedily and, without a word, he offered her his face so that she could lick my honey from him. As she did so, I reached down and felt Alex's prick which was as hard as stone.

I slipped from the chair onto my knees, eager to feel Alex's hardness inside me. His trousers slipped off easily and I stroked his cock tenderly, making him moan. In a moment Suzanne was beside me, her gleaming eyes fixed on the same beautiful flesh as my own.

'Let's share him,' I suggested wickedly. She agreed and we fell forward, our mouths going together over his prick. It felt wonderful, the softness of a woman's lips worshipping the hardness of an erect prick. We kissed and sucked, managing to share that pulsing rod with joyful abandon. My hands slipped under her dress and I felt a thrill of excitement when I realised that she wore no panties. Her pussy was small and tight but dripping deliciously. I was tempted to leave her with Alex's cock so that I could eat her from behind, but I felt his prick throbbing, pulsing, getting closer to release.

I used my fingers on Suzanne, stroking and loving, teasing her pussy lips apart, while at the same time kissing her on the mouth over Alex's cock. I heard him moan urgently, his body tensing. Suzanne and I both released his cock, pulling back an inch, our mouths open, joined together. His thick cream burst forth, spewing from his glans into our waiting mouths. The spray covered our faces, our lips, chins, our mouths. We swallowed quickly then turned towards each other and used our tongues to clean every drop of spunk from the other's face. I climaxed again, my fingers frigging my hot pussy while I swallowed Alex's come from Suzanne's delicately shaped lips.

Alex stood up, his face beaded with sweat, his prick still wet with spit and come. Suzanne was breathing hard, her face was flushed pink, her lips tender from all our kissing and sucking.

'That was so good,' she sighed, taking my hand and breathing the bouquet of sex on my fingers. 'I can see that

Amelia was right, you will do a grand job with us here.'

'Thank you, Suzanne,' I smiled.

'Do you want Alex for the night?' she asked, standing up and wiping the sweat from his brow with her long painted fingers.

I suddenly remembered that Charlotte was upstairs waiting for me. 'Another night, Alex,' I told him, not wishing to take him from Suzanne.

We all three kissed good night and then I went up to bed, my body still tingling, the taste of come still in my mouth.

I awoke with the most pleasant sensation in the world: a lovely pair of feminine lips kissing me all over. I turned languidly, opened my eyes and was greeted by a vision of loveliness. Charlotte, her nakedness framed in bright Alpine light, was showering me with butterfly kisses with her full rounded lips. She did not see me waken, her eyes were gazing in silent adoration of my breasts. I shifted again, turned onto my belly and pulled one leg high. I could feel that my bottom was lifted perfectly, my prone position naturally parting my bottom cheeks. The windows were open and I could feel the soft breeze lightly caressing the soft flesh between my pussy lips.

Charlotte traced the long curve of my back with the very tips of her fingers, careful lest she wake me. My eyes were closed again, I was floating dreamily, enjoying the sexy sensations of lightness and darkness on my body, of fingers and lips playing with me in the softest, most erotic way possible.

'Excuse me, Miss Melissa,' a voice asked suddenly, startling us both and forcing me to complete wakefulness.

'What is it?' I snapped, turning to find Rudi at the door, his eyes all over Charlotte and myself. I waited a moment, enjoying the sensation of being looked at, then sat up.

'There is someone to see you, miss,' Rudi snapped, in his clipped Germanic way.

'To see me?' I was surprised. Who possibly knew that I was here?

'Shall I send him away?' Rudi asked, and I could tell that it was something he would have enjoyed doing. Rudi and the others were in paradise, the last thing they wanted was a stranger turning up at the door.

'No, I shall be down at once. Do you have a name?'

'No, miss,' he shook his head. 'Miss Amelia sent me here directly.'

'I'll be down in a moment. Tell whoever it is to wait.'

Rudi went and I turned to Charlotte. We kissed lovingly but I could see that her eyes were clouded with concern. 'What is it, Charlotte?' I asked her, hugging her close.

'I am afraid, miss,' she said softly. 'You're not going to leave are you Miss Melissa? Do not let this stranger take you away . . .'

'Don't be silly,' I said gently. Poor Charlotte, she was in love already and my poor darling was afraid that she would lose me.

I dressed quickly, all the time trying to figure out who the stranger might be. There was only one thing that I was sure of, I wanted to see none of my old friends again.

My past was dead and I did not want any of it to come back to life.

My aunt was waiting for me by the stairs, a worried frown on her face. 'I don't want him here,' she hissed. 'I don't like strange men here, not ever.'

'I'm sorry, auntie, I didn't tell anyone I was coming,' I said, seeing her bad temper for the first time ever.

'Obviously you told someone or else he wouldn't be here,' she said coldly.

'Did he leave a name?'

'No name, he would only say he was a friend. A very close friend.'

I shook my head. 'I'm sorry, Amelia, I honestly can't think who it can be,' I explained apologetically.

'I apologise for snapping at you like that,' she replied softly, running her fingers through my hair. 'There's something about this man that I don't like, there's something very false about him. Please, Melissa darling, get him out of here.'

I went down the stairs quietly, hardly daring to breathe, afraid of who I would meet at the bottom

'Mel!' I hardly had time to register my surprise when Russell scooped me up in his arms and spun me round, laughing.

'Russell, I never thought I'd see you again,' I said.

'Oh come on, did you really think I'd let a catch like you slip away?'

'I waited at the airport, I waited ages,' I lied.

'I knew you would and I'm sorry. There was some damned problem to do with visas and papers, you know what the bureaucracy can be like sometimes. Anyway, I'm here now. How's the school?'

'Fine. Look, Russell,' I said taking his arm and leading him towards the door, 'I'm not working today. How would you like to take me out for lunch?'

'Lunch? Excellent idea! Are there any good restaurants close by?'

'I was hoping you could tell me,' I laughed.

'I'm staying at a hotel a few kilometres north of here,' he explained, stepping out into the crisp breeze. 'The food is excellent, absolutely first class.'

'And of course a hotel is quite convenient afterwards,' I added, remembering the feel of his stiff cock inside me. He looked better than ever, his dishy blue eyes flashing me a look that made me go weak at the knees.

'Yes, very convenient,' he agreed.

'I'll just get a coat,' I said, giving him a peck on the cheek and then running back inside.

'Well, who is the mystery man?' Amelia asked, in a good mood once again, her eyes shining knowingly.

'Someone I met on the plane,' I said sheepishly.

'The man with the cigars?' she said, raising an eyebrow. I nodded. 'What does he want?' she asked.

'Auntie!' I laughed, and she laughed too, it was obvious what Russell wanted.

I grabbed a coat and met him outside, waiting for me beside an expensive sports car. He slipped behind the wheel and in a second we were accelerating away, through the twisting mountain roads to his hotel. The mountains were breathtaking, a view that was always different and always the same, and never boring. The highest peaks were fringed with wisps of cloud but otherwise the sky was a clear crystalline blue.

'Have you finished with your business meetings?' I asked Russell, turning in my seat to face him, my skirt hitching up a fraction. I saw him glance at my bare thighs and smiled, happy that he was still interested in me.

'Yes, pretty much,' he said. 'You know how dull these things can be. Luckily I've a few days spare before I have to fly back. I thought I'd take some holiday while I'm here.'

'Good. You can help me explore the countryside, assuming we've both got the time.'

'Believe me, Mel, there are other things I'd rather be exploring,' he said.

The hotel was ringed by solid outposts of rock, fringed with a few trees and some greenery. It was low and deep, as if carved from the rock itself. A stream gushed and roared close by, the pure spring water throwing a rainbow into the air.

We ate al fresco, enjoying a simple meal and chatting about nothing in particular. The weather was lovely, the crisp breeze invigorating without being cold.

'Do you think you'll stay here?' Russell asked me after we had finished eating.

'Yes. I think it's lovely, I really do.'

'I'm happy for you, Mel, it's not often we find what we want in life.'

'Thank you, Russell,' I said, touched because I could

tell he was sincere, 'I really appreciate that. How's your room?'

'You tell me,' he said, taking me by the hand and pulling me up. We walked through the hotel lobby, the girl at the front desk smiling familiarly to Russell as we passed.

His room was on the second storey and overlooked the stream. I ran out onto the balcony, leaned across the handrail and breathed the crisp fresh air.

'You're beautiful,' Russell said softly, coming up behind me and taking me by the waist. His breath was warm and exciting, I could feel his hardness pressed against my thighs. I took his hand and put them on my breasts, thrilling to the touch of his fingers on my nipples.

'Russell,' I sighed, 'did you really come all this way just to see me?'

'No, I came all this way to fuck you,' he whispered, his voice low and guttural. I turned and we kissed passionately.

'Fuck me here,' I told him, wanting the breeze in my hair and the sun on my skin.

'With pleasure.'

He was naked in a second, his thick prick standing stiffly to attention, and in a moment I was naked too. We joined suddenly, impulsively, arms and legs everywhere. He was already fingering my sex, touching my wetness, opening me, stimulating the petals of my cunny. I put my arms around him and he lifted me high, holding me under the bottom and pressing his shaft into me. I cried out, the force of penetration like an electric shock. I clawed at him wildly, jigging up and down on his wet cock. I climaxed almost instantly, out of my mind with the sudden inrush of pleasure.

He put me down and kissed my quivering mouth. There was a table on the balcony and he spread me on it, I lay back and opened my thighs, my fingers playing with my nipples. Russell began to kiss my thighs, his feverish mouth eating every inch of smooth glassy flesh. I felt like a queen, worshipped, loved, devoured by an eager lover.

I moaned, turned to one side and opened my eyes. A face smiled back. I made to move but the woman on the balcony opposite put her finger to her lips. Russell's tongue was entering me, sucking my hard throbbing clit into his mouth. I closed my eyes and felt a wave of pleasure pulse through me. I opened my eyes again and got a better look at the person opposite. It was a young blonde, her eyes fixed on Russell and myself. I smiled at her and she came to the edge of her balcony and blew me a kiss. I sighed and moaned loudly, I was going to come again. Russell was fucking me expertly with his mouth.

The woman moved and I saw that she was dressed only in a robe. It fell open and I saw her pale breasts exposed. I blew her a kiss too and she responded by letting the robe fall from her shoulders. She had small breasts with hard red nipples, a slim waist and a neat bush of hair. I tried to sit up, to see her nakedness as much as possible. Russell was still eating me and the pleasure came in pulses, making me sing with ecstasy.

My blonde voyeur realised that I was trying to look at her for she stepped back from the handrail and mounted a chair. She sat on her heels and parted her thighs so that I could see her exposed pussy. I climaxed again, my cries carrying across the gap between the rooms.

'I want your prick inside me,' I whispered, driven beyond endurance by Russell's skilful mouth.

He laughed. 'And I want to feel that lovely tongue of yours,' he said.

I moved quickly, not wanting Russell to see his neighbour, half afraid that he would want her instead of me. I positioned him so that his back was to her while I could still see her.

She laughed but the sound of it was taken by the breeze, the same breeze that had her hair flowing and shining in the sunlight. Russell's prick was wet and slippery with my juice. I swallowed it, relishing my own taste, relishing too the droplets of silver fluid pouring from the glans.

I saw that our erotic display was too much for the blonde. She was reaching across to the table on her balcony, to the bowl of fruit that sat there. I watched her with mounting excitement. She slowly peeled a banana, wet it with her lips and then gently inserted it into her sex. I imagined the feel of it inside her, cool and firm, the flesh of it moistened by her own sweet juice.

The image of the woman frigging herself with the banana excited me beyond measure. I was moving up and down Russell's prick, enjoying its masculine hardness against the inside of my mouth, the throbbing heat of it in contrast to the coolness of the banana in my distant companion's sex. Russell held my head in place. He was fucking me now, forcing himself into the back of my throat. I shifted round to accommodate his full length and closed my lips tightly to form a mouth-pussy for him to fuck.

My secret companion had her eyes closed. Her mouth was open and I recognised that she was close to orgasm. Her hand was working furiously, spearing her quim with the wet sticky fruit. I half envied her, my own fingers were alternately playing with my pussy or with my nipples. Somehow I managed to keep my eyes on her, even though I sometimes felt dizzy with the surges of blissful sensation that coursed through me.

Russell's thrusts became more urgent, he held me tightly, his fingers digging into my shoulder. He bucked hard and then the explosion happened in my mouth, his cream driven right to the back of my throat. I swallowed it, enjoying the sinuous feel of it going down. I caught sight of the woman across the way arching her back, her mouth open, her eyes closed. She held the chair for support as if afraid that it would give way under her – she had climaxed too.

I could feel myself on the edge, my own pleasure certain to blossom soon. I looked up, Russell had stepped away, and I saw the woman take the banana from her sex and place it to her mouth. She smiled to me, blew me a kiss and then began to eat it, the white-fleshed fruit dripping with her honey. She savoured every mouthful, closing her eyes and swallowing as if it were the rarest delicacy. The image was too much and I too climaxed, crying out with joy as Russell's fingers teased my nipples.

'Who's that?' Russell asked as he turned round and saw the woman smiling at me, she was wrapped tightly in her robe once more.

'I don't know, she just stepped out,' I lied, grinning at her, too, as Russell led me back into his room.

I collapsed on the bed, still thinking of the woman across the way, trying hard to imagine the sexy taste of banana and sex-cream. Russell flopped down beside me, cradled me in his arms, tracing a finger down the curve of my back. 'Are you glad I came back for you?' he asked, sitting up on one elbow and gazing into my eyes.

'Sure, but I have to admit that I'm a bit surprised.'

'Don't be,' he whispered. 'I really enjoyed our time together.'

'Even that time in the airport, when the guard caught us?'

He chuckled. 'Yes, especially then. Mel, do you remember I left something with you just before we parted?'

'The smelly old cigars,' I smiled.

'Hey, they were very expensive,' he laughed, drawing slow patterns on my flat belly with the very tips of his fingers. 'Do you still have them?'

'I suppose so,' I shrugged, not quite remembering what had happened to them. Were they still in my room?

'I'm going to see the old man again before I leave, do you think you could find them for me?'

'But I didn't get what I wanted,' I teased him petulantly, puckering my lips like a sulking child.

'And what was that?' he asked seriously, his voice losing its good-humoured tone.

75

'Hey, I was only joking,' I smiled, at a loss to understand how his mood had changed so quickly. His fingers were frozen into place, his eyes had darkened, his voice hard and brittle. It was a complete change of personality and it frightened me a little.

'Of course you were,' he laughed, but the darkness in his eyes was real. 'Now, what is it that you didn't get?'

'Nothing,' I mumbled. I had wanted to feel his prick fucking me, filling my sex and not my mouth with its creamy reward, but my mood had passed. 'I'd better get back,' I said looking at the clock on the wall above us.

'Sure, I'll drive you,' he said, too keenly for my liking. I had expected him to try to persuade me to stay but his manner had changed for good and I had no idea why.

As we walked through the hotel lobby I saw the delicious blonde standing by the front desk, dressed in a staid business suit, her long hair tied in a tight bun. I paused for a moment, intrigued to find out who she was, wondering whether to talk to her or not.

'What is it?' Russell asked impatiently.

'Isn't that the woman we saw on the balcony?' I whispered, nodding towards her. She was in profile, talking in hushed tones to the female receptionist.

'No, it can't be,' Russell told me. 'She's the hotel manager, what would she be doing in one of the guest rooms?'

'It looks like her,' I insisted, certain that it was her.

'That woman had to be a guest, she was in a robe, wasn't she?'

'Yes but . . .'

76

'Come on,' Russell urged. I allowed myself to be pulled along, certain that I was right. As we reached the door the woman turned, our eyes met and she waved. I smiled back but already Russell was jumping into the car.

The return journey was made in strained silence, neither of us picking up on the other's attempt at conversation. I remembered what Amelia had said about not trusting him and I couldn't help thinking that she was right. It had been such an inconsequential conversation but his mood had switched from playfulness to a coldness that I didn't like.

'Will you get me those cigars, please,' he said as he steered the car round to the entrance to the house. 'I may as well pick them up while I'm here,' he added jauntily.

'Sure,' I said. The jaunty manner did nothing to convince me that his mood had changed, there was still something wrong.

I ran into the house and up to my room, not bothering to stop and talk to anyone. I wanted Russell out and away, I knew he was never going to come back and I was glad. I looked in the drawers and in my bags but there was no sign of the damned box of cigars and I wished that he had never given them to me.

'You are back, madame,' Charlotte cried happily, running into the room to greet me with a kiss.

'Charlotte, have you seen a box of cigars?' I asked, going over to the window and looking down at Russell, pacing up and down impatiently by the car.

'*Oui, madame,* they are in the top drawer,' she said, going over to it and looking inside.

'I looked,' I told her, exhaling forcefully.

'But I put them here myself,' she insisted, searching again.

'You didn't put them elsewhere?'

'*Non, madame,* I put them here, I am sure of it.'

'Would anyone else come into this room?'

Charlotte shook her head. I hadn't seen the cigars but if Charlotte said they had been in the top drawer then I was willing to believe her. The only possibility was that someone had taken them and that was not something to fill me with joy.

The door was open but Suzanne knocked before entering. I knew what she wanted even before she said anything. 'I'll get rid of him as soon as possible,' I told her.'

'It's nothing personal,' she hastened to explain, 'you do understand.'

'Of course I understand, Suzanne,' I said, recognising that her concerns were real and justified. 'He's just waiting for some gifts that I was looking after for him.'

'Good,' she smiled, looking relieved.

'Not good,' I corrected. 'The stupid cigars are missing. Charlotte put them in the top drawer and now they're gone.'

'Are you certain, Charlotte?'

'*Oui, madame, absolument,*' Charlotte insisted, her dark eyes looking to me for support.

'Look, this is silly,' I decided. 'I'll tell him to forget

the cigars. If they're that important I'll buy him another box.'

His smile disappeared when he saw me approach empty-handed and the cold hard look returned to his face.

'I'm sorry, Russell, but I can't find them. The box seems to have been mislaid. I'm sure that you'll find something better in Zurich, and if you let me know how much they cost I'll pay you.'

'It's not the money,' he snapped, turning away from me. 'It's not the money. This old man is very fond of these cigars, he can't find them at all in Switzerland. And I promised him, gave him my word that I had a box with me.'

'I'm sorry.'

'Do you think they've just been mislaid or are they gone for good?' he turned to face me, real anguish in his eyes.

'What is it, Russell? This isn't about cigars, is it?'

'Of course it is, what else could it be? You saw me buy the bloody things. I could lose a lot of face here, Mel, this could cost me a lot of money.'

I looked back, saw Amelia standing in the doorway, watching me closely. 'I don't believe you, Russell. What was in the cigar box?'

'Cigars! Look, Mel, promise me you'll find them, promise me, please.'

'I promise I'll find them for them for you.'

'I'll be back tomorrow,' he promised.

'No, let me call you. It's better that way,' I said, watching him get back into the car. I felt cold, shivering.

I had been so sure of him, certain that I had judged him well but now I knew I was mistaken. The car roared off and I watched it go, angry with myself for being so stupid. I trudged back to Amelia disconsolately, on the verge of tears but vowing to find out what Russell was really up to.

5

I sat and told my darling aunt everything, from the moment Russell had appeared to rescue me at the airport to the moment his mood suddenly changed in the hotel, not sparing any of the details. My aunt listened in appalled silence, sitting next to me, her legs crossed so that my eyes were constantly drawn to her silky smooth thighs.

'I've been very stupid, haven't I?' I mumbled when I had finished.

She smiled comfortingly. 'Not at all,' she said, 'you've been a bit naive, nothing more.'

I was glad that she was giving me the benefit of the doubt, it was not a luxury I would allow myself however. My main concern now was to find out what I had unwittingly smuggled into the country for Russell – if that was his real name, for now I could take nothing for granted. 'What do you think is in the cigar box? Diamonds, drugs, money?'

'It could be diamonds,' Amelia mused, 'certainly the box was too small to hold any amount of drugs or money. But it could be anything, electronic micro-processors, plans, documentation, anything.'

'This is awful,' I gasped. 'If it gets out it could ruin

the school for you, as well as landing me in jail.'

'Well darling, sitting here worrying is not going to solve the mystery. I suggest we start looking and asking questions. I cannot believe that any of my girls would steal the cigars, my young women wouldn't be seen dead smoking those things,' she laughed, and her good humour cheered me up too.

'What about Rudi or Erich or some like that?'

She considered for a moment then shook her head. 'I trust them completely. They've never let me down before, and I can't see why they would do that for a box of cigars. There has to be some completely innocent explanation.'

'Or some more devious explanation,' I reminded her.

'Such as?'

'Russell was bringing the box into the country for somebody. Could it be that they, or their enemies, got the box before he did?'

Amelia looked mortified, her face drained of colour, her eyes wide. 'I hope to God that's not true,' she whispered. 'A break-in by gangsters . . . If that ever got out we would be ruined.'

I took her in my arms and kissed her on the cheek, wishing that I had never met Russell and hoping that my fears were totally ungrounded. We kissed on the lips and then I got up, returning to my room with all the worries of the world on my shoulders. I felt guilty, certain that my naivety was going to lead eventually to absolute disaster, far worse than it had done in England.

I collapsed on my bed and began to weep, all the anger and frustration boiling over suddenly. Why did things have to always go wrong? Why was it always me?

'Please don't cry, madame,' Charlotte whispered, appearing as if by magic at my side. I turned to her and she cradled me in her arms, my tears falling onto her soft brown skin.

'I've caused so much trouble,' I sobbed.

'It's not your fault, Madame Melissa,' Charlotte whispered, her voice a soft Caribbean lullaby. I looked up into her dark eyes and felt a sudden flaring of desire, hot and passionate. Charlotte really was the most adorable being, her full lips always ready to be kissed, her eyes full of sadness and joy at the same time. I reached up and kissed her softly on the mouth.

'You're a good girl,' I told her, wiping the tears from my eyes.

'Everything will soon be sorted out,' she said optimistically, kissing my fingertips.

'Yes, I'm sure it will Charlotte,' I agreed, willing myself to feel as hopeful as I sounded. 'Come on, we need to search this room from top to bottom.'

We looked through my bags and suitcases, just in case the box had been put back by mistake. Charlotte and I searched diligently but with no result, the cigars were not there. Next I suggested we look under the bed and under the mattress, and I couldn't help caressing Charlotte's lovely backside as she bent down to search. Her bottom cheeks were nice and round, firm, well-shaped, lovely to touch and caress, and she loved it too, hollowing her back and pushing her bottom out. She was wearing a loose skirt and when I put my hand under it and stroked her bare thighs I heard her moan softly, her eyelids fluttering like butterflies in the breeze. She was lovely and the feel of her in my hands made me forget my worries for a moment.

'Any luck?' Amelia asked, coming into the room.

'Not yet,' I laughed, a little embarrassed to be caught fondling Charlotte instead of concentrating on the search, but Amelia didn't seem to mind.

'I asked Rudi but he can only remember that you had them at the airport,' Amelia reported. She went to the window and looked out wistfully and I wondered whether she was afraid that she was going to lose everything that she had worked for.

'Nothing here, madame,' Charlotte said, sitting up and smoothing down her skirt.

'Where did you last see them, Charlotte?' Amelia asked, turning from the window to face us.

'In the top drawer, madame, where I put them after unpacking Madame Melissa's things.'

'This drawer?' Amelia walked across, her high heels banging hard on the varnished floor. Charlotte nodded vigorously. 'And the box, it was here?' Amelia said, pulling the drawer open.

'*Oui, madame*,' Charlotte said.

'Is it this box?' Amelia asked, pulling a small package from the drawer.

Charlotte and I both jumped up at once, staring open-mouthed at the small box in Aunt Amelia's elegant hand.

'But I don't understand,' I cried, rushing across to take the box from her. It was the same one, the same silly box that Russell had given me to take through Customs.

'We looked there many times,' Charlotte said, shaking her head in disbelief.

'It seems then, that it has returned as mysteriously as it was taken,' Amelia said, sounding as surprised as the rest of us.

'The seal's broken,' I noted, carefully opening the box. The hinged lid opened and beneath it was a row of five long slim cigar tubes, with space for a sixth. 'One's missing.'

I passed the open box to Amelia who took out one of the cigar tubes. She held it up to the light, examining it closely, her eyes scanning the smooth object for any sign of tampering. 'This one looks unopened,' she commented, putting the box on the chest of drawers.

'Open it anyway,' I urged, taking another from the box.

We both carefully unscrewed the base, tearing the gummed paper label that sealed each tube. The rich ripe smell of fine tobacco soon filled the room, as each cigar case was found to contain one very long, very round cigar.

'Inside the cigars?' I suggested hopefully, knowing full well that if there was anything at all suspect in the package it had to be in the single missing tube.

Amelia shrugged, she took one of the cigars and carefully crumbled it into the empty box, the fine papery tobacco falling to pieces before our very eyes. 'Nothing. The question is who took the box and then returned it?'

'Well,' I said, 'that rules out anyone from outside.

They'd hardly put the box back again, would they?'

'How true,' Amelia acknowledged, looking every bit as relieved as I felt.

'Madame,' Charlotte said cautiously, 'I have just remembered something.'

'What?' we both asked, turning towards her.

'I mentioned the cigars to Antonia and Philippa, they were the only other girls to know about them.'

'When was this?' Amelia demanded, her face darkening.

Charlotte swallowed hard, she shrank back, obviously fearing Amelia's anger. 'On the first day, I mentioned that Madame Melissa had many fine perfumes and also a box of cigars for her lover. Did I do wrong?'

'No, of course not,' I assured her, rushing over and planting a friendly kiss on her cheek. 'Did you also tell them that we were looking for the cigars?'

'*Oui madame*, this morning when the gentleman arrived.'

'Right! I'm going to have to have a stiff word with these two!' Amelia declared, straightening her back, her face a picture of anger.

I was sure that the girls, and I hadn't met them yet, had meant no harm and I wanted to spare them a good telling-off on my account. 'Please, Amelia, would you mind if I dealt with this?'

She looked at me for a moment then she broke into a smile. 'Yes, that's a good idea, Mel. I'll leave them in your capable hands and I imagine that they'll be able to tell us what happened to the missing cigar. In the meantime, I'll give your friend Russell a call and arrange a visit.'

'He's not my friend, auntie,' I asserted. 'And I suggest we let him sweat a little. I'll find the missing cigar and then we can call him tomorrow morning. A sleepless night might do him some good.'

'As you wish,' Amelia agreed. 'And well done, Charlotte, you've been very good. I'm sorry if I snapped at you earlier.'

'I am sorry too, madame,' she smiled shyly. 'I wish I had remembered earlier.'

'Now, Charlotte, it's time I made the acquaintance of Antonia and Philippa.'

Antonia and Philippa both lived in the chalet nearest the main house. Antonia was the daughter of a Swiss banker, a native of Geneva, very vivacious and anxious not to live up to the Swiss reputation for dullness. Philippa was a year younger, her mother and father were both officials in the United Nations and frequently on opposite sides of the globe. The two girls were completely infatuated with each other and it was rare that they spent the night apart, even when they were joined by one of the men.

Charlotte explained all this and more as we crossed the grounds to their chalets. The sun was going down and the sky was suffused with a soft pink glow.

'Please, madame,' Charlotte said, stopping at the door to the chalet, 'it would be better if I were not here.'

'Of course, I understand,' I said. 'But there is one favour you could do for me, Charlotte.'

87

'Anything.'

'Madame Amelia has had a very trying day today. She is probably preparing for dinner at the moment, would you be a treasure and look after her for me?'

She smiled, her eyes lighting up at the idea. 'Of course, madame,' she agreed. I kissed her on the lips and patted her on the bottom, grateful for all her help. She returned to the house excitedly and I knew that Amelia would be glad to have her back, even if it was just for a short period.

I had only been in the chalet once before and then only very briefly. I was struck by the relaxing atmosphere, by the beautiful simplicity of construction and decoration. The door opened into a hallway, a wide open space with doors to all the rooms. I waited for a second, trying to remember which member of staff lived with the girls. I had only met them for a few moments but I seemed to remember that it was Monique who stayed here.

I found the door and knocked softly, waited for her to answer before going in.

'Melissa! How nice to see you,' she smiled, looking up from the desk where she was working.

I apologised for disturbing her and told her about the missing cigars, without going too much into the sordid details. She took off her glasses and looked at me for a second. 'That sounds like Antonia's doing,' she decided. 'She has a friend that she sees in Zurich sometimes, one of her father's friends. We tried to put a stop to it but she has her mother's permission so we can't prevent her.'

'You think she has taken the cigar for him?' I asked, downhearted.

'It is possible. To be honest, Melissa, the situation is not to our liking. Both the mother and the daughter share the same lover and the father knows nothing. We are in a difficult situation, the best we can do is to limit the number of trips she has to Zurich.'

'Has she been there recently?' I asked, hoping to God that she hadn't. Monique smiled and shook her head, for once luck was on my side. 'Where are they now?'

'Probably in Antonia's room,' Monique said, rising and taking me by the hand. Monique looked lovely, she had dark curly hair and a soft round face, slightly girlish in a bookish kind of way. She wore small round glasses that made her look like a pretty young student, a very sexy student at that.

We listened at Antonia's door for a moment but heard nothing. Very carefully Monique opened the door a fraction and looked inside. 'Not there,' she said, opening the door fully to show me.

'What next?'

'Perhaps they are bathing,' Monique suggested. I followed her down the corridor to the bathroom, we could hear the hissing jets of water from the shower and the soft murmur of voices.

'Shall we let them finish?' I asked quietly, putting my ear to the door.

'No,' Monique replied. She turned the handle of the door very slowly and pushed the door open an inch. She looked inside first then gestured for me to follow suit. I saw the two young women under the shower, the streaming water coursing down their naked bodies. They were lost in each other, oblivious to everything but the feel of their closely entwined bodies. The shower curtain was partly drawn so we could not see what they were doing, though it was obvious they were enjoying themselves.

'Quietly,' Monique whispered and managed to slide cat-like into the room. I followed, carefully easing the door shut after me. We tiptoed to the other side of the room, shielded by the curtain and certain that we had not been spotted by the young women.

'Tony . . . Tony . . . Bite my buttons again, I want your lips on my titties . . .' one of them, Philippa, sighed.

'Ask me nicely,' Antonia teased, her voice low and sultry, her English accented a touch to make her sound deliciously sexy.

'Please, please, please . . .' Philippa begged, the ache in her breasts and in her sex reflected in her anguished voice. She sighed, a long low moan of pleasure that had Monique and I smiling, both of us imagining the dreamy feel of feminine lips on our nipples. We edged closer, the rushing of the water and the sighs and moans of the girls drowning all other sounds.

We were beside the shower, we could see the dark forms behind the plastic curtain, could see the shadowy movements, hear the mingled voices, and see the water splashing to the floor at our feet. I carefully pulled the corner of the curtain aside but I was too close and the gap was too small to see properly. Monique tapped my shoulder and then pointed to the mirror across the room.

Philippa had her head thrown back, her long red hair bathed in the jet of water. Antonia's face was between Philippa's gorgeous twin globes, her mouth greedily sucking on an engorged and fattened nipple.

Monique and I also saw ourselves, two voyeurs spying on the young lovers in the shower. I stifled my surprised laughter and together Monique and I found a more suitable position, where we could see the action more clearly and where we could be sure our own reflection was not so obvious.

'Now my darling,' Antonia whispered between sucks of Philippa's nipple, 'I want to play with that lovely little bumhole of yours.'

'But you said you were going to taste my cunny,' Philippa complained, but her complaint turned into a murmur of pleasure as Antonia's lips pulled on a nipple.

Obediently Philippa turned around to face the wall, bending over to thrust out her very pert and attractive backside. The shower gushed water down her back. It fell in ripples and rivulets down her glistening spine, down between her lovely round bottom-cheeks. From our position we could barely make out the reddish hair that guarded her pussy lips.

Antonia knelt down in the water. Her own breasts looked tempting, the nipples hard and glistening under the droplets of water that splashed onto her chest. She massaged Philippa's bottom, moulding her hands onto the full globes, her fingers pressing deep into the firm flesh. The look of rapt concentration told us all we wanted to know, she was certainly in love with her best friend's delightful *derrière*.

'What a lovely picture they make,' I whispered to Monique, the excitement making me feel hot and sexy too. I wondered if Monique felt the same, hoping that the two of us could make love once we had dealt with the two young women.

'We can interrupt them now,' Monique suggested, 'and have them apologise to us in the most voluptuous way.'

'No, let's watch for a few moments more,' I said, turning back to the erotic view in the mirror, curious to see what was going to happen next.

'Push out your bottom more,' Antonia commanded and Philippa obeyed, bending lower, moving languidly, her eyes half-closed and her mouth open. She was the image of pleasure, lost in the swirl of rushing water and the feel of her lover's fingers and mouth. Antonia used her thumbs to carefully pull the buttocks apart, marvelling at the tight round treasure she found there. I felt my heart pounding, the sight of Philippa's bottomhole and the parted pussy lips made me feel suddenly wet between the thighs.

'Philippa,' Antonia whispered hotly, 'you have the most scrumptious bumhole in the whole of the school.'

'You should know, darling,' Philippa giggled, 'you play with it often enough.'

'I do not!'

'Yes, you do!' Philippa insisted. 'Why, you fingered me there all the way through this afternoon's lessons.'

'So that's the reason for her lack of attention this

afternoon,' Monique whispered. 'The little minx will have to learn not to play games when she should be working.'

'I can't help it,' Antonia admitted. 'I just love you to distraction. You know I can't resist this . . .' She swept down quickly and planted a long slow kiss between Philippa's parted cheeks. Philippa moaned, pressed her rear out more, took her buttocks in her hands and opened herself fully. Antonia twisted and turned, giving her a throaty French kiss deep in the rear hole. I watched, fascinated by the way both girls enjoyed every movement, every whisper of sensation. Antonia was sucking and kissing, her head moving feverishly between the enticingly parted buttocks.

'I'm going to explode!' Philippa cried, moving her bottom sinuously. She was almost squatting over Antonia, her knees bent and her back arched. Antonia was stroking Philippa between the thighs, her fingers teasing open the wet pussy lips while she tongued the tight rear hole.

'I'm going to make you scream the house down,' Antonia promised, moving away for a second and then returning with something in her hand, something I couldn't make out. She resumed her tonguing, mouthing Philippa's behind with absolute abandon. I watched, transfixed by the beautifully erotic image; two attractive young women, their sexy bodies naked and glistening under the running water, engaged in feverishly abandoned lesbian sex.

Antonia's hand was moving something in and out of Philippa's pussy. It was partly hidden and we could only see her hand moving in and out, faster and faster, deep into Philippa's opening. And all the while Antonia was making love to her rear hole, her tongue snaking into it, tickling, lapping, sometimes playfully biting Philippa on the thigh. Antonia was intent, her own pleasure was real, we could see that from the look of concentration on her face and in her aroused nipples, but she wanted to give the utmost pleasure to her lover. And Philippa's cries were indeed growing louder, higher, her face contorted, ecstatic. At last she did scream, a piercing cry that filled the room and marked her powerful climax.

'Now it's my turn,' Philippa said, her voice strained after her thunderous orgasm. 'I want to see if I can make you scream with this too.'

Monique and I both stood up at once, our eyes wide with fascination as we watched Philippa pulling the silver cigar tube from her sex, where Antonia had used it to such good effect.

'Actually it's our turn,' I said, stepping forward, enjoying the look of horror that crossed the errant young ladies' faces.

'Miss Melissa! Miss Monique!' the two friends cried, quickly trying to hide the cigar tube.

'Where did you get that?' I asked, retrieving it at once. The silver tube was warm and wet, still sticky with Philippa's love cream.

'I'm sorry,' Antonia mumbled with head bowed. 'I borrowed it for a while. I didn't mean to cause any trouble, miss. I returned the box as soon as I could, I didn't think you would miss one cigar. I just wanted to show Philippa what it was like.'

'But why a cigar tube?' I asked, unable to see why she had gone to so much trouble when there were other things available – the image of the women with the banana came unbidden into my mind.

'It was what I used the first time, when I was sixteen and wanted to see what a man felt like,' Antonia said, managing a half-smile even in her red-faced embarrassment.

'I . . . I helped her too,' Philippa said, taking Antonia's hand in hers. 'We both borrowed it.'

'I think Miss Monique has a few things to discuss with you,' I said sternly, turning to Monique. I could see from the fiery look in her eyes that the shower games had not finished.

'That's right. I wondered why you two were so inattentive this afternoon,' she said, not managing to hide the playful smile that gave the lie to her anger. 'If the feel of a finger in the behind is so appealing I think it only right that you both investigate it after hours. And perhaps Miss Melissa might join in the investigation?'

I shook my head sadly, much as the idea appealed to me I had more important things to worry about. 'I'm afraid you are going to have your hands full, Monique,' I said apologetically. 'Both hands full.'

'In that case, girls,' Monique smiled, 'I think you ought to get back under the showers and bend over. I'm going to make you ache with pleasure but there'll be no release until you've learned your lessons.'

I waited for a moment and watched the two delightful girls bend over, their bottoms ripe for frigging. Then I left, my heart sinking at the thought of what I was missing. I consoled myself with licking Philippa's sweet pussy emissions from the cigar tube, enjoying the taste as it filled my mouth and slid down my throat.

I rushed back to the house, clutching the tube as if it were my most treasured possession. It was the key to everything, my only hope of finding out what Russell was doing and hence the means of ridding him from my life. Amelia was up in her room, I was so keyed up that I remember rushing in without thinking. I also remember the sight that met me – darling Charlotte was drinking lovingly from Aunt Amelia's pussy, while Rudi was fucking Charlotte furiously in her beautiful dark sex.

'I'm so sorry,' I blushed, retreating back to the door.

'Nonsense, darling,' Amelia sighed, closing her eyes momentarily as Charlotte worked her tongue deeper. 'Join us . . .'

I shut the door and leaned back against it. My sex had still been tingling after what I'd seen the shower but now it was wet and aching to be loved. I put the cigar tube down on the nearest available surface and in seconds I was naked and stepping towards the bed, my eyes fixed on Rudi's firm backside rising and falling as he thrust deep into Charlotte, his hands snow-white on the dark brown of her chocolate skin.

My aunt kissed me on the mouth, her lips sending a spark of electricity that pulsed right through to my nipples and my sex. I had always found her the most highly charged woman I had ever met, she had initiated mc into the pleasures of sex and I still worshipped her for it. Her lovely breasts were free, her nipples rouged where Charlotte had no doubt been feasting, and I couldn't resist taking them in my hands.

'Auntie . . .' I kissed her lovingly on one nipple and then the next, my lips teasing the hard round node. I felt so happy at that moment, so thoroughly sexy, that my pussy was flooded by a torrent of love juice that poured forth, dripping down my thigh. I watched my aunt tease it onto her fingertips, tracing the little river up to the source then take it to her pretty lips. She smiled, poked her tongue out and licked her fingers slowly and deliberately, her eyes on me all the time.

'Lovely, my darling,' she whispered.

'*Madame Melissa*,' Charlotte cried joyously, seeing me for the first time. She smiled and then moaned, Rudi was thrusting harder, pistoning his prick deep into the velvet wetness of her sex. She cried out, arched her back and climaxed, her body taut with the sudden pulsating pleasure.

Rudi withdrew, his prick still strong and hard, and liberally coated with the divine emissions from Charlotte's cunny. I looked at him and he smiled, moving closer to me, his tool stiff and inviting. My body was tingling all over, I wanted him inside me, in my sex, in my behind, in my mouth.

'Aren't you going to clean him?' Amelia asked me, pulling Charlotte up so that they could exchange a long slow kiss.

I turned, knelt down on the bed and began to lick away

Charlotte's taste from Rudi's lovely prick. I sucked every inch of his beautiful tool, from the thick round base to the silky softness of his glans and the silver fluid that poured from the little slit. I had my hands on him, wanting to touch his thighs, his behind, under his balls.

I moaned – someone, Charlotte or Amelia, had pushed a finger into my sex. I moved back, opening myself, eager to have my throbbing clitty stroked. Rudi was moving rhythmically, screwing me in the throat, knowing that I could take him, that I enjoyed his immense cock filling my mouth. Waves of bliss washed through me, starting from the fingers tingling my bare clitty and surging like a tidal wave into my body.

The taste of Charlotte was mingled with the taste of cock, the two merging deep in my mouth and making me feel dizzy with excitement. I cupped his balls, squeezed gently, cradled him, loving the feel of him. My sighs were stifled, I was too busy with Rudi's lovely cock, licking under the glans, grazing my teeth ever so lightly as he thrust into my mouth. All the time I could feel fingers going into my sex and I had no idea how many or whether it was my aunt or the lovely Charlotte. It added something, a delicious feeling of mystery and excitement. I climaxed, not once but several times, and each time I felt the cream pour from my cunt onto those skilful fingers.

I thought Rudi was close to climax too so I pulled away, wanting to share the pleasures of his ejaculation with my aunt and Charlotte. I sat back and was cuddled by the two women, their mouths all over me, on my breasts, on my belly, on my mouth. Rudi stood between the three of us and fondled his enormous cock, his eyes closed. I had never watched a man stroke himself like that and watched, fascinated and incredibly turned on.

Suddenly he grunted, forcing his hand back so that his prick was hard and tight, and then he spurted thick wads of come over us. It sailed through the air, spurt after spurt of spunk, spraying onto all three of us, wave after wave until there was no more. I turned and looked at Charlotte, her dark breasts wet with sliding pools of come, and at my aunt, her face glistening with it. I could feel it on my neck, a warm viscous cream. Suddenly Charlotte was on me, sucking and biting, and I was kissing my aunt, licking it from her lips, while she smeared juice all over Charlotte's nipples.

Charlotte sat back, cupped her breasts and offered a nipple to each of us – large chocolate-coloured nipples that glistened with a thick coating of spunk. I gave my aunt one last lingering kiss and then we licked Charlotte clean, making her climax as we did so.

I dressed quickly while Charlotte and Rudi attended to my aunt. In a moment we were both ready, our eyes glittering still, and our faces flushed but ready to finally crack the mystery.

'You've found the cigar tube I take it?' Amelia said, brushing her long golden hair.

'Yes, being put to very good use,' I said.

'In what way?'

'As a dildo,' I said, holding up the phallic-shaped object. 'Philippa seemed to enjoy the way that Antonia handled it.'

Amelia laughed indulgently. 'My girls are always original, if a little perverse at times. Is it intact?'

'The sealing paper is gone but the bottom is still on tight,' I said, only then really having a proper chance to examine it. I turned it over and began to unscrew the flat end, holding it carefully lest it fall to pieces in some way. I felt a dark cloud of foreboding, afraid that I would find either nothing or something truly horrible. The bottom came away and I peered into the tube. There was no cigar this time.

'What is it?' Amelia asked, coming over to look at it. I turned it over and carefully tapped the contents out.

'Documents . . .' I whispered, taking a rolled-up polythene bag from the tube and spreading it out. A thick scroll of documents had been pushed into the tube and I had smuggled them into the country without a care in the world. I made a slit in the polythene wrapper and pulled the papers out. They were completely dry, even after the shower scene.

'Bankers' drafts,' Amelia said as I handed her the papers. 'Worth millions by the look of them. It looks like our friend Russell has been moving large sums of money about for somebody.'

'No wonder he was worried sick about his blasted cigars.'

'Tomorrow morning I think we'll give him a call. And it's high time we both paid a visit to him. Don't you think?'

The sly smile on my aunt's face was infectious. I laughed, certain that in some way we were going to get our own back on Russell Cross once and for all.

'Amelia?' I asked later on at dinner. 'When we were all making love earlier . . . Was it you that . . . that . . . or was it Charlotte?'

'Who would you like it to be?' Amelia smiled enigmatically, gazing warmly into my eyes. I blushed, unable to answer her question. I had wanted it to be her. I still ached to have her in my arms, to make love to her the way she had taught me so many years before.

6

Russell called early the next morning, while I was still fast asleep, with Charlotte cuddled up in my arms. My aunt nonchalantly instructed Suzanne to inform him that we were in conference and to call back later, thus prolonging the agonies of doubt that he was surely experiencing. Amelia and I breakfasted together, enjoying fresh croissants and piping hot coffee on the terrace that opened from the dining room. The sky was so clear that the clouds seemed to come alive as they skated majestically across the blue surface.

'Well, Amelia,' I wondered, 'what have you got planned for Russell?'

'I think we ought to go and see him together,' she grinned. 'But there are certain discussions that I think should be in private.'

'You mean the two of you?' I asked, not at all certain what Amelia was getting at.

'Yes, darling,' she explained. 'There are certain assurances that I need as regards the good name of my school. Would it hurt you terribly if you left us alone for a while?'

'Of course not,' I said, trying to fathom her motives

behind the happy smile. Russell was an attractive man and I wondered whether she was going to fall prey to his charming manner and suave good looks just as I had.

I took the call from Russell a few moments later. Rudi brought the telephone out to the terrace and Amelia listened in on another extension.

'How are you, Mel?' Russell asked, trying desperately to sound unconcerned and failing miserably.

'I'm fine, Russell, and you?' I asked innocently, winking at my aunt who beamed me a delectable smile.

'Fine, fine. Mel, did you have any luck with the matter we discussed yesterday?'

'A matter we discussed yesterday?' I repeated forgetfully.

I heard him inhale sharply. 'The cigars,' he hissed, his voice icy cold.

'Oh the cigars,' I laughed. 'Yes, we did find a box of the smelly old things. These are the cigars that you promised to your old friend. The cigars that are just cigars and nothing else.'

'Stop playing with me, Mel,' he said. 'Did you find them or not?'

'Yes, Russell, we found a box of cigars. You'd like them back, I suppose.'

'Of course I'd like them back!' he spluttered. 'I'll be down to pick them up now.'

'No, it's all right. I fancy a day out, I'll come to see you. Would you like that, darling?'

'Yes, okay, bring them to me. When will you be here?'

'My aunt and I should be leaving soon,' I let drop casually.

'Your aunt? What has this got to do with her?' he demanded.

'But, Russell, how else do you expect me to get there? She'll drive me down, we could both do with getting out for a few hours.'

'How much does she know?' he asked suspiciously.

'There's nothing *to* know,' I teased. 'You told me yourself, it's just a box of fine old tobacco, nothing more.'

'I'll be waiting for you then,' he said, putting the phone down.

'Good girl!' Amelia cried rushing over to give me a lovely kiss on the lips. 'He just didn't know what to do or say.'

'Well, auntie,' I smiled, 'if I was a little bit devious then it's only because I have had an excellent teacher.' We both laughed at that, then I went up to my room to dress for my trip across the mountains.

I looked at Amelia as she drove; rosy lips, slightly pouted, eyes hidden behind dark glasses, long hair swept back. She looked adorably sexy and I felt my love for her swelling inside me, beating with the same rhythm as my heart. We were both silent, and when I wasn't gazing at Amelia I enjoyed the countryside as we drove in the direction of Lake Wallen.

'Do you ski?' Amelia asked as we entered the picturesque village of Wildhaus, in view of the snow-capped peaks.

'No, I've never tried,' I said, looking in admiration at the figures zig-zagging down the slopes, the bright blues and pinks of their ski clothes in contrast to the blue-white surface of the snow.

'You must get Rudi or Erich to teach you,' she smiled, 'they're both excellent skiers. They teach all the girls at the school, though most of them are pretty good already when they arrive.'

'I'd like that.'

'And you should try making love in the snow too,' she added, 'it really is quite an experience.'

'A quick one I would hope.' I laughed at the thought of rolling around naked in the freezing cold.

Russell was waiting for us in the lobby of his hotel, pacing up and down impatiently, wearing a distracted look on his face. He greeted us without a smile, his eyes searching for just one thing.

'It's in my handbag,' I explained, allaying his fears.

'Have you opened the box?' he asked expressionlessly.

'Yes,' I told him.

He waited for me to say more but I smiled, rather enjoying my new role as tormentor in chief. It was revenge of sorts, revenge for the way he had used me and for the worry he had caused us.

'Shall we go up to your room?' Amelia suggested, her formal manner perfect for the occasion.

'Yes, of course,' Russell agreed, making way for us to go to the elevator.

'I'll see you in twenty minutes then,' I said to her, opening my bag and handing the prized box to her.

'What are you talking about?' Russell demanded suspiciously. For a moment I thought his anger was going to explode, but he controlled himself, aware of the people around us.

'I would just like a few words alone with you,' Amelia explained, taking her sunglasses off and looking directly into his eyes. She smiled slowly, coquettishly, and he followed suit, the expression on his face becoming more relaxed, more like the Russell who had seduced me at the airport.

'As you wish, dear lady,' he smiled, oozing charm and sophistication once more. It made me shudder to see the way he could turn the charm on and off at will, so convincing and yet so very false.

'I'll be up to see you shortly,' I said, kissing Amelia tenderly. There was no way that she would allow herself to be seduced by a shallow trickster but for a moment I doubted her and fear gripped at my heart. I watched them go, he taking her by the elbow and leading her to the elevator, whispering to her softly so that she had to lean closer to him to listen, closer to his bewitching blue eyes.

I found the bar and ordered myself a glass of white wine, noting the time by the clock in the church across from the hotel. Not for the first time I found myself reflecting on my life and on the way that things invariably went wrong. Was it something about me that attracted trouble? My mood was already turning bitter, much as I had tried to be optimistic about my new life.

'You are English?' a voice asked, I looked up and found the hotel manageress standing beside me. She was dressed in a sombre blue skirt and top, her golden hair pinned in a tight bun, somehow making her look cold and severe. Only her eyes gave her away, eyes that sparkled brilliantly, hinting that underneath the staid exterior she was wild and incredibly sexy.

'Yes, and you are Swiss,' I grinned, licking my lips as I remembered her frigging herself to orgasm with the banana while she watched Russell and I make love.

'Alone today?' she asked.

'For the moment,' I told her, my eyes meeting hers then looking down coquettishly.

'My name is Erika. Do you like my hotel?'

'And I'm Melissa. To be honest, Erika, I've only really seen the one room,' I hinted, recognising the excitement in her voice.

'Then you must allow me to show you another,' she insisted, taking my hand in hers.

We walked out of the bar arm in arm, as if old friends. In a sense I felt that I already knew more about her than I did of many of my real friends. The barman nodded as we walked out and I wondered whether he knew what his boss did to amuse herself during the quiet afternoons when business was slow.

We engaged in polite chit-chat as she escorted me to a room on the first floor, both of us pretending that all we were interested in was the hotel. I half-hoped that she would show me to the room opposite Russell's, so that I could stand on the balcony to see what he and Amelia were up to. But instead Erika escorted me to a room on another floor. She opened the door and let me go in, brushing against her as I did so.

'Do you often bring people up to show them empty rooms?' I asked, walking straight through the room and out onto the balcony.

'Only pretty young English girls,' she teased.

I turned to her, saw her letting her long blonde hair fall over her shoulders, shaking it free from the austere bun that added a dozen years to her age. Her blue eyes were pencilled and her eyelashes were painted with mascara, so that her eyes seemed at once to be clear blue and yet dark. 'Why do you keep your hair up? You look so much lovelier like this,' I told her, brushing my fingers through her luxuriant locks.

'My husband prefers it like that.'

'Perhaps he's jealous,' I suggested. 'Perhaps he thinks that you would be irresistible if your hair was left free?'

'Do you find me irresistible?' she whispered, her pretty lips only inches from mine, her warm breath caressing my lips as she spoke. My reply was to kiss her softly, to touch my lips against hers, while at the same time my hand stroked her belly.

'Will you do to me what I saw you do yesterday?' I asked, looking round for the basket of fruit on the table. She took my hands and pulled me back into the room, suddenly quiet, her breathing hard and fast. I sat on the bed, my heart pounding.

She began to undress, very slowly, unbuttoning her skirt and letting it fall to the ground, a neat bundle around her ankles. Her top came off next and she undid each button slowly, increasing the tension while I watched her. She wore stockings, suspenders, black lacy panties and a black basque, a vision of loveliness that had me growing moist between my thighs.

'Am I still irresistible?' she asked, standing before me, looking at herself critically.

'Even more irresistible,' I cried, leaping up to take her in my arms. Her mouth was electric, we kissed for an age, our tongues searching, touching, licking. She undressed me quickly, pulling off my clothes in a sudden lustful frenzy. Her hands were on my breasts, her fingers pinching my nipples so that I cried out. My sex was burning, aching for her fingers to touch that jewel of passion that would drive me mad with pleasure.

We fell on the bed, my mouth still glued to hers. I felt dizzy as she sucked in my breath and arousing me with her fingers at the same time. I moved a hand between her thighs, over the sheer filmy stockings onto warm bare flesh. Her black panties were wet and I pulled the material to one side and slipped a finger into that lovely well of desire. I felt her spasm, her body pressing against mine, and I knew that she was already close to peaking.

'Let me kiss your sex,' she pleaded, releasing my nipples and sitting up. I lay back and parted my thighs, feeling a silver nectar sliding down between my crack. Very gently she parted my pussy lips with her fingers and

I watched her gazing adoringly at my open sex. She licked her lips slowly, running the tip of the tongue enticingly around her open mouth.

'Suck me . . . suck me . . .' I implored her, opening myself further, impatient to feel her tongue tickling my clit.

She bent down between my legs, her breath kissed the inside of my thigh, and then I felt the top of her tongue enter me. She licked me slowly, tracing an unknown pattern in the mouth of my sex, and then she went into me. I struggled hard to control myself but my sighs of pleasure were impossible to hold back. I wrapped my thighs around her and pulled her closer, lifting my bottom up to meet the darting attacks of her tongue, as soft and sweet as a feather touch. She sucked me expertly, built up the sensations to a peak that had me screaming, then snapped her luscious lips around the aching bud inside my sex. I creamed all over her mouth in waves of pearly juice which she lapped up greedily.

I released her, opening my thighs and stretching back against the bed languidly. How lovely to climax under the tongue of an attractive woman, to know that your thrills of pleasure are appreciated by her the way they could never be by a man. We kissed and I thrilled to the taste of myself on her lips.

'Let me kiss you too,' I said, sitting up, eyeing her greedily. Her skin looked virginally pale against her dark lingerie, nipples partly obscured by the lace, long legs wrapped in silk stockings.

'Not yet, my English rose,' she said, kissing me tenderly

on the mouth. 'Close your eyes. I have something for you.'

I did as I was told, sitting up naked in bed, closing my eyes tightly and not daring to peek. I heard her skip away and then she was near me again. 'Can I look now?' I asked excitedly.

'Not yet,' she laughed, putting a hand over my eyes to stop me looking.

I cried out, a little alarmed, and then I fell into her welcoming arms. A cold tongue had touched the inside of my thigh and then I knew. I opened myself, pulling my pussy lips apart with my fingers, opened myself for the cool banana flesh to slip into the lush warmth of my cunt. I kissed her on the mouth, grateful for the pleasure that she was giving me, happy to be sharing my body with her.

She pushed the fruit deep into me, let it rest for a moment and then began to draw it out. She moved slowly, out and then in again. I could feel my sex-honey lubricating the path, smothering the firm flesh with a sexy coating. It felt divine, pressing firmly against the walls of my sex, rubbing tendrils of erotic sensation through my body, from my quim right through to my tender nipples.

'It's good, yes?' she wanted to know, whispering in my ear as if it were a great secret that she was sharing.

'Yes, lovely,' I admitted, closing my eyes. I moved my hand between her thighs and found my second surprise. Her lovely pussy was already full, the familiar cool touch of a banana meeting my fingers. I laughed joyfully and she laughed too, hugging me close to her.

Together we began to frig each other, with the same rhythm, in the same way. When I sighed with pleasure I heard it echoed on her tongue, when she cried I felt the ecstasy flare up in my sex. The sensual lyricism of it all added another dimension, an erotic extra that heightened the pleasure. The rhythm was growing faster and more urgent, our mingled cries louder. My body was pierced with sudden surges of blissful energy and I knew that Erika felt the same.

We sat up on our knees and leaned against each other, breast to breast, my head on her shoulder and hers on mine. I had an arm around her back and one between her thighs, playing the phallic object in and out, faster and faster, my fingers dripping with her juices. We were a mirror image and when I arched my back and cried out with the force of orgasm, Erika did the same.

I fell back on the bed, the banana still protruding like a little penis from the soft mossy hair of my sex. Erika kissed my toes, then my knee, a chaste kiss on the sex, a lick of a nipple and then her mouth was on mine. Our gaze met, locked together, and I saw the pleasure she had experienced shining like a light in her eyes.

'Now we must finish, my English rose,' she whispered. She moved up over me, and I looked up and stared at the beautiful image of the fruit pressed deep into her pussy. She bent down and arched her back so that her lovely round bottom was offered to me. I lifted my head and brought my trembling lips to the sensitive lips of her sex. Reverently I kissed the tight little bud between her rear cheeks, just flicking my tongue over her anal hole so that she sighed joyfully. Then I lapped at the dewdrops of her come, at the sweet nectar laced with the taste of the banana. I opened my mouth and sucked the banana from her cunt, eating the fruit as it slipped from her folds wet with her sex-cream.

I swallowed it all and then I sat up on hands and knees, my posterior sticking out seductively. She sucked the banana from my pussy and the feel of it was so good that I climaxed again, my juices sliding down the length of my thigh so that Erika had to chase every last drop with her tongue.

Erika used her pass key to let me into Russell's room. I was late but I knew that they were waiting for me so had no qualms about entering without knocking first. By the time I was inside it was too late to change my mind.

I heard Amelia's voice, a coaxing whisper too low for me to make out any words but I recognised the tone well enough. Russell's murmured reply was also indistinct. It was obvious that I had caught them during an intimate moment. Normally I would have turned away, retraced my steps and pretended that nothing had ever happened, but not this time. I crept forward quietly, my voyeuristic instincts aroused to the full.

Amelia and Russell, both of them naked, were on the bed. He was on his knees facing her, his eyes closed and his face a picture of ecstasy. My darling aunt had her back to me but I could see that she was enjoying his prick in her mouth, her head bobbing up and down, her hair shimmering in the sunlight which streamed through the open windows. Her back was long and straight, flawlessly smooth, swelling into a gorgeous *derrière*, her bottom cheeks round and slightly parted so that I could glimpse the mat of hair between her thighs.

'Just relax, darling . . .' Amelia whispered, releasing his prick for a moment to look into his half-closed eyes. Russell moved his lips, mouthed something, but no sound emerged, as if a great wind had blown his words away. His face was dappled with droplets of perspiration on his lips and forehead, tiny jewels of sweat that caught the light.

I moved further into the room, intrigued by what I was seeing. What was it that so filled Russell with pleasure that it left him speechless? Amelia took his prick into her mouth again, her lips closing tightly around the purple-headed dome. I saw that she was stroking him with one hand, massaging his long hard shaft as she sucked it, playing on it a symphony of fingers and lips and tongue, guaranteed to make any man moan ecstatically. I knew she was an excellent fellatrice and she had Russell in agonies of heightened pleasure. He kept opening and closing his mouth, wordlessly, as if the sound could not escape.

'Relax, darling . . .' Amelia repeated and I saw a sharp movement of her hand. Russell winced visibly, his face screwing up with a look of pain that subsided into pure pleasure.

I moved closer, aware now that Amelia was using both her hands, that she was doing more than sucking

Russell's lovely shaft. I stopped by the chest of drawers, on the opposite side of the room. Glancing down I saw the bankers' drafts, an unprepossessing pile of paper worth an absolute fortune. At that moment I wanted to pick them up rip them to shreds, to tear up the cause of all our anxieties. I remember wishing that life could be so simple, that a dramatic gesture like that could rid us of our troubles.

Russell moaned deliriously, I looked up and saw something glinting in the sun, something between his thighs. 'Auntie!' I cried, putting my hand to my mouth, utterly shocked.

Amelia turned to me and smiled indulgently, looking very happy indeed, as if she expected to see me there and had been waiting for just this moment. At the same instant Russell's face blazed red with shame and he turned away from me. I looked down and saw the long silver cigar tube being pushed into his rear hole.

'I was just showing Russell what our girls had been using the tube for,' Amelia explained proudly.

Russell moaned, a guilty moan of pleasure. His prick was throbbing, glistening with spit where Amelia had been mouthing him. I moved closer to him and stroked his cock, delighting in the feel of it under my fingers. Amelia pulled away, making space for me to sit in front of him. He was near orgasm, his glans dripping droplets of pre-come that I swallowed eagerly. I could feel Amelia frigging him in the rear, sliding the tube in and out slowly, deep into his rear hole. He moaned with every stroke, his prick jerking deeper into my mouth, his body

'Just talking with the hotel manageress,' I explained, looking innocently at the Alpine scenery.

'Just talking?' she laughed sceptically.

'Perhaps more than just talking,' I admitted with a short laugh. 'I was doing my bit for Anglo-Swiss relations.'

'Were you now,' she laughed, stroking my leg, her hand barely touching my skin but still making my heart beat just that little bit faster.

My blouse was open at the top and my breasts were bare. I leaned forward coquettishly, wanting her to see the deep cleavage and the soft untanned skin at the slope of my bust. 'Yes,' I drawled sexily, winning a glance from Amelia, her eyes surely scanning my breasts. 'She was awfully nice too and very friendly,' I added. 'What happened with you and Russell? I've never seen anyone so dumbfounded after a sexual encounter before.'

'We reached an agreement,' Amelia said after a pause.

It was the sort of enigmatic reply that was guaranteed to arouse my curiosity. 'What sort of agreement?'

'A financial one,' she said cagily.

'Oh stop it! Tell me what happened,' I begged her, unable to stand the tension.

'I negotiated a fee for our services. You acted as a courier, you brought the documents into the country and then looked after them for a few days. I think all that deserves a fee, don't you?'

'Yes but what if . . .' I spluttered, thinking of all the possible sources of the money – drugs, smuggling, crime.

'Don't worry,' Amelia said calmly. 'I did a little

checking up on our Mr Cross. The money was smuggled out of one country in contravention of local currency laws. It was gained quite legally so we don't have to worry too much. This is the sort of thing that Switzerland is famous for.'

'But how did you know? How did you find out?'

'It just so happens that a number of very senior Swiss policemen have daughters at our school. And of course they are very grateful to me . . .'

'You clever old thing,' I laughed happily, glad that it had all ended so well. 'And what about the other thing?'

'What other thing?'

'The little game with the cigar tube,' I reminded her.

She laughed, her lips parted, head thrown back, hair caught by the breeze. 'I just wanted to teach Russell a lesson. It took him quite by surprise, I can tell you.'

'I'm sure it did,' I agreed, trying to imagine the look of horror dawning on his face.

'He tried to push my hand away at first, but once I started it seemed to grow on him. In the end he was enjoying every confusing second of it.'

'I could see that alright. His prick was as hard as stone in my mouth. Do you think we'll ever see him again?' I asked, my tone serious again. Now that it had ended I never wanted to set eyes on him. The whole episode had soured my first few days in Switzerland and I would never forgive him for that. Even now, when I look back on it, I cannot find it in myself to forgive and forget, though I cannot deny the pleasures that we shared together.

'I don't think so, darling,' Amelia assured me, giving

my thigh a gentle squeeze, my cleavage mirrored in her dark glasses as she looked at me. My pussy was wet and with every touch of her fingers I felt the fire spreading through me. I fervently wished that it was Rudi driving us home because, at that moment, when I was fired up with passion, I felt a great desire to seduce my aunt no matter what.

'Good,' I said, trying to put the lascivious thoughts from my mind, 'now I can get on with starting my new life.' Amelia smiled and I felt myself go weak at the knees. Did she feel the same way about me? How I longed for her to make love to me, to recreate that first time when I had melted in her arms, when my body had hummed with pure sexual pleasure.

7

In retrospect, the affair with Russell was an annoyance but once it was over I remember the feeling of optimism coming to the fore once more. I chided myself for being so negative, for letting it get me down when I had so much to look forward to. We learn from experience and yet we never welcome it, we just wish that things were naturally right instead of trying to set them right ourselves. There is only one future, the one that happens, and yet the present always seems so fraught. I promised myself then that I was never going to let myself down again, that I was going to be positive and to hell with the consequences. Easy promises to make but I remember that those few simple words felt like a revelation, as if my life had finally changed direction – for the better.

I had a day to settle down before the first of the new girls started and, to tell the truth, I didn't know who was going to be more nervous, the new girl or myself. Amelia told me a little about her, though I remember thinking that she was being a little cagey. If she was, I put it down to her not wanting to get in my way too much. And that was just how I wanted it. I wanted room to develop and if

I made mistakes I wanted the room to rectify them on my own.

Isabella Bertolusci was the only daughter of wealthy Milanese parents but the family now lived in Paris. She had been at a private college and had fancied a change. She suffered a little from shyness. I was unable to get anything else out of Amelia, she just smiled and told me to let my instincts guide me. My instincts told me that something was not quite right but I didn't push it.

On the day that Isabella was due to arrive I woke up before dawn, the excitement and nerves churning over inside me. The sun had only just clipped the horizon, the first rays of dawn still weak in the crisp mountain air. Charlotte was asleep beside me, curled up into a tight ball of loveliness, her eyes closed and lips pursed, breathing soft and deep in a rhythm that had matched my own. I kissed her gently on the cheek, brushing her frizzy hair from her face. She looked delightfully innocent, an incendiary kind of innocence that ignited fires in everyone that sets eyes on her.

I smiled to myself, it would be too bad of me to wake her so early and have her suck my pussy no matter how much I longed for it. I wrapped her tightly in the coverlet and slipped out of bed, knowing full well that if I stayed a moment longer my fingers would soon find their way between her dusky thighs.

The sun rising between the mountains always made me feel so peaceful, the shafts of light spearing the darkness as the colour of the mountains shimmered and changed moment by moment. Every morning was different, every sunrise unique and spectacular. I watched the sun clear the horizon, shivering in the cool morning air but certain that it was going to be a brilliant day.

I pulled on a robe and slipped out of the room, the smell of coffee rising up through the house tempting me. I was careful not to break the silence, enjoying that as much as anything else. I crept downstairs and into the kitchen, stopping at the door for a moment to listen for voices. Apart from the bubbling of the coffee machine, I heard nothing so I went in, my robe hanging loose, my breasts bare.

'Hello . . . it's Pierre, isn't it?' I smiled, happily surprised to find myself face to face with one of the male members of staff. I had only met Pierre once before and, apart from the fact that he was French, I knew nothing else about him.

'Good morning, Miss Melissa,' he said, turning to face me. He was dressed in jeans and a loose cotton shirt open to the waist, revealing a smooth chest apart from dark rings of hair around the nipples. I suddenly realised that he was studying my bare chest as intently as I was studying his.

'That coffee smells good,' I commented, leaning against the worktop, my robe falling open further. His eyes swivelled from my breasts to my face.

'Yes,' he agreed, 'it does smell good. You are awake early – is it an early start or a late finish?'

I laughed. 'An early start. And you?'

'A late finish. Monique and I have been working all night.'

125

'Oh yes?' I laughed, easily able to imagine the sort of things they had been getting up to.

'No, it's not like that,' he smiled. 'I mean real work.'

'What sort of work?' I asked dubiously, knowing that in that situation I would have mixed it with a little play.

'Computer work. We needed to connect one of our computers with a network in New York. Miss Amelia is very eager that we keep up with all the technology. We can link up with the most up-to-date financial systems in the world,' he explained proudly.

'Is it really that important?'

He looked slightly offended by my question, as if I had cast doubts on the value of what he'd been doing all night. 'Very important,' he said. 'It's what makes this institution different. It's part of Miss Amelia's vision.'

'But I thought this was what made this place different?' I said, cupping my breasts, covering the nipples coyly with my fingers.

'Of course, that too,' he smiled. 'But not just that. The mind needs as much exercise as the body. But you are right, it is the combination . . .'

I was feeling very horny. I had done my good deed for the day and let Charlotte get some sleep but my body worked to its own rhythms. I squeezed my breasts, pressing my nipples hard so that they began to throb delightfully. 'Are you so very tired?' I asked him playfully, watching the bulge in his jeans get bigger.

'Yes, very tired indeed,' he complained, unbuttoning the top button on his jeans.

'Let me perk you up, you poor thing,' I whispered,

pulling the cord from my robe and letting it fall open completely. His hands were on my breasts as our lips touched, his tongue between my teeth. The feel of his fingers tweaking my nipples soon had the juices oozing from my hot pussy.

He slid the robe from my shoulders and let it fall to the floor. I was naked, the early morning rays of light warming my skin. I smiled, he had stepped back and was admiring my body, his greedy eyes tracing a path from my toes, up my long silky legs to the triangle of fine hair between my thighs to my erect nipples and to my face. I looked back at him with fire in my eyes.

He must have read my mind for he pulled his clothes off, the shirt joining my robe on the floor. His body was smooth, sinewy, with a wide chest and a smooth flat belly. His prick was long and thick. Amelia had selected her young men with a connoisseur's eye, each of them was good enough to eat.

'I think you've perked me up already,' he said, looking down at the stiffness poking out from his abdomen.

'I need to check,' I said, taking his prick in my hand, enveloping the silky hardness in the warmth of my fingers. The feel of a firm cock is special – soft skin pulled tightly over the hardness, the glans as smooth as silk, the pulse throbbing like a heartbeat . . . And Pierre's cock felt absolutely divine. I rubbed my fingers up and down slowly, teasing him, making it stand harder.

We kissed again and this time his hands sought the heat between my legs. I wrapped my leg around him, lifting and opening myself, enjoying the feel of his nakedness on mine. His fingers rubbed between my pussy lips, stimulating the oozing flow of pussy cream. I sighed, brushed my nipples against his chest, my mouth sucking at his lips again.

'Let me suck you,' I whispered, driven mad by the feel of his hardness in my hand and pressing into my belly.

'No, I want to feel you properly,' he whispered hotly.

'That's not fair,' I sulked, stroking his prick harder, wanting the lovely thing deep in my mouth, rubbing the inside of my cheek, my tongue playing with the slit pouring out its juices.

He lifted me higher so that both my legs were wrapped around him. I put my arms around his shoulders and held on tight, knowing that my pussy was open and ready for fucking. He supported me by sliding his hands under my bottom and lifting me higher, his prick nestling against the slippery warmth of my cunny lips without going in.

'Hey!' I cried, surprised and disappointed that he hadn't entered me yet. He was playing with me, rubbing me against his hardness, maddening me with sensation, building the pleasure to a peak without giving me the ultimate thrill. His hands pulled my backside apart, opening me still further. His fingers were pressing against the smoothness of my rear cheeks, he was manoeuvring me, playing with me.

Suddenly he seemed to shift me forward and his hands were under my sex, a finger placed up against my rear hole. He put his mouth over mine and then began to press his finger into me. My sighs were smothered, my words sucked into his mouth in a passionate kiss. His finger was playing with my anal hole, pressing in a little way, sending spasms of pleasure pulsing through me, lightning strokes of purest bliss. It was the first time I'd ever been fingered in the rear and the sensation was unbelievable.

'Shall I stop now?' he whispered, smiling wickedly.

'Don't you dare . . .' I sighed, wriggling my backside so that his finger penetrated further.

'You like this?' he asked innocently, beginning to frig me in the behind. Did I like it? I was out of my mind with desire, it felt so good. I answered by kissing him furiously on the mouth, my lips burning into his. He began to move rhythmically, rubbing his prick against my dripping pussy while finger-fucking me in the rear. The pleasure was growing in intensity, and when at last he forced his prick into my sex I screamed to a rapturous orgasm.

He carried me to the table, and set me down on the edge while I caught my breath. I looked down at his glistening prick and felt the desire surge through me again. I fell on my knees and took that lovely piece of masculine flesh between my lips, sucking hard, swallowing the taste of my sex so that I could get down to the taste of him. I licked under the glans, wanking him with my fingers at the same time. It was as if I had never had a prick before, as if I were sucking a man for the first time. I held his tool by the base, pulled it towards me and licked it like a candy, my tongue tracing the thick vein running along its pulsating length.

I knew he was close to orgasm, I felt him struggling to hold back. Quickly I stood up, turned and leaned across the table, parting my thighs at the same time. He grabbed me by the waist and drove into the moistness of my cunny. The thrill of having him drive into me made me come again, arching my back, lifting my chest from the table so that the nipples dangled free of the cool pine surface.

He fucked me with a wild passionate rhythm, his ardour making me sigh and moan deliriously. I climaxed again, my whole being shaking with tremors of delight. My nipples were hard and red, rubbing delightfully against the polished table, adding more sensations to the rousing wave of pleasure.

Pierre cried out, then froze, his body moulded to mine. I felt his huge rod deluge my pussy with thick wads of cream, waves of it filling my sex as I was carried over the threshold of pleasure too. As I sighed, the door opened and for an instant my mind flashed back to the day I had been caught with two men by Lady Agatha. Then Charlotte walked in, looking as if she had just seen the most beautiful thing in the world.

'Let me cleanse you, madame,' Charlotte cried excitedly, kissing my rosy nipples as I turned to her. Pierre was leaning against the table, his prick dripping pearls of thick cream mixed with the juice of my pussy nectar.

I leaned back against the table too, opening my thighs as Charlotte knelt down before me. Her eyes were wide, admiring my freshly fucked sex, red and wet, the folds of skin glistening invitingly. I watched her stick out her pink tongue and lap through the mat of wet hair before going into me. I closed my eyes, the feel of her hot tongue applied so expertly to my throbbing little clit made me swoon. She licked me, building me to orgasm so that my juices would mingle with Pierre's and slip into her hot little mouth.

Pierre kissed me, already his prick was building to erection again and I knew that he and Charlotte wouldn't be happy until we all three climaxed together.

There could be no greater contrast between mother and daughter than that of Isabella and her mother, Maria. I had entered Amelia's office after the formal interview had finished, and as soon as I set eyes on them I knew that this difference between mother and daughter was part of the problem.

Maria was stunningly elegant, wearing a clinging lace dress, her white skin obscured by the fine dark mesh, her breasts high and taut, the nipples dark disks clearly visible under the tight lace. She was petite with a heart-shaped face and delicate features, her eyebrows finely delineated over dark eyes, her mouth small with full lips. When she held out a hand I didn't know whether to shake it or fall to my knees and kiss it. She had the kind of beauty that is pure and yet remote, creating a space around her, a reserve that you were afraid to breach.

In startling contrast, Isabella was dressed in a heavy woollen jumper and a long loose skirt, clothes that were deliberately dour and baggy, covering her from head to foot. Her long curly hair was tied loosely at the back, wisps of it flying loose, adding to the overall look of untidiness. Her face was plain with no sign of lip gloss or pencil about the eyes, and she wore a hideous pair of glasses, the sort that were designed to keep people away. It was plain that she was deliberately dressing in opposition to her stylish mother, trying to set herself as far apart as possible. Clearly, she was succeeding.

'This is Melissa,' Amelia said as I shook hands with Maria. 'She will be looking after Isabella while she settles in.'

'I'm looking forward to it very much,' I said, unable to keep my eyes from Maria. I was close enough to breathe her perfume, Paloma Picasso or something from *la maison Patou*.

'I'm sure Isabella is looking forward to it too,' Amelia said, flashing me a dirty look and steering me towards Isabella.

'I'm sure we'll get on like a house on fire,' I said, 'I'm still very new here myself. We can explore the place together,' I suggested, smiling hopefully.

'Yes,' Isabella mumbled, staring at the ground rather than look me in the eye.

'There have been some problems,' Maria began to explain, her voice soft and low, almost a whisper, and as alluring as her looks. 'Isabella had some bad experiences at her last college . . .'

'Mother!' Isabella snapped, looking up angrily.

'I was just going to explain to Miss Melissa . . .' Maria said, chastened by her daughter's angry rebuke.

'Well, just don't,' Isabella warned. 'I don't want her to know. I don't want anyone to know. It's nothing to do with you, not any of you.'

'I think it's time I left,' Maria said, turning to look at me, her eyes filled with tears.

'Perhaps that's a good idea,' Amelia agreed, putting a consoling arm on her shoulder and leading her towards the door. Maria tried to kiss her daughter on the cheek but Isabella turned away sharply.

'Goodbye, Bella,' Maria said, turning to look back sadly. 'You will write or telephone, won't you?'

'Yes, yes!' Isabella hissed irritably.

'Goodbye, Maria,' I smiled, 'I'm sure that everything will be fine,' I lied, trying to hide my own anger. How dare Isabella treat her mother so badly? I was furious, my instinct was to give the girl a slap in the face and a good talking to, but I knew that that was the last thing the mother wanted.

'What shall I call you? Isabella? Bella? Isabel?' I asked calmly, turning to the sulking girl, looking down at her feet once more.

'Call me what you like,' she shrugged.

'Bella, I like that,' I told her, not rising to the bait. 'Come on, I'll show you to your room.'

She followed, a few paces behind me, dragging her feet along as if she were exhausted. Outside I heard the roar of a car and the squeal of tyres and guessed that Maria was off, leaving with Isabella's cruel words still ringing in her ears.

Isabella's room was strategically placed opposite my own, her cases had already been carried up and the room was warm and bright.

'Well? What do you think?'

'It's all right,' she shrugged, slumping down on the bed, hunching herself down, staring emptily at the ground again. She was playing to perfection the withdrawn and difficult adolescent role, a role I had played for myself years earlier.

'Where were you before?'

'At home,' she mumbled.

'And before that?'

'With my grandmother,' she mumbled, though this time I caught a sly smile that she couldn't quite conceal.

'And before that,' I repeated, sounding as bored as I felt.

'At some crappy girls' college near Paris. It was a dump.'

'Is that why you left?'

She looked up at me sharply. 'I don't think it's anything to do with you,' she said coldly, her grey eyes sparkling with defiance.

'If that's how you want it, Bella,' I shrugged.

'Yes, that is how I want it. And don't call me Bella. It's what she calls me and I hate it.'

'What do you want me to call you then?' I asked curtly. She was annoying me, which was the whole point I knew, but I couldn't help myself.

'What you like,' she repeated.

'Well, Bella, I'll let you get on with your unpacking,' I smiled, walking out of the room, glad to see her scowling.

I returned to Amelia's stately office, pondering the new arrival. I had wanted a challenge and a challenge was what I had before me. Isabella had already shown herself to be difficult and unruly. Her behaviour was carefully designed to provoke and to hurt. If that was how she had behaved at her last place then I wondered whether she had left of her own accord or whether she had been expelled. I thought about it for a moment and realised that there was no way she could have been expelled. For a girl in her frame of mind, expulsion was a victory of sorts and not a guilty secret. No, there had to be something else, something that she was ashamed of and didn't want her mother to talk about.

'Well, what do you think?' Amelia asked, a drink ready in her hand for me.

'I remember being like that once,' I sighed, taking the glass of sherry. 'It wasn't much fun, even though I was trying to be horrible to everyone else at the same time. I remember that the more I hurt people the more it seemed to hurt me.'

Amelia nodded. 'I remember that too. And do you remember how you snapped out of it?'

'Of course I do,' I whispered, blushing. 'But I was much younger than Isabella, only sixteen.'

'Do you think the same thing will work with her?'

I shook my head. 'No, there's something else here. Do you notice how she dresses and how she holds herself?'

'How could you not notice?'

'It's obviously a reaction against her mother's beauty. It's like she's chosen to rebel by dressing in opposition to her mother, hiding herself in those awful shapeless rags. And her posture, drawing herself in, turning her body into armour to keep us all out.'

'Well, Melissa darling,' Amelia said soberly, 'no one ever said your job was going to be easy.'

'What's the secret? What did Maria want to tell us?'

'I was hoping you'd find out and tell me,' Amelia laughed. 'Maria had promised not to tell. All I know is that Isabella had a rough time at her last college and asked to leave. She wasn't kicked out by any means, in fact the college did their best to keep her there but Isabella insisted on leaving.

'And we have no clues?'

'None.'

'Oh well, I guess I'll have to find out from her.'

'Though I imagine you'd prefer to find out from Maria herself,' Amelia said.

'I think it'd be worth the effort,' I agreed, smiling. Amelia was right, Maria had me licking my lips greedily. I could just imagine myself lapping her nipples, or on my knees sucking from her pussy, running my hands over those shapely thighs.

'Perhaps when all this is over,' Amelia suggested.

'Now, that's what I call an incentive!'

'Where is Isabella now?'

'Unpacking. I think I'll send Charlotte in to say hello, perhaps she views me as just another uncaring adult.'

'Good idea,' Amelia agreed.

'She was horrible,' sobbed Charlotte, crying on my shoulder, her tears falling down her cheeks onto my bare breasts.

'What did she do?' I asked soothingly, rubbing my

hand up and down Charlotte's silky thighs.

'She called me a spy, said I was only pretending to be friendly so that I could betray her,' Charlotte sniffed.

'And?'

'And she told me she would never be my friend, told me I was a lying cheat, a sneak . . .'

'It's okay, don't cry,' I whispered, ashamed to say that I was enjoying the trickle of her tears down the slope of my breasts, the warm jewels of liquid dripping softly from my hardening nipples.

'But it's not true,' Charlotte complained bitterly. 'I really did want to be her friend, I didn't just go there to pry.'

'I know that darling,' I consoled her, kissing her softly on the forehead. Her face was wet with tears, her lips quivering with emotion. Strong emotion is always sexy and this was no exception, I wanted to rip Charlotte's clothes off and make love to her, to suck the tears from her eyes and the juices from her quim.

'But why did she have to be so nasty? What have I ever done to her?' Charlotte asked, kissing me softly on the neck, her lips cool against my skin.

'Because she's angry about something and the only way she knows how to react is to lash out at the nearest available target,' I explained, a good deal more charitably than I actually felt but the last thing I wanted was two girls at each other's throat.

'But I haven't done anything . . .' Charlotte started to complain again but I took her chin in my hand and turned her mouth to mine. Her words died as our lips met. I felt her melt into my arms, the anger in her body turning into hot desire. Slowly I unbuttoned her blouse, letting it fall open.

I kissed her madly, on the lips, on the throat, on the shoulder, between her heavy round breasts. Her tears were tingling in my mouth, salty droplets that I lapped up lovingly. My hands were all over her, smoothing up and down her supple body, touching, exploring, teasing. She kissed me on the back as I licked her breasts, taking her dark nipples into my mouth one at a time, sucking hard so that she sighed and moaned softly. I spent an age just teasing her nipples, biting, sucking, licking them like little lollipops. Each ripe berry seemed to grow in my mouth, hardening like a baby penis as I played. She cried out, her whole body shook and I heard her sigh as the orgasm took her.

I kissed her on the mouth again, shifting her round so that she was lying on the bed beside me. Her thighs were slightly parted and when I brushed my fingers against her mound I felt the damp heat. I just touched a finger into her slit and thrilled to the sticky warmth. 'Not so fast,' I cautioned as she tried to open herself further, jerking up so that my finger went deeper.

Her hands were stroking my breasts, playing with my nipples while I toyed with her quim. The feel of her fingers lightly grazing the exquisitely sensitive peaks made me gasp for breath. We kept kissing on the mouth, our lips joining, forging together then parting for breath before joining once more. I dipped a finger into her well and brought it to my mouth, we looked at it, at the stickiness on the end, at the glistening musk from her sex. At the same instant we pressed our lips together, sharing the delicious dab of pussy cream.

The taste of her made me hungry for more. I pushed her back on the bed and parted her thighs so that her dark body was spread out before me, feminine, beautiful, *mine*. I showered her with kisses, my mouth worshipping her from the toes, to the ankle, to the finely turned calf, to the back of the knee to the thigh, to her sex. I kissed her reverently, almost chastely, on the mouth of her sex. She sighed deeply and opened herself to me, her sex wet and pink between the dark folds of skin and jet black curls of hair. I used the fingers of one hand to open her up, pulling apart the petals to see the nectar glistening within.

I lapped at her open pussy, my tongue traversing her sex with one slow lingering swoop. I felt her shiver, her body responding to the thousand blissful sensations of being worshipped. Her clitty was hard and I toyed with it playfully, making her moan. Her cries seemed to goad me, making me suck the hard clitty between my lips. I sucked and licked and bit, making her thrash wildly, lifting herself up to my mouth. She climaxed and my face was wet with her essence.

I was sorry for sending her to Isabella and causing her to be upset. I wanted to wipe away the memory and replace it with something good and loving. I sat back, licking my lips, still gazing in adoration of her red-hot pussy. A trickle of her juices was leaking from her, meandering slowly from her slit and down between her rear cleft. I watched, fascinated by the rivulet of pussy come, caressing her softly as it journeyed between her rear cheeks.

'Turn over, lovely,' I commanded, still greedy for her body.

She obeyed instantly, turning over onto her belly. Her back was flawlessly smooth, tapering to a slim waist and then opening at the hips. Her bottom was beautiful: pert round bottom cheeks, deep rear cleft, the dark hair of her pussy visible from the rear. I palmed her backside softly, enjoying the sensation of her under my fingers, wondering how on earth I was going to feel when the time came for Charlotte to leave.

I kissed her on the shoulder and she turned to me. 'Your face is wet,' she said, smilingly, her eyes no longer wet with tears but filled with joy. She put out her tongue and licked away the traces of her pussy cream from my mouth and lips.

'Now, lift up your beautiful *derrière*,' I told her, kissing her on the mouth.

She lifted her bottom up and I slipped a pillow under her belly, sitting behind her so that I could admire the view. I massaged her bottom softly, opening her behind gently and rhythmically, eyeing the rear bud and glimpsing the tears of pleasure weeping from her sex.

'Does this feel good?' I asked softly, sitting on her legs, pressing my wetness against her.

'*Oui, madame*, it feels lovely,' she sighed in her sing-song way.

'Not as lovely as this,' I said, parting her rear cheeks and gazing admiringly at her tightly puckered anal hole.

The oozing pussy cream had completed its journey, a little reservoir of juice glistening enticingly on the rear opening. It was irresistible, I bent down at the waist and scooped it into my mouth, my tongue pressing firmly into her arse-pussy. I shivered, it felt so sexy, so intensely erotic that I almost creamed myself.

I kissed her bumhole, a long hard kiss, my lips pressed between her beautiful bottom-cheeks, my tongue pressing into the tight sheath of muscle. She sighed and I felt her press her backside high, offering herself to me. I began to rub back and forth, moving my sex against the calves of her legs. I was wet and smearing her also, my clitty pressing against the slippery skin. At the same time I was feasting on her rear, sucking and tickling, entering her from behind.

We moved like animals, with an urgency and passion that knew no bounds. Her legs were soaking, wet with my sex cream, the honey coating the smooth dark skin of her legs. She was moaning, lifting herself, arching her back impossibly so that I could suck her deeper. My mouth was glued to her anal hole and I had never sucked anything so beautifully tight before. She screamed, her cries torn from her throat by an intense orgasm that made her body freeze into position. Her cry triggered my own climax. I felt as if I were falling through space, without body, without soul. I was nothing but pure blissful sensation.

8

That first week with Isabella was a trial. She was wilful,
uncooperative, withdrawn. All our efforts to coax her to
life were met with unbridled hostility and the situation
showed no signs of improving. Relations with the other
girls began badly and grew worse and, of course, the
worse things became the more she felt justified in her
own unreasonable conduct.

If her attitude towards other females was bad, her
behaviour towards the males was utterly inexplicable.
She avoided any contact with them completely, to the
extent that she would lock her bedroom door every evening
just in case Rudi or any of the others tried to drop by. I
suppose I might have been partially at fault here – on the
second day I had sent Rudi into her room early in the
morning, hoping that the sight of a nearly naked male
would arouse something other than hostility. How wrong
I was. She screamed at the top of her lungs and had us all
running, thinking something terrible had happened. We
found her curled up in the corner of the bed, screaming
abuse at poor bewildered Rudi.

Amelia didn't say anything. The problem was mine to
deal with, though I was aware that the situation had an

unsettling effect on all of us. Suzanne too was discreetly silent about the problem, though I was sure her patience was wearing pretty thin. It would have been easy for me to turn to the two of them for advice, but I could be as stubborn as anybody and I wanted to solve the problem without my aunt or Suzanne. I was convinced that doing a good job with Isabella was going to make my reputation at the finishing school.

I had one particularly fruitless session with her, trying to persuade her to join one of the skiing classes setting out for Wildhaus. I tried every trick in the book, from outright pleading to subtle threats to promises of treats to come. Nothing worked, she stood by the window looking down, adamantly refusing to have anything to do with skiing, with the school or with me. I asked her if she wanted to go home but, much to my relief, all she did was shrug her shoulders and turn away.

'Any luck?' Amelia asked, catching me leaving Isabella's room.

I shook my head, feeling that I had failed. 'She doesn't want to leave but she doesn't want anything to do with anyone else.'

'She can't just vegetate in her room. What are you going to do?'

'If I don't make any progress soon I'm going to have to talk to Maria. We need to have some idea of what's at the root of this problem, otherwise we're working in the dark.'

Amelia paused, her face flickered with doubt. 'I'd

rather you didn't talk to Maria without talking to me first,' she said slowly.

'You think it's an admission of failure?'

'Isn't it?' she asked reasonably.

'I suppose so,' I admitted. It was true, we were admitting to failure in a sense. But it would have been an even bigger failure just to give up.

'Look,' Amelia suggested helpfully, 'why don't you just go for a walk? Have you been up into the forest yet? It's a great place to just get away from it all and to sit and think. Try it, you never know . . .'

'That sounds like an excellent idea,' I said. She gave me a quick hug and then continued on her way.

I ran up to my room and pulled on a quilted jacket and a pair of rough jeans. The sun was still up and the day was pleasantly warm, the breeze hardly stirring. I looked out of my window and saw that there were paths leading from the school grounds up into the nearby hills, thickly wooded but not too high. My climbing skills were nonexistent and hill walking had never been my idea of physical exercise but a good long walk was all I was after.

I picked a path at random and headed into the forest, breathing in the pure mountain air and already feeling better for it. The area was fairly rocky but the paths up into the hills were clearly marked, with spindly wooden handrails to hold onto and suitably placed benches, damp and mossy, set aside to rest on. I didn't want to rest, I climbed higher and higher, suddenly aware of the pure silence and clear air. The trees seemed to be growing out of pure rock, emerging at all angles, the branches mingling together as if to support each other. The rocky ground was muddy in places, slippery at times, the rock sheared into large geometric slabs.

I stopped once and turned to look down at the school, at the chalet buildings and the main house, at the lakes not too far away and, as always, the panoramic view of the mountains. The school looked so small it was hard to believe that anything could possibly be wrong with the world. The silence felt strange, almost unnatural. When I looked up into the sky the clouds seemed to sweep past, turning and swirling as they traversed the crystalline sky.

Why was Isabella being so difficult? Wasn't this a glorious day? Wasn't this a lovely place? Why couldn't she just enjoy it? The questions kept going through my mind but now it was without emotion, without that passionate feeling of commitment that can impede clear thought. I leaned back against a tree and gazed out at the world, wondering dispassionately about Isabella Bertolusci and her adorable mother, Maria. It couldn't be easy, being the daughter of a mother so glamorous and so attractive, a mother who looked like an older prettier sister and not a mother.

That had to be part of the problem. I was sure Maria wasn't aware of it, she was simply a beautiful woman and the idea that she was overshadowing her daughter had probably never occurred to her. I remembered walking into the room and seeing the two of them. I was instantly drawn to Maria, even though I knew that it was Isabella I should be attending to. Perhaps that was why Isabella didn't want to go home, why she preferred to remain miserable with us rather than return to the warmth of the family home.

I started to make my way back down when I heard a soft humming carried by the breeze, someone was singing softly close by. I stopped and listened, not sure where the sound was coming from, though I was certain that the voice was vaguely familiar. It seemed to originate from an area a little below me, an area where the trees were especially close. I waited, certain that the sound was getting nearer, I could even make out the tune, a French love song that many of the girls used to sing.

'Monique!' I cried, happy to see her emerging from the trees. She looked as surprised to see me as I had been to hear her.

'Melissa, what are you doing up here?' she exclaimed.

'I was going to ask you the same question.'

'I often come up here, it's so very relaxing,' she explained, putting her arm in mine. 'Will you join me for a walk?'

'Of course I will. You're not going skiing with the others?'

'The girls don't want me getting in their way,' she laughed. 'They'll be well looked after by Alex and Pierre. What about you? Do you ski?'

'I tried once but I ended up on my backside too many times.

'You should get the boys to teach you, they are very good. And if you do fall down who better to pick you up again?'

We walked back the way I had come, chatting amiably, admiring the view. She pointed out the different lakes and the highest peaks, telling me a little about the area. I listened without really concentrating on what she was saying but enjoying the sound of her voice. I liked the way she kept brushing her curls away from her face and her happy smile made such a change from Isabella's frosty face.

'What is it, Melissa?'

'Pardon? Sorry, Monique,' I apologised, 'I was miles away.'

'It's the Bertolusci girl, isn't it?' she guessed.

'I just don't know what to do, she won't let me or anyone else get close to her. I want to help, but she won't let me.'

'Maybe you are trying too hard,' she suggested helpfully.

I turned to here and looked into her soft round face. She was concerned for me and I was glad. 'If only it were that easy,' I sighed. 'I tried leaving her alone for a couple of days but it made no difference. It's not healthy for a girl that age to lock herself away like that.'

'That's true,' Monique agreed, 'but it is also not healthy for you to worry so much about it. Relax, you'll work it out, I'm sure you will.'

'Are you really so sure?'

She pulled me close and kissed me softly on the mouth, her generous lips pressed against my own. I was taken by surprise, I opened my lips, let her tongue go deep into my mouth. We kissed like lovers under the trees, the sun trickling through the canopy, dappling us with patterns of light and dark.

'Come on, I'll show you something,' Monique said excitedly, releasing me then pulling me by the hand. I allowed myself to be dragged along, wishing that she hadn't stopped. My heart was pounding and I was breathing fast, aroused by her passionate kisses.

She led me away from the path, through the thickest part of the forest, ducking under branches and fighting through the undergrowth. Her enthusiasm was not shared on my part but I followed silently, hoping that she would turn and kiss me once more.

'Just through here,' she said breathlessly, pointing to an impenetrable tangle of roots and branches, the ground a cold dark slurry of mud and rock.

'What is it?' I muttered, stepping very carefully in Monique's tracks, certain that I was going to end up flat on my face in the mud. I kept my eyes firmly on my footing and didn't look up until I was clear of the weave of undergrowth. 'Wow . . .' I whispered, looking around with outright amazement at the clearing we had entered.

The mountain face was a sharply sloping wall of stone in front of us, its face a rusted brown. A grove had been etched into the stone, carved by a tiny stream of water splashing down from the heights. The water fell down into a small rocky pool and was channelled through the rock, meandering to one side before disappearing into the trees. The waterfall was in a tiny clearing on its own, the wall of trees blocking it in, turning it into a secret haven that could not even be imagined outside the thick circle of vegetation.

'Isn't this lovely?' Monique said delightedly, as if the place belonged to her. 'And so private too.'

'Good,' I said, taking hold of her wrist from behind and giving her a long slow kiss on the neck.

'This is my special place,' she sighed, taking my hands and putting them on her breasts. 'When things get too much for me I come up here to relax in my own sweet way.'

I unzipped her padded jacket and slipped my hands inside. 'You haven't got anything on underneath,' I whispered, my hands rubbing blissfully against her naked breasts.

'And nothing on underneath my trousers,' she giggled. 'I told you, I relax in my own special way. Ohh . . . that's good,' she sighed as I clamped her lovely nipples between my fingers.

'And what's this special way,' I teased, squeezing her full breasts, my hands cupping them firmly.

'Taste this water,' she suggested, reaching out to put her fingers under the spring water splashing down against the rock.

'I'd rather taste you,' I complained, aching to suck her nipples and to have her suck mine in turn.

'No, taste this first, feel the rush of water through your fingers. It really is very sensual,' she insisted, taking my hands from the inside of her jacket. I looked at her with exasperation, my pussy was wet and all she wanted to do was play with spring water. I cupped a handful of the cool water and drank from it.

'Doesn't it feel good?' Monique continued, looking at me hopefully, letting the water splash onto her fingers.

I was missing something. 'Yes, it feels good,' I admitted, letting the jet of water force my fingers apart, the cool water foaming and spraying as I blocked it.

'It feels much better between the legs,' Monique smiled, pursing her lips wickedly.

'And that's how you relax,' I laughed, the light finally dawning. The feel of it on my fingers acquired new meaning, the force of the cool water and the way it foamed and sprayed.

'Yes, do you want me to show you how?' she asked, putting her shoulder bag down by her feet.

'You don't expect me to say no, do you?' I laughed, completely unzipping her jacket, and then slipping it off. The sun was high above us and the light shone on her tanned body, on her tight round breasts with the copper-hued nipples standing stiffly to attention.

'This will be our secret, won't it?' she asked, looking to me for confirmation.

'I'll never tell a soul,' I promised. It was her place, she was right about that, her secret spot where she could forget about everything else in the world. How could I deny her that? I was privileged to have even been let into the secret.

She pulled her boots off, standing by the rock pool where the stones were washed clean. I watched her pull her jeans off and then stand under the sun, defiantly, beautifully, nude. The dark hair between her thighs was trimmed, a perfect triangle of tight black hair hiding the opening of her sex.

'Isn't it cold?' I asked, noticing that she was shivering a little, her nipples were puckered up hard.

'Yes, the water is always cool but that adds to the enjoyment,' she explained, stepping into a rippling pool of water only a few inches deep and barely large enough for her to stand in. She sat back in the water, her body already glistening with a thousand liquid diamonds on her tanned skin. She smiled to me then lay back, facing the sheer wall of rock. Very slowly she positioned herself, edging closer to the rock wall, her thighs spread, lifted high. It took an instant and then she was in place, resting flat against the slippery rock wall, a flesh shaped V against the stone. Her thighs were wet and shiny, the droplets of water coursing down her smooth skin.

'Nearly there,' she gasped, shifting slightly more. I heard her sigh and knew she was ready. I stepped up close to her, my face against the smooth rock, following the path of the clear mountain water as it fell down in a straight line to the dark opening between her thighs. She was using her fingers to open her pussy, now glistening pink and fleshy against the dark hues of rock and stone.

'Is that good?' I asked, fascinated by the way the water fell straight into her sex, splashing and foaming marvellously in the reservoir formed by her body and the stone. I could imagine the cool jet crashing down onto her hard pussy-bud, making it throb yet cooling it too, washing over it with a million touches and sensations.

'You must try this ... Ohh ... Lovely ...' she sighed, arching her back, pressing herself against the rock, opening herself to the rushing flow of water. She seemed to be on the verge of peaking and I couldn't help but sit beside her and kiss her mouth, her lips were parted and too tempting for me to resist.

I leaned back and pressed my finger into the reservoir, my fingers guiding the water into her sex, making her moan and arch her back even more. She cried out, her breath rising and falling with the force of orgasm. I kissed her again, cupping her breasts, flicking my fingers over her rubbery points.

'Do you want more?' I whispered, kissing her again. I was keen on trying the experience for myself but was enjoying watching Monique at the same time.

'I usually lie here until I can't take any more, I come and I come and yet the water is always so strong, so refreshing ...' She sighed, a poem in its way, her voice faraway as if the feelings running in her beautifully open sex were carrying her away with them.

I kissed her again and then began to suck her nipples, so hard and cold. I bathed them with my warm mouth, my tongue rubbing insistently over her teats while she ran her hand through my long golden brown hair. I felt her shudder again, her breath escaping in a long sigh. As she arched her back her breasts were forced into my face. I kissed and sucked deliriously, my own sex wet with longing and close to orgasm.

'You know,' she whispered, recovering her dreamy voice once again, 'that a person is only truly naked under water, bathed in the element that symbolises life and purity.'

'That's it!' I shrieked, jumping up excitedly.

'What? What's it?' Monique asked, closing her eyes to the feel of the water, arching her back once more in readiness for the wave of pleasure about to engulf her.

'The key to my problem with Isabella, you've found it!' I laughed. I knelt down and kissed her on the mouth again. 'We've got to get back, we've got to get back,' I gabbled excitedly.

'But the water . . .' she said, sighing.

I stood up and kicked my hiking shoes off, in a moment I was naked from the waist down. 'I don't have time for that,' I told her. 'But we do have time for this.' I padded over to her, careful not to stumble on the slippery rocks. The water was cold and I wondered how Monique could stand it, she was hardier than she looked. I stood over her, smiled, then squatted over her face. Her breath was hot on my skin, brushing with like an invisible hand against the damp flesh of my quim.

Monique moaned loudly, pushed herself up and buried her face between my thighs. Her lips and tongue teased my pussy lips open, I could feel droplets of liquid drip down onto her face. It was my turn to sigh as her tongue slipped into me, into the welcoming warmth and cloying taste of my pussy. She sucked me, drawing out my juices with an expert tongue. She lapped at me, licking me from the tight rear opening up into the heart of my sex.

I closed my eyes to the sensation. All I could hear was the rushing water and the rushing of my breath. It felt exquisite to be locked away behind a barrier of trees under the afternoon sun and cooled by the purest spring water in the world. Monique was sucking fervently, pushing herself against my sex, her lips caressing and teasing while her tongue explored. She found my clit and I moaned loudly as the pleasure passed through me like a spear of lightning.

I climaxed, crying out loudly, shattering the calm with my cry of pleasure. Monique climaxed too, caught between my thighs, her tongue still inside me, while the cool water rushed through her sex.

After that I dried her quickly, amazed that the cold water hadn't frozen her solid. I kissed her sex and marvelled at how lovely it felt, so cold and yet so warm at the same time. She tasted different too, as if the mountain waters had suffused her body, mingling with her essences.

'Aren't you going to tell me?' she complained as I zipped up her jacket, after kissing her nipples goodbye.

'No, I want to see if I'm right first,' I said cautiously, though in my heart of hearts I was sure that Monique had unwittingly given me the clue that I required.

The school was empty, the silence hanging in the warm afternoon air. It was one of those rare sunny afternoons when everyone goes to sleep, or flicks lazily through a book, or watches the sky roll and swirl, changing and unchanging at the same time. I went up to my room quietly, stripped off and stood for a moment by the window, letting the sun colour my body with its soft golden light.

I looked out towards the lakes and mountains, glad that the stillness was there too, a blanket of serenity that extended from my heart to the heart of the mountains. My breasts touched the window, my nipples pressed against the cool glass, and I felt part of it, part of the big wide world that always seemed to be outside of me. Or maybe I was outside of it.

Only naked under water. How right Monique had been. I found a loose silk robe, a dragon breathing red fire down the back and put it on, tying it around the waist with a bow. I passed the mirror and caught sight of myself, the robe covering me to my thighs, my face serious but not unhappy, my hair still sparkling with droplets of water.

As I had expected, Isabella's door was closed. It had become a habit, to keep herself inside and others out. But today the house was empty and there was no one to keep out, only herself to keep in. I listened at the door, waiting for the right moment, for there could only be one right moment that day. There was silence. I waited, straining to hear but there was no sound. I returned to my room, the lazy afternoon giving me its fund of patience in return for my silence. I sat on the bed, half-dozing for a while. The clock moved slowly and I followed its progress sleepily.

The second time I listened at the door I was certain that the time was right. I tried the door and found that my gamble had been correct, Isabella had been lulled into a feeling of security, certain that none would violate her privacy on such an idyllic afternoon. I pushed the door open and peeked inside, she wasn't on the bed and I could hear the sound of rippling water.

I went in, quietly shutting the door behind me. Her bathroom door was open, the light pouring from the bedroom window passing through the open door to light the bathroom too. Isabella's discarded clothes were on the floor, a black bundle of clothes in a neat pile by the bed. As I crossed the room I heard a gentle splash of water, as of someone turning over in the bath, or turning a page in a book, or sinking lazily into the hot water – the sound of someone enjoying a long hot soak.

The door was open and I waited for a second, standing flat against the wall, wondering how to announce myself. I turned and looked down into the bath, at Isabella resting in the steaming water, her eyes closed, her face relaxed. How right Monique had been. I saw at once what the problem was, the key to her ugly clothes, the key to the feelings of hostility.

Isabella was a slim girl, she had the same slight frame as her mother, the same long limbs, frail arms, delicate features. But she had the breasts of a woman twice her size. I watched, fascinated by the way her huge breasts bobbed gently just below the surface of the water, her round nipples rising and falling as she breathed. They were beautiful – large, round, with jutting nipples and a naturally deep cleavage.

That was why she wore loose shapeless clothing, that was why she walked as if collapsed in on herself. I hadn't noticed it before, but now I remembered how she would sit with her arms folded tightly across her chest when we spoke. I had taken it as defiance, not camouflage. The poor girl was self-conscious, afraid that her ample charms were somehow ugly, something to be hidden and not exposed.

My silent contemplation was shattered by a sudden splashing of water and a cry from Isabella.

'What are you doing here?' she demanded furiously, trying to cover her breasts with her small elegant hands. She turned over in the bath, pressing herself up against it so that I couldn't see her chest at all.

'You're beautiful,' I said softly, stepping into the room properly.

'Go away, I don't want you here,' she said coldly, her face hard and hostile once more. It was a familiar face and I was used to it.

'You have such a lovely bust,' I said calmly, leaning back against the wall, letting my robe fall open to reveal my own breasts.

'Go away,' she repeated, though without the conviction this time, because she finally recognised that I wasn't going to budge an inch.

'You know, when I was at school some of the other girls used to laugh at me because my tits were bigger than theirs. I used to feel so hurt. I didn't want to be different, I didn't want my body to be bulging out all over the place but it just happened. What I didn't realise was that they were all jealous. They wanted a figure like mine. They used to pad their bras and put make up between their breasts to try and make their cleavage look deeper.'

'So?' Isabella asked defiantly.

'It took me a long time to realise that they were jealous

and, until I did, I used to feel horrible. I felt as if there was something wrong with me. They used to call me a freak, isn't that terrible?'

She looked at me for a long time, her eyes scanning my face, searching for some clue as to my feelings. 'That is terrible,' she finally agreed, almost whispering.

'But once I realised that they were envious I felt different. I felt proud of my body, confident, relaxed. I felt sexy, too, because my breasts made me look like a woman. They were part of me, part of my femininity. How do you feel about your body?'

'I feel all right,' she mumbled.

The robe slipped from my shoulders and I stood before her, totally naked. She looked at my shyly, her face colouring with embarrassment, her eyes partly shielded by loose ringlets of jet black hair.

'You see,' I said earnestly, 'there's nothing wrong with the naked body, nothing wrong at all.' I smiled, posed before her completely naturally, legs together, one bent at the knee, arms at my side, chest pushed forward and shoulders back. I wanted to display myself, to expose myself to her bitter scrutiny. I cupped my breasts, moulding my fingers around the firm mounds of flesh, lifting the nipples so they stood out.

'It's all right for you,' she said softly, 'you're beautiful.'

'That's not how I felt when I was being teased. I felt ugly and I wished my breasts would shrink, that they would disappear overnight. But now I love my body, it gives me so much pleasure.' I tweaked my nipples with my fingers, making them redden and stiffen, offering them to Isabella's shy inspection.

I turned round, wanting Isabella to see all of me, not just my breasts and pussy. I twisted round and could see her admiring the rear view of long thighs and round buttocks. 'My legs are a little too fat,' I sighed, smoothing my hands down the back of my thighs. 'And my bum's too flabby. I could do with some exercise, but then you can see that, can't you?'

'That's not true, your legs are lovely,' she assured me quietly, her voice still guarded.

I bent over at the waist, touched my toes, parting my legs so that I could look through them at Isabella. 'Are you sure?' I asked, smiling at her. My legs were taut and I could feel that my buttocks were slightly parted, my pussy lips were touched by the very slight breeze that flowed through the room.

'No, I mean, yes. You look good, much better than I do. I can't believe that you were ever teased.'

'But I was and that's what happened to you, isn't it? That's why you try to hide yourself in those loose clothes.'

'Did you speak to my mother?' she asked suspiciously, but it was a question and not an accusation which was the first hopeful sign I'd seen since she'd arrived.

'No, I guessed. Maybe it's because I was there, because I experienced it for myself. You are beautiful and you should never let the spiteful jealousy of others stand in your way.'

'I'd like to get dressed now,' she said.

'I'll help you,' I offered, smiling hopefully.

'No, I just want to be alone . . .' she mumbled, turning her eyes to the ground.

So near, yet so far. The situation called for some dramatic action, something to prove to her once and for all my good intentions. 'I want you to love your body as I love mine,' I told her. 'And I want you to see how comfortable I am with myself, to show you how you could be too.'

I put one foot on the edge of the bath, to one side of her head, and the other I kept flat on the ground. From where she lay she had a clear view of the dark bush of my pussy mound, she was looking up directly at my sex. The sun was warm on my back, and the stillness of the afternoon had yet to completely dissolve. I pinched my nipples, making them stand out, red and hard, poking out from the milky white globes of flesh. I couldn't help but close my eyes to the mounting pleasure, my nipples are always so sensitive, and I had no doubt that Isabella's would prove to be the same.

While she watched, silently enraptured by my display, I cupped my breasts and stretched my neck down as far as possible. I flicked my tongue onto my nipples, the tip barely brushing against the target but still passing thrills of delight through me. It had been years since I had kissed my breasts but I still had a supple body and my breasts were lovely and large. I licked myself, first one nipple and then the other, using my fingers to excite my hard rosy buds. The pleasure was amplified by Isabella's presence, as if my exhibitionist instincts were being aroused by her intense gaze.

The pleasure was growing and, much as I wanted to concentrate on my breasts, I couldn't help passing a hand down between my thighs. I was pressed forward, leaning heavily on the bath so that I could suck my own nipples, but the position also allowed me to part my fleshy pussy lips with my fingers. I was wet and the feel of my finger entering the damp heat made me sigh audibly, the breath escaping from my open mouth.

'Isn't this beautiful?' I whispered, pressing two fingers into my pussy, in and out slowly. Isabella made no reply but I didn't care any more, the feelings welling up inside me were for nobody but myself. I was enjoying the feel of my fingers exploring my sex, playing with my clit, swimming in my juices. I caught a nipple in my mouth and sucked hard, pressing the fleshy node between my teeth, flicking my tongue over it at the same time. My body was pulsing with sensation, from my nipples to the raw sexual pleasure of frigging myself with my soaked fingers to the sensual feel of the warming sun on my back.

'Yes . . . yes . . .' Isabella whispered, her voice full of joy and hope, urging me along until I cried out, my pleasure exploding inside my sex and inside my mind at the same instant.

For a moment I felt dizzy, not quite sure what was going on. I was standing by the bath, breathing hard. Down in front of me, Isabella was holding my hand in hers. It took a second, but then I realised that she was sucking my fingers into the warmth of her mouth, her hot tongue licking the cunny juices from each finger in turn.

The desire returned quickly, a sudden flash of fire in the belly, the heat in my sex fired up once more.

'Let me see you,' I whispered.

Silently she stood up, the water falling from her body like a thousand stars falling from Aphrodite as she emerged from the sea. She was stunning, a fragile waist, lithe thighs and a magnificently full pair of breasts with nipples that stood begging to be sucked and fingered.

'You are beautiful,' I whispered and reverently bent down to kiss each nipple in turn.

9

The dam had burst and all of Isabella's hurt and anguish came pouring out, a flood of pain and anger that was washed out with her hot bitter tears. I took her by the hand and led her into the bedroom. I towelled her body softly, drying away the water that ran with her tears. She was weeping, heaving for breath, trying to speak but unable to form the words. My heart went out to her. I knew what she must have felt like, understood the suffering that she had gone through.

'It's okay now,' I whispered soothingly, taking her in my arms. I cradled her, rocking her gently, kissing her on the head.

'It's been horrible . . . They all hated me . . .' she sobbed.

I sat her on the bed, knelt down in front of her, brushing back wet curls of hair from her face. 'It's over now,' I assured her softly, smiling encouragingly. 'No one here hates you.'

'They hurt me,' she said, surprised, as if only just admitting it to herself.

'They were stupid people, cruel and stupid. You're much better than they will ever be.'

'But why did they do it?'

'Because you're beautiful and they were jealous of you, it's as simple as that.'

'Is that true?' she asked, looking at me earnestly, the tears still twinkling in her eyes. She looked so sweet and innocent, so unlike the hostile and aggressive young woman that had made life difficult for all of us.

'Yes, darling, it is true,' I smiled sadly. 'They were jealous, and I can see why. But you've no need to worry, we're not like that here. Here we'll all love you, you can be yourself and not worry what others think.'

'But I was so horrible to you,' she said guiltily.

I kissed her on the cheek, just touching my lips against the coolness of her skin. 'I forgive you. It's true,' I added, 'everything I told you about what happened to me. I don't want you thinking I made all that up.'

'Am I really beautiful?' she asked doubtfully.

'Of course you are!' I smiled. 'Come and look at yourself.' She let me drag her across the room to the mirror. I stood behind her, looking over her shoulder at the full-length reflection framed in golden sunlight. Her tears had gone and now she was smiling.

'But look at me,' she said, her hands down at her sides, afraid to touch herself.

'Yes,' I agreed, 'look at you. Look at your thighs, so slim and well formed, and your skin so soft and smooth.' I ran my hands along the outside of her right thigh, my fingers massaging her firmly. She watched my hand going up and down, as if her body was something distant, disconnected from her being. 'Touch yourself,' I said firmly. She hesitated then began to copy me, using her hand to rub up and down her left thigh.

'That does feel good,' she admitted with a shy laugh. I kissed her on the shoulder, proud that she had admitted it without prompting from me.

'And your stomach,' I suggested, pressing my hand there, caressing her smooth round belly, my fingers grazing the silky hairs on her mound. She followed suit, touching herself gingerly, watching herself in the mirror at the same time. 'And such a tight waist, so lovely,' I sighed wistfully, beginning to press my bare breasts against her smooth flawless back. I wanted her to feel my nakedness against hers, to make the sensual connection between her body and feeling good.

'I'm sorry for being so horrible,' she repeated, twisting her head round to look at me remorsefully. Our faces were close, our eyes meeting head on, her breath and mine mingling. She moved closer, twisted her face to an angle, her mouth open, lips ready and waiting. We kissed and the feeling was electric. I felt the thrill pass between us, a fire that touched us to the core. My tongue was tracing the inside of her lips, entering her mouth. She took my hands and placed them on her breasts and I squeezed softly.

'Doesn't this feel good?' I whispered, cupping her lovely breasts, her flesh filling my hands, her nipples poking through the gaps in my fingers. She turned and looked in the mirror, at the picture of the two of us together, her breasts in my hands, our legs touching, my mouth on her throat.

'I've never felt this way before,' she sighed, sounding surprised.

I massaged her breasts, flicking my thumbs over her rigid nipples, watching her close her eyes and throw her head back, the breath whistling from her lips. How lovely she looked – ecstatic, joyful, innocent. Her hands were on mine, shadowing my movements, exploring her body with me.

'Back to the bed,' I whispered hotly, the heat in my sex raging. I wanted her. She had never been touched by a woman, never been touched by a man, and I wanted to initiate her into the joys of sex. I took her hand and we walked to the bed, each of us glancing at the reflection in the mirror; two naked females, bathed in sunlight, bodies roused and ready to make love.

She lay back on the bed and I climbed in beside her. I couldn't keep my eyes off her breasts, so round and firm, the aureoles a mouthful, with a deep valley that drew the eye. Was she as sensitive as I imagined? I knelt above her and put my lips to one nipple, eager to explore her properly. She cupped her breasts, offering them to me, her desire making her forget her self-consciousness. I kissed her softly, then lapped at her nipple, licking it slowly, feeling it press back against my wet tongue. She sighed and I turned my attention to the other nipple. I sucked, pulling the sweetmeat into my mouth, playing my tongue back and forth over it. Her sighs told me all I wanted to know.

'Isn't that the most delicious feeling?' I asked, releasing her breasts for a moment. She nodded eagerly, her eyes wide with excitement. I sucked again, this time tugging playfully at the teats, guided by the song of sighs and moans that accompanied the action. I was building up her excitement, licking, sucking, soothing, licking again. She was mine, I knew her body better than she did, I knew how to excite her, how to stimulate her.

My hunch had been correct, she was blessed with unduly sensitive breasts, each touch on her roused nipples sent spasms of pleasure pulsing through her. She was the sort of woman that could climax just by having her breasts stimulated. Quickly I forced her nipples together, rubbing the berries against each other then sucking them hungrily into my mouth. She cried out, her voice as full of surprise as of pleasure. She forced her chest forward, arching her back, her sigh stuck in her throat. I sat back on my knees, looked down at her breasts and chest patterned red by the force of the climax that had shaken her.

'That was fantastic . . .' she whispered, still gasping for breath, her eyes full of joy. For the first time she had enjoyed pleasure as a woman, at the hands of a woman.

'You're so lucky,' I told her softly. 'There's so much for you to learn and I'm honoured to be the one to teach you. Now, are you beautiful?'

She hesitated and looked me in the eye. 'You make me feel beautiful,' she replied shyly.

'Good, that's a start,' I smiled. The first lesson had ended – the first of many.

That first time with Isabella was a turning point, from

then on she was different and, on reflection, I think I
changed too. I made her climax several times, always by
playing with her nipples, forging the connection in her
mind between her lovely breasts and the ultimate
expression of pleasure. She was eager to learn. She
wanted to make love, she begged me but I resisted. I
didn't touch her sex and I did not let her touch me at all.
My plan was to concentrate just on her breasts, to make
her love herself properly so that she would never again
look at her body with a feeling of shame.

I left her exhausted, lying naked on the bed, her body
flushed pink and beaded with jewels of perspiration. She
closed her eyes and I knew that she would sleep and
dream the most joyful dreams, the heaviness lifted from
her heart once and for all.

I dressed quickly and then flew down to Amelia's
office, rushing in without thinking. As always, I had
blundered in without thinking. Suzanne and Amelia looked
round guiltily.

'Oh . . .' I said lamely, 'I'm sorry . . . I'll come back
later . . .'

'It's all right,' Suzanne smiled, getting up off the desk
and buttoning up her blouse. She moved to one side and I
saw Amelia fixing her blouse too, her face colouring
slightly.

'I was just so happy,' I explained, closing the door
behind me, 'I didn't think.'

'That sounds like good news,' Amelia smiled, standing
up, using her fingers to wipe away a smudge of red
lipstick from Suzanne's face.

'Yes, it is. I think I've finally solved the problem with Isabella,' I stated proudly.

'Excellent!' Suzanne laughed, clapping her hands together.

'What was it?' Amelia wanted to know, the relief clear to see in her happy smile.

'The poor girl had some sort of complex about the size of her breasts. It seems that the girls in her last school made her life a misery because she was so well-developed.'

'So that's why she was so poorly dressed,' Suzanne realised.

'How did you get her to tell you?' Amelia asked.

'She didn't. I guessed this afternoon and checked up on her in the bath to see if I was right. I've just spent some time with her, she seems much better now,' I explained, unable to keep the wicked smile from my lips.

'Does that mean what I think it means?' Amelia laughed.

'It does,' I admitted proudly. 'She has lovely sensitive tits and I want to make sure she learns to love them properly.'

'Well done.' Amelia stepped forward and kissed me on the cheek. 'I knew you would do it.'

'Yes, very well done,' Suzanne agreed, also giving me a peck on the cheek. I felt so happy I wanted to scream. My intention had always been to solve the problem myself, to prove once and for all that I was at the finishing school to do a job and not because my aunt felt sorry for me when I was in trouble. At last I felt vindicated and my joy was mixed with a tremendous feeling of relief.

'What are you planning on doing now?' Amelia wanted to know, sitting back at her desk and flicking through a large diary in front of her.

'I want to spend more time with her, just the two of us for a while. I think if I suddenly lose interest she'll get the wrong idea. Once I'm happy that she's in a better frame of mind I want to get her and Charlotte together. And if that works . . .'

'Not if,' Suzanne corrected me instantly, 'when.'

'. . . When that happens I want to set her up with one or more of the young men.'

'It sounds like you've got a whole programme worked out for her,' Amelia commented approvingly, picking up the phone and tapping out a number.

'I have. I want Isabella to forget all those bad experiences, I want her to enjoy her stay at the finishing school.'

'Good, that's exactly what I'm going to tell Maria,' Amelia smiled, holding the phone to her ear. 'Hello? Maria? Hi, this is Amelia. Yes . . . I have some excellent news for you . . . Yes . . . Melissa tells me that she has made excellent progress with Isabella . . . Very good news . . . Yes, she is here . . .' Amelia put her hand over the receiver and looked up at me. 'Maria would like a word with you,' she said, handing me the phone.

'Hello, Maria,' I said nervously, not quite knowing what to say to her.

'Amelia tells me you have made friends with Bella,' she said softly, the line was clear but her voice sounded muted.

'Yes. I understand now what the problem was at her old college,' I said, not at all certain that Maria knew the full story. 'But now I think she'll be okay.'

'She told you?' Maria asked disbelievingly.

'Only after some guesswork and a lot of prompting,' I assured her.

'And how is she now? Is she still feeling very depressed?'

'I don't think so. She looked very . . . very elated,' I said, struggling to find the right words.

'Elated? Did she let you touch her?'

'Er . . . Yes,' I confessed. 'She let me caress her, I think it was very important,' I added quickly.

'Good, I'm glad. She has a lovely body, hasn't she?'

'Yes, Maria. You have a lovely daughter. And I think she's very sorry for the way she acted.'

'Perhaps she will call me?' Maria asked hopefully.

'Yes. I'll try to get her to call as soon as she is ready.'

'Thank you, Melissa. I'm very happy, and I hope that you and Bella learn to love each other very much. I think she will turn into a very sensual young lady with your guidance.'

'Thank you, Maria,' I said, slightly flustered by Maria's frank words. 'I'll get her to call soon.'

'Goodbye, and thanks again,' she said softly.

I handed the phone back to Amelia. 'That was a bit tricky,' I said. 'I mean how do you tell a mother that you're making love to her daughter?'

'The mother already knows,' Suzanne smiled. 'That's why Isabella was sent here. Maria wanted Isabella to grow up without any hang-ups. She wants her daughter to be happy with herself.'

'Good girl,' Amelia beamed. 'I knew you'd do a good job. I'm proud of you, and I'm sure that this is only the first of many.'

'Thanks,' I said. 'I'm just glad that I could help Isabella, the poor girl really did need it.'

After the relative solitude of the finishing school, Zurich seemed all hustle and bustle. The streets were full of life and buzzing with people, though in reality it was nothing compared to London where I had been only days earlier. I sat in the car, with Rudi at the wheel and Isabella at my side, both of us girls looking forward to an extended shopping exhibition.

I had decided that the new Isabella was in need of a new wardrobe, the dreadful rags she wore wouldn't do any longer. She agreed with me readily, the shapeless and the baggy were to be disposed of forever. She had spent hours making up lists of what she wanted, with all the excitement of a child waiting for Christmas day. Of course, as soon as she decided what she wanted she changed her mind. Now that she was no longer ashamed of her body the possibilities seemed endless. Everybody remarked on the change in her personality, she was acting like any other young woman of her age and not like a manic depressive.

Rudi drove us to one of the smartest shops in the town, a very chic boutique with the latest Paris fashions displayed in the window. For her trip Isabella had selected the best of her clothes, but they still looked very downbeat. When we stepped out of the car into the street I couldn't help wondering whether we would even be allowed into the boutique, she hardly looked like an advertisement for their wares.

'Do you think they'll have anything in my size?' she asked doubtfully, looking at the sylph-like mannequins in the display.

'I'm sure they will,' I assured her, taking her by the hand and dragging her inside.

We entered timidly, both of us slightly in awe of the stylish atmosphere inside. It was warm, the air scented, light jazz played softly in the background. Two young women assistants stood side by side, barely deigning to look at us.

'I hate places like this,' I whispered, giving the assistants a dirty look.

'Shall we go?' Isabella suggested, not daring to move further into the shop.

'No, this is the place we've chosen,' I said decisively. 'Now, where do we start?'

'Where do you think?'

I sighed, she still lacked confidence, and was looking to me to supply it for her. 'Come on, let's have a look at what they've got,' I said.

'*Bonjour*,' one of the assistants said perfunctorily, looking at us as if we had just stepped in something nasty.

'We're just looking,' I told her airily, putting on my best posh English accent.

'Of course,' she smiled, her attitude changing, 'if I may be of assistance . . .'

'The waistcoats,' I said, pointing to a rack of dark leather garments.

'But you said no black,' Isabella protested as the assistant, a good-looking blonde, went to fetch one of the waistcoats.

'But this is leather,' I pointed out with a smile. 'This isn't dowdy, this will look fantastic.'

The assistant brought one over for us to look at. It was made of very dark fine-grained leather, with tight stitching at the seams, a row of black buttons down the front and a single strap at the back. It felt cool to the touch, the bouquet was rich and sensual, just the way leather ought to smell.

'Try it,' I suggested, turning to Isabella.

She looked at it hesitantly, as if unable to imagine herself in it. 'Do you really think it would suit me?'

'If *madame* would like to follow me,' the assistant said, 'I'll show you the changing room.'

All three of us retreated to the back of the shop, to an open area that was hidden from the rest of the shop. The walls were lined with mirrors, I watched a thousand copies of myself looking at a thousand copies of Isabella. She took her jacket off and reached out for the waistcoat. The assistant looked at her open-mouthed, scandalised by Isabella's behaviour. My laughter took both of them by surprise.

'Not like that,' I smiled to Isabella, giving her a friendly peck on the cheek. She was wearing a thick

woolly jumper, tighter than most of her clothes, but still
with all the style and finesse of a hearty peasant costume.

'*Madame*'s right,' the assistant agreed, smiling, her
blue eyes filled with amusement.

'Take your jumper off,' I said.

'But . . . but . . .' Isabella stuttered, her face going
bright red. Showing her lovely breasts to me was one
thing, showing them to a pretty young stranger was
something else altogether.

'If *madame* is shy . . .' the blonde said quietly, sensing
that it was time to retreat.

'No, *madame* is not shy,' I asserted, smiling
encouragingly.

Isabella swallowed hard and then turned away from
the assistant. She lifted the jumper over her head and
handed it to me. I smiled, Isabella's gorgeous breasts
were reflected all around us, from every angle, firm and
round and suckable. The assistant smiled too, she turned
to me and I saw that she was enjoying the view as much
as I was.

'Shall I help you on with this?' the blonde asked
quietly, standing directly behind Isabella and looking
directly at her reflection.

'Yes please,' Isabella agreed, her face still flushed
pink but with a smile on her lips.

The blonde opened the waistcoat and Isabella put it
on, slipping one arm in and then the other. The dark shiny
leather was in stark contrast to her pale white skin,
untanned and untouched by the sun. The assistant had her
hands on Isabella's shoulders, holding her delicately.

They kept looking at each other, their eyes meeting for a moment then looking away shyly. It was an interesting situation and one that I liked the potential of. The assistant was very pretty, her blonde hair fell in carefully cut layers, soft curls that sprang as she moved. The blue eyes that had been cold and hard were now warm and exciting. A familiar feeling of desire flashed through me, making my heart pound and my breathing quicken.

'Well?' Isabella asked, buttoning the waistcoat up quickly.

'No,' I decided, shaking my head decisively.

'No, *madame*,' the assistant agreed.

'I told you,' Isabella said, sounding hurt by our emphatic decision. She turned to face me, the waistcoat was buttoned up tightly, squashing her breasts almost flat, making her lose shape and definition.

'If *madame* would permit?' the assistant gestured.

'Her name's Isabella,' I said, wondering if she and I had the same idea.

'And I am Marie,' she said, stepping in front of Isabella. Very confidently she undid the top three buttons and pulled the front open, then she carefully cupped Isabella's breasts, lifting them up a little. Isabella's face was red, but her eyes were wide with excitement. In a second Marie was finished and she stepped back to admire her creation.

'You look perfect,' I whistled, unable to believe the miracle that Marie had effected, totally transforming the way Isabella looked. The waistcoat seemed to funnel her breasts, lifting them, so that the deep valley was clear, the eye drawn magnetically to the white flesh against black leather. Her nipples were impressed on the leather, undulations in the smooth black surface that caught the light, creating two haloes that positively begged to be touched and stroked.

'Doesn't that look better now?' Marie asked, smiling proudly, knowing that she had transformed Isabella's look completely.

'Is that really me?' Isabella laughed happily, putting her hand to her mouth, turning to look at herself from every angle. 'Thank you, thank you,' she cried ecstatically, taking Marie by the shoulders and giving her a soft kiss on the cheek. They looked at each other for a moment, eyes together, sharing something, then they parted. Isabella gave me a kiss too, but I held her close, kissed her softly on the mouth, our lips touching in full view of Marie, Isabella held back for a second then melted into my arms, opening her mouth to my hot eager tongue.

'Now, Marie,' I said, turning to her, glad that she was still smiling excitedly. 'What do you think would go with this?'

'I have just the thing,' she said. 'Shall I wrap the waistcoat?'

'No!' Isabella squealed. 'No, I'm wearing this. Have you got a bin? Then put the jumper in with the rubbish.'

Along with the waistcoat Marie picked out a pair of stylish jeans, a pair of tight leather trousers, a silk shirt to wear under the waistcoat, a skirt that was long and tight. Isabella tried all of them on enthusiastically, twirling like a marionette in front of the mirrors. I watched indulgently, sharing in her happiness, enjoying also the fact that Marie was surreptitiously touching her as much as possible. Marie was rubbing Isabella's backside, flicking her fingers over the erect nipples as often as she could, a touch here, a caress there. I don't know if they imagined I hadn't noticed, but I took great delight in the way they secretly flirted with each other.

'Do you sell lingerie?' I asked, wanting to see Isabella's charms in black lace or silk, and eager to see how far she and Marie would dare to go.

Marie looked crestfallen. 'I am sorry, Melissa,' she sighed apologetically.

I shared her disappointment and so did Isabella. 'We don't have to buy lingerie,' she said.

'Not even stockings?' I asked hopefully.

'No, not even stockings . . . But wait!' she suddenly remembered something. 'We were sent some items just recently, I will ask the other assistant . . .' and she skipped off excitedly.

'How are you enjoying your day out?' I asked Isabella softly, kissing her on the lips again now that we were alone.

'It's fantastic. And Marie's so helpful,' she smiled innocently.

'And very pretty,' I teased.

'Yes, she is very very pretty,' Isabella admitted. 'Do you think she likes me?'

'Surely you don't need to ask me that? Do you think I haven't noticed the way her hands are all over you. Do you think I didn't see the way she was massaging your backside? Or the way her lips brushed your shoulder?'

'You're not jealous?' Isabella asked, her face becoming dark and serious once more.

'Jealous? Why ever should I be jealous? No, you are very beautiful and so is she, I think you should enjoy your body. Does it feel good when her fingers brush your nipples?'

'Very good,' Isabella sighed dreamily.

'We were sent some lingerie samples a few weeks ago,' Marie explained. 'We do not sell lingerie but apparently the samples are still in the stockroom downstairs. Would you mind going downstairs?'

'No!' both Isabella and myself said at the same time, then laughed. Marie led the way, her short skirt clinging tightly to her round backside, her arse cheeks wiggling sexily with every graceful step.

The stockroom was down a narrow flight of stairs, the way partially blocked by cases and empty clothes racks. Isabella followed Marie, with me following a few steps behind. It had already turned into a far more exciting shopping trip than I had planned and my feverish imagination was going into overdrive.

The stockroom was stacked chaotically with boxes and crates. Clothes were hanging from the walls, wrapped in cellophane, piled high in corners. There was a full-length mirror on one wall and Marie took Isabella there at once.

'I'll only be a minute,' Marie explained. 'I just need to find the right box.'

'I want to see you naked,' I whispered to Isabella,

holding her by the waist and kissing her on the mouth. This time there was no hesitation, she turned to the mirror, took one long look at herself, her prominent breasts cupped sensuously by the black leather, her long legs swathed in tight shiny leather trousers.

Isabella unzipped her trousers and slowly wriggled out of them, pulling them off and pausing to look at herself again. I felt that she was seeing herself for the first time as others saw her – sensual, attractive, a little exotic. She was wearing white cotton panties, the bulge of her pussy standing out, the dark bush of hair partly visible through the thin cotton. Next she unbuttoned the waistcoat, one button at a time, very slowly, enjoying the tantalising display as much as I did.

Marie returned with a brown cardboard box. She watched as Isabella finally removed the waistcoat, standing totally naked in front of the mirror, her eyes looking to us for our response.

'Isn't she lovely?' I asked Marie. I stood behind Isabella, crossed my arms over her chest and cupped her lovely bosom, weighing each globe, lifting and separating, my fingers pressing down on her rubbery nipples.

'So sexy,' Marie whispered wistfully.

'Do you really mean that?' Isabella asked, not daring to believe it.

'I see a dozen gorgeous women every day,' Marie assured her positively, 'and none are as sexy as you are.'

'Thank you, thank you,' Isabella gushed happily. She turned and planted a long slow kiss on Marie's mouth. They were positively eating each other.

Marie still held the box so she couldn't respond further. 'You don't mind?' she asked me nervously, turning towards me after she and Isabella parted.

I laughed. 'Mind? Why should I mind? I think it's positively wonderful. Now, aren't her lovely titties ripe for sucking?'

Marie dropped the box and embraced Isabella again, this time they held each other close, their faces locked together in one long sensuous kiss. Marie began to stroke Isabella's breasts, running her fingers between the valley, touching her nipples, pulling gently then stroking once more. Isabella was in rapture, eyes half closed, enjoying the exquisite sensation of being explored by another young woman.

There was no way I could stand and watch without joining in. I stood behind Isabella and kissed her throat while my hands held her breasts, offering them to Marie's eager lips. Isabella's soft moans of pleasure were my true reward. I felt her sighs as hot breaths on my face, we kissed, and all the time I was holding her, feeding her delectable body to Marie.

My pussy was wet and I could feel that my silk knickers were soaked through. I pulled my skirt up and my panties down, letting the red silk garment rest at knee level. Isabella's round arse cheeks were against me, I could feel the softness on my belly, the shape of her moulded against me. The feeling of her naked rear pressing against my belly was tremendously arousing. I began to rub myself against her, a trickle of golden liquid from my sex smearing onto her behind.

Isabella was sighing and crying, her body assailed by sensual pleasure from both sides. Marie was feasting on the hard and erect teats, sucking them deep into her mouth, her lipstick rouging the soft white breast flesh. From behind I was grinding my abdomen into her behind, and she in turn was pressing herself back to meet me. My clitty was rubbing against her and in the delirium of sensations I felt as if I was fucking her, going into her body to the pleasure of us both.

My cries of pleasure rose and became part of the same song as Isabella's. My head was spinning but as I opened and closed my eyes I saw Marie's reflection in the mirror, her short skirt tight around her ankles, while she frigged herself joyfully with her painted fingers. Isabella was almost bent at the waist. I was grinding my sex into her tight round posterior and her breasts hung down into Marie's lovely red mouth. Isabella climaxed first. I heard the breath catch in her throat as she arched her back, straining her bottom up, her hands clutching at Marie for support. Marie cried out a second later, burying her face in Isabella's chest as the pleasure took her over the edge.

When I climaxed, I felt as if my sex were open and pouring juice against the parted arse cheeks of Isabella's rear. I stepped away, dizzy with the excess of feeling. Marie crawled round and I watched her lap up my cream that was smeared so erotically against the snow-white flesh of Isabella's rear.

After that we bought the entire box of lingerie, not really caring what was in it, not even bothering to look inside. Before we left the boutique I saw Marie pass her phone number to Isabella, who clutched it tightly as if it were the most treasured possession she had ever had.

We breezed into other boutiques later, flirting outrageously with the staff, male and female, laughing and joking like silly school girls. I watched Isabella slowly growing in confidence, excited beyond measure as all eyes turned towards her, lingering glances that she returned or ignored at will. When she went in to buy some high heels she practically had the male assistants fighting amongst themselves, so eager were they to fall at her feet and look up at her breasts cased in fine black leather.

Rudi picked us up in the car to drive us back. Suddenly alone again we both became more serious. Our laughter was gone and we sat in silence as the car left the city. I think she was going over all that had happened, all the little incidents of the day that had been like a revelation after her self-imposed isolation.

'Thank you,' she said, turning to kiss me on the lips, her face dark once more. I kissed her back, recognising the gratitude swelling up inside her. We kissed and kissed, and gradually the gratitude turned to arousal. We made love in the car, stripping ourselves naked and wrapping our bodies tightly together. Until then I had concentrated on her breasts, wanting her to get over her complex, but that session in the car was the last time I made her climax just by concentrating on her nipples. I remember deciding afterwards that the time had come to move onto the next lesson.

10

The shopping trip had been a great success. Now, Isabella not only acted differently, she also looked different. The dowdy black rags had been replaced by snappy new skirts and bright sexy tops. It showed in her personality too, she had become a new person and was now very popular with the other girls. It wasn't all good news though, I did notice that she was still shy in front of the men. But I wasn't bothered by her timidity, in fact I deliberately did nothing to dispel the cool reserve she displayed.

Charlotte was the first to tell me that she had been 'playing games' with Isabella, as she so charmingly put it. I smiled indulgently, glad to see that Isabella was making up for lost time. The fact that most of the games seemed to revolve around breast-sucking and stroking was also a good sign, she now saw her body as an asset and not a liability. I asked Charlotte what else she and Isabella had been up to but she grew strangely reticent, as if embarrassed to be questioned about what she and another girl had been doing together. It didn't bother me though, I still had my programme to go through, I wanted Isabella to receive a full sexual education, so that the arts of love would appear both natural and joyous.

One morning, Amelia came to my room. I had just emerged from the shower and the water was still dripping from my body. As soon as I saw her I pretended to be shy, modestly covering myself with the towel, though there was no way I could hide my smile of delight. Being so close to her was becoming quite a problem, every time I set eyes on her I felt desire throb inside me. I wanted her so much, yet I did not have the words to invite her into my bed. Because she was my aunt, and not just an employer or friend, I found myself waiting for her to make the first move. And several times she had almost made that much-longed-for move. We would kiss, tease each other with caresses, expose our bodies to each other, yet it never seemed to lead to the loving I ached for.

'Auntie, how nice to see you,' I said brightly, brushing my wet hair back from my face. I was holding the bath towel in front of me to cover my breasts, but I was naked at the back and I knew that Amelia could see that in the mirror.

'I saw Isabella this morning,' she said, flashing me a smile. 'I must say, darling, you'd never believe that it's the same girl who arrived here two weeks ago.'

'Isn't she lovely now? Have you two spent some time together?' I asked.

'No, do you think it's a good idea?' Amelia asked, also clearly intrigued by the prospect.

'Certainly. She should take her turn looking after the staff just as the other girls do,' I decided. Isabella had yet to be given any duties but I liked the idea of sending her to Amelia, as if by making love to my aunt in my place she would somehow draw Amelia closer to me.

'Good, I'll look forward to it then. But I came here for something else. I'd like your advice.'

'My advice?' I repeated, flattered beyond question.

'Yes, both Suzanne and I thought it a good idea to talk to you. We have a young man we'd like to join us, but we'd like your opinion first.'

'Of course,' I said, certain that this was the first real sign that my success with Isabella had been recognised. 'Has he been interviewed?'

'There have been discussions,' Amelia explained. She moved closer to me, took the brush from my hand and began to comb it through my wet hair. I turned my back to her, glad to have her so close, secretly turned on by the fact that my bare back was to her and that she was openly eyeing my glistening thighs and bottom cheeks.

'Do you want me to meet him?'

'That's up to you. He knows a little about what goes on here, but obviously we can't let him have the full details. Staff selection is always a difficult process.'

'Except when it's your niece,' I added softly.

'Don't be silly,' she said, patting my wet bottom softly with the brush. 'You've proved to be an excellent choice, not that there was ever the slightest doubt of that. Rudi and the others came by word of mouth, or personal recommendation. Luis is neither but he had a girlfriend who had been one of our girls, he learned something of our school from her.'

'You've spoken to her?'

'She speaks highly of him, both as a friend and as a lover. But the fact is that we do not know him. Suzanne had met him but she has her doubts, she is not at all sure that he will fit in here.'

'What did you think of him?'

'How do you know that we've met?' she asked, pursing her lips girlishly.

'You must have,' I laughed. If she hadn't met him then I would have been too shocked for words.

'I like him,' she admitted. 'But it might just be because I'd like to add another virile young male to my team.'

'In that case I'd like to meet him too,' I said, turning to face her. 'And I'd like to take Monique with me.'

'As you wish, darling,' Amelia agreed. 'Let me know what you want me to arrange. He's in Switzerland at the moment, we've had him fly over from Spain, so the sooner you let me know the better.'

Amelia started to move towards the door. I released the bath towel, letting it fall to the ground. I stepped forward, took Amelia in my arms and drew her close. We kissed instantly. I breathed in her scent and it made me dizzy with excitement. My nakedness was moulded to her body, her hands were on my waist, holding me hesitantly, not at all sure whether to pull me close or push me away.

'You've soaked my clothes through to the skin,' she laughed, pulling her mouth from mine. I looked into her eyes and saw the desire there, but also the doubt. She stepped away from me, her smart clothes dark with wet patches where I had impressed myself against her.

'I'm wet too,' I said to myself, watching her retreat,

the fire in my belly raging unquenched. Why did she not make love to me? The expression in her eye was full of desire, why did she not act on that desire and satisfy us both? The question was a dark cloud that marked the end of the summer. I looked out of the window and noticed that the sky was white with cloud, the sun partly hidden, it matched my own feelings completely.

I had asked for Monique to join me for the meeting with Luis on the spur of the moment. I had no particular plan in mind but it helped the impression I wanted to give and I'm sure it worked. I liked Monique and trusted her a good deal, more so than any of the other women working at the school. I had no doubt that between us we'd find a way to fathom the personality of the young Spaniard who had divided the opinions of Amelia and Suzanne. That afternoon, while I was still thinking about the meeting with Luis, I asked Isabella to come up to my room for a chat.

She arrived promptly at three, wearing a short flared skirt, a scarlet top and a happy smile. Her long hair was tied with white ribbon at the back, so that she looked more like a child than a young woman. In greeting she gave me a friendly peck on the cheek, then sat down comfortably on the end of the bed, tucking one leg under her bottom while swinging the other over the edge.

'You look happy,' I remarked cheerily, sitting opposite.

'That's because I am,' she smiled. 'I've made so many new friends here, it's still hard to believe that any place could be so wonderful.'

'I know what you mean,' I agreed. 'I feel the same way, I wake up in the morning and can't believe how lucky I am to be here.'

'I'm glad you are, I don't think anyone else could have helped me the way you did.'

'Well, that's all over now,' I said firmly, thankful for the gratitude but wanting her to forget all that had happened in the past. 'I hear you've been making some very close friends,' I teased.

'Yes,' she admitted, her pretty face flushing pink with innocent embarrassment.

I laughed gently, then kissed her fingers resting on her knee. 'Good, that's what I want you to do. Don't they simply adore your body?'

'Yes,' she nodded proudly. 'They just love the size of my breasts. They can't wait to touch them. I never imagined that having big breasts could be so much fun.'

'Do you do anything else but let them play with your breasts? Do you let them touch you between the thighs?'

She looked mildly astounded. 'No. Some of them want to, but I don't let them, it doesn't seem right. I watch them touch themselves though, it makes me feel very strange.'

'Excited?' I suggested, putting my own feelings to her.

'Yes, excited. I feel very hot inside, a kind of sticky heat that feels so very wicked.'

'Do you touch yourself? When you're feeling very hot and sticky?' I ventured softly.

'Yes . . . yes . . .' she cried, throwing herself flat on the bed, burying her face so that I could not see the shame burning in her eyes.

'Good, then you're like most young women,' I assured her. 'I did it when I was younger. In fact, I still do. I give myself pleasure when I want to. There's nothing to be ashamed of.'

Isabella wouldn't move, she scrunched up the bed cover and hid her face from my gaze. I stroked her hair, pulling the ribbon away to release the dark locks. To tell the truth, I was amazed that she hadn't let the other girls finger her. It was what I would have done if I had been in her shoes. Perhaps she was waiting for permission, waiting for me to tell her it was good, as I had done with her breasts.

'It's okay,' I repeated, 'there's nothing to be ashamed of.' My entreaties were not working but there was something else that was certain to succeed. I lifted her skirt from behind and looked at her backside. She was wearing lacy black panties, pulled tightly between her buttocks by the position she had adopted. I slipped my hand under the skirt and began to massage her bottom firmly, running my hand up and down her thighs, pressing a finger between the cleavage of her rear cheeks, smoothing a hand round to the inside of her thighs.

She made no move but I felt the change come over her. Her body became less tense, her breathing gained in depth and the first involuntary sighs escaped from her lips.

'Let me touch you now,' I whispered to her, my teeth playing with the lobe of her ear. She twisted round to face me at last, her eyes wide and round. Without prompting, she began to unbutton her top, opening the garment to reveal soft white skin, her breasts squeezed into a silky black bra that lifted and parted her gorgeous titties.

I put my tongue out and licked between her breasts, pushing my face into the enveloping warmth of her chest, and at the same time passing my hand fully up her skirt. She parted her thighs and I palmed her pussy mound, filling my hand with her flesh, squeezing together her plump pussy lips. She was wet, the dampness soaking through the silk wetted my hand. I brought my hand to my face and breathed in the bouquet of her sex. She watched me, fascinated, as I licked the traces of her wetness from my palm. I touched her again and this time I put my hand to her face.

'Taste yourself,' I urged, using my other hand to rub my own pussy. She sniffed my hand then licked away her essence that was smeared on my palm. 'Now taste me,' I said, giving her the other hand. She did the same, breathing my scent then tasting me with the tip of her tongue.

'We taste different,' she observed, with a note of genuine surprise.

'Of course,' I smiled. 'Every woman is unique, all of us are sexy.'

I pulled her panties down a few inches, wanting to tease her a little. She parted her thighs, caught in her underwear, stretched tight like a band of silk that bound her together. My fingers roughed up and down her pussy lips, opening her, tickling her, teasing her without entering her special place. She moaned and lifted herself, trying to push her thighs apart. I caught a trickle of pussy juice sliding down between her bottom cheeks and traced it with my finger.

'I bet you taste wonderful,' I said, taking my wetted finger and sucking every drop down, swallowing as if it were the finest wine in the world.

'Can I taste?' she asked nervously. I dipped a finger into the river flowing from her sex and put it onto her lips. Her tongue lapped it up, then pulled my finger into her mouth. She swallowed it, then nodded happily.

She shifted round, pulling her own panties down to her knees, eager for me to explore her fully. I pressed my finger into the delicate tightness of sex, feeling the wet heat and the fleshy walls of her sex. She cried out, afraid that I was going to hurt her. She really was untouched and I was to be the woman honoured to initiate her into the pleasures of woman-to-woman loving. The thought made me shiver with lust. I seized her in my arms and kissed her violently, sucking away her breath, her girlish sighs, all her resistance.

I pushed her back on the bed, placed her hands on her breasts and closed her fingers around her nipples. 'Touch yourself there,' I commanded, excited by the view of her teasing her gorgeous nipples to erection. She obeyed, the pleasure from her fingertips making her close her eyes. I parted her thighs and looked down at the precious jewel that was mine to enjoy.

I lay beside her, my hands playing over her body. I pressed a finger deep into her sex and felt her stiffen anxiously. I played with her, moving my finger up and down softly, wet and sticky with her juices, playing with the tight bud. A second finger went into her pussy, now sufficiently wet and open. Her face was furrowed and I was afraid that I was hurting her.

We kissed and then my mouth sucked in a nipple, pulling it deep so that it filled my mouth almost to the back of my throat. The pleasure flooded her pussy with cream and I pressed my fingers deeper. She began to cry out but her pain soon turned to pleasure. She moaned suddenly and I was inside her, touching her like a woman. Her sighs became deeper, more fulfilled. I had taken her with the loving touch only a woman can supply.

I frigged her lovingly till she arched her back and screamed with pleasure. For the first time I had made her climax by playing with her sex and not with her breasts. It was pleasure of a sort she had never experienced before and from her ecstatic sighs I knew that she loved it.

We kissed once more and the longing in her eyes matched my own feelings of desire. I licked my fingers clean and then began to touch her again, exploring her pussy with a dexterity that had her rolling from side to side, parting her thighs and arching her back. I made her climax again, her wetness pouring onto my fingers thickly. My free hand caressed her breasts, her thighs, wiped the jewels of perspiration from her face and lips.

She lay beside me, her body bathed in sweat, exhausted, glowing pink with pleasure. 'That was good, wasn't it?' I whispered, letting her lick the last droplets of her pussy cream from my fingers.

'Is it always this good?' she asked, dazed by the experience.

'It can be,' I said. 'Now, it's your turn. My pussy is as wet and as hungry as yours was earlier. I want you to touch me, to give me as much pleasure as I gave you.'

She sat up on one elbow, looked at me eye to eye. 'Isn't it a miracle,' she whispered, 'how our bodies can give so much delight?'

'It is a miracle,' I sighed, opening myself to her tentative fingers as they slid into the velvety warmth of my pussy.

Having shown Isabella the pleasures of having her pussy sucked and fingered, and of mouthing another woman in turn, I let her loose on the other girls. It's true to say that for a whole week she seemed to be permanently dazed, her body glowing with the special luminosity of a woman well fucked. Her progress was phenomenal. Several times she came to my room and we made love furiously, her tongue like quicksilver in my sex, proving herself adept at making me come again and again.

Of course, the other girls taught her much too. I well remember my cries of delight when she began to finger my rear hole with one hand while fingering my sex with the other. That wasn't something I'd taught her but it was a lesson she'd learnt and taken to heart. She did it so well that she spent the night with me, I just couldn't allow her to stop. And always there was the gratitude, she was so thankful that I had shown her the way.

But there was still one big step for Isabella to take

before I could be satisfied. Although she wasn't aware of it, I was regularly checking to see how she reacted to the young men. Where she was confident and flirtatious with the other girls and the female staff, she was shy and retiring when confronted by Rudi or Erich or one of the other men. If there were still some doubts lingering inside her, they were all to do with the opposite sex.

We were taking a walk through the forest when I first broached the subject. The autumn had fallen quickly and the weather was growing cooler and wetter. The colour of the world was changing, imperceptibly at first and then by the day. But I liked the change and I took every opportunity to go out to the hills or down to the lakes to watch the movement of the seasons. That afternoon, Isabella and I were out in the trees behind the school. She had been telling me about Milan and Paris, about the fashion houses, designers and models. I only half listened, not that I wasn't fascinated by the chic and exclusive world that she knew from the inside, but because I wanted to talk to her about men.

'Bella, I know you might not want to discuss this,' I said, stopping in the middle of our walk and pulling her round to face me, 'but why are you so nervous in front of the boys?' I had been searching for a way to ease the question into conversation but had failed dismally.

'I'm not nervous,' she said defensively, the unexpected question throwing her for a second.

'Yes, you are,' I insisted. 'You haven't said more than a dozen words to Rudi, have you?'

'We just don't have anything to talk about,' she said

petulantly, turning to tramp back towards the school.

'Let's just talk about this,' I cried, catching up to her and grabbing her by the sleeve. She pulled her arm away and started off again. It had started to rain, the sky had gone from pale blue to grey to black and the wind was picking up speed, whipping up a flurry of leaves.

'There's nothing to talk about,' she maintained, in a voice at once so stubborn and hard that I was tempted just to forget the whole thing.

The rain was falling diagonally, cold heavy drops splashing forcefully onto our faces. Isabella started to run, swinging her arms and kicking through the dead leaves lying on the ground. I watched her for a second, cursing my bad timing, then started after her, running for my life as the rain got heavier. I followed her to the nearest chalet, not bothering to go back to the main building. We swung through the front door as a peal of thunder broke above us, an explosion of sound that echoed through the valley.

I was breathing hard, trying desperately to catch my breath, my chest heaving from the unexpected exertion. I looked round and saw Isabella laughing. The rain had slicked back her hair but her face was flushed red and speckled with droplets of water.

'What's so funny?' I wheezed.

'You,' she laughed. 'I thought that with all the physical exercise you get that you'd be fit enough to run a few metres in the rain.'

I laughed too. 'You know,' I said, standing up straight, 'you look lovely when you're wet.'

We kissed. Her lips were cold against my mouth. The rain on our faces merged and cool droplets flowed over our wet skin. I was right – she looked very sweet. Her face was glistening with jewels of rain picked out on pale skin.

'Do you want to make a run for it?' she asked, standing at the open door and gesturing to the main building across the way. The rain was steady now, swept along by a steady breeze that threw it diagonally. It wasn't far but I didn't fancy it, not when I knew that I'd be gasping for breath every step of the way.

'Let's stay here till it stops,' I replied, closing the door on the foul weather.

'You ought to get fit,' she said, wagging an admonishing finger, regarding me with a joyful smile.

'I'll do a deal with you,' I suggested. 'Tell me what your problem is with boys and I'll get fit.'

'That's not much of a deal,' she said coolly, the smile wiped from her face.

I sat on the floor, too tired to stand any longer. 'Why not?' I offered. 'You tell me about boys and I'll let you get me into shape.'

'But I thought Andrea was here to get us all into shape,' Isabella pointed out, referring to the dance teacher who also took the keep-fit classes.

'That's not for me,' I mumbled, gym classes had never been my thing, not even as a schoolgirl.

'You're ever so lazy,' Isabella stated disapprovingly. I nodded, she was right of course, there was no denying that. 'But you'll let me get you fit again?'

'That's right,' I confirmed. 'I'll give up my boycott of the keep-fit classes, if you talk to me about why you won't go anywhere near the men.'

'It's a long story,' she warned.

'Have we got anything better to do?' I asked, listening to the rain crashing against the door.

'It's no big deal,' she began, sliding down the wall to sit next to me, her legs pulled up, resting her chin on her knees. 'I was always a bit shy, you know that, and you know why. But I was trying to sort myself out, I was doing my best, and for a while I thought I was doing well. People always tell you to pull yourself together or to try and be outgoing, but it's never easy to do it. Like I say, I was trying very hard. I spent my sixteenth birthday with my grandmother in Milan and I felt comfortable with her, my mother was in Paris and I was just allowed to do things my way and in my own time.

'My grandmother's villa is a big place and she had people working there, looking after the house and the grounds. One of them had a son, Mario, about the same age as me. He was very friendly, he made me laugh and I liked that. I liked that a lot. He was a good-looking boy, he looked like one of those young Italian gangsters in *The Godfather*. You know, short hair, thick eyebrows, always laughing but with a hint of something dark and dangerous behind those big brown eyes.

'One day we were walking in the grounds. It was a summer afternoon, siesta time, it felt like we were the only people on earth. There was a fountain in the grounds and we watched the water gushing and splashing in the heat. It looked so inviting and we had often joked about pushing each other in. He splashed me and I splashed him back, and before we knew it were both soaked to the skin. I was wearing a thin tee-shirt and once wet it clung to my body and became almost transparent and the cool water made my nipples stand on end.

'I was hardly aware of it, we were having such fun. He pushed me hard and I fell headlong into the water. I came up laughing and spluttering but my shirt was see-through and my breasts were clear for him to see. He stopped laughing and put a hand on one of my tits. It felt good, I sort of half smiled, not certain what to do next. He wasn't laughing any more, the look in his eye was quite frightening, menacing in a way that I didn't understand.

'He told me to take my shirt off. He didn't ask, he ordered me. I said no but didn't push his hand from my breast. What I really wanted was for him to kiss me, to be nice to me, to cuddle me. Instead he ordered me to undress and began to unzip his trousers. I started to climb out of the water, I didn't like him any more. He grabbed me from behind, pulled me back into the water and pushed my head under. I came up screaming blue murder but he didn't care. He was naked, his prick was hard, his body lithe and muscular, the water sparkled on his skin.

'We struggled and he swore and told me it was my fault for arousing him. He said that I had breasts like a cow and that I needed to be taught a lesson for leading him on. He said lots of things, cruel horrible things, and all the time he kept going on about my breasts. He said that I was monstrous, deformed, that I had the tits of a whore. We struggled in the water but I managed to get away, my shirt ripped, shaking like a leaf. I ran away and all the time his taunts followed me, in my mind, so that even when I was back safe in my room his words echoed round and round in my head.

'That did it for me. I just withdrew back into my shell. I went home to Paris that same day, unable to tell anyone about what had happened. It was my fault, I shouldn't have led him on, I shouldn't have excited him. Looking back now I know that it wasn't my fault but at the same time that was all I could think of. It was my fault . . .'

I looked at her, her voice a whisper, staring straight down at the floor, reliving the nightmare. I took her in my arms, cuddled up to her, wrapped her in the warmth of my body. 'It *wasn't* your fault,' I whispered. 'It was never your fault, never in a million years. If only you'd spoken to someone! The little bastard should have been taught a lesson,' I spat angrily. 'How terrible for you Isabella, I'm so sorry.'

She smiled. 'Don't worry,' she assured me. 'I know now that it's not my fault. I realise that he just wanted to shame me into doing what he wanted. The truth was I would have made love with him. I loved the feel of his hands on my breasts. I wanted to, but not the way he wanted. He didn't want love, he just wanted to prove he wasn't a little boy.'

'That's the only thing he did prove,' I said. 'He just confirmed that he was a stupid little boy and nowhere near a man.'

'Since then I've always felt very nervous when I meet

a nice-looking fellow,' she admitted sadly. 'I can't help wondering whether he'll turn out to be another Mario. Good-looking but nasty.'

'Don't worry,' I assured her confidently. 'None of the boys here is anything like that. Do you trust me?'

'Of course,' she nodded vehemently.

'Then let me fix up a little time with Rudi.'

'Can it be Pierre or Alex?' she asked, looking up at me slyly.

'Sure,' I agreed readily. 'It'll be Pierre *and* Alex.'

'And you?' she added hopefully.

'And me,' I agreed, liking the idea very much.

'Then I can start on my side,' she said firmly, standing up.

'Pardon?'

'Your keep-fit programme,' she reminded me, taking my arm and pulling me up. I sighed, I had forgotten about that.

11

The idea came to me in my sleep, not as a dream exactly but it woke me up in the middle of the night – the idea of what to do about Luis. I didn't want just to talk to him, that would really give me very little idea of what he would be like when let loose in a building full of sexy young women. It's every man's dream, to live in a world of available young women, so how could we turn that dream into reality and be certain that Luis would know how to handle it? No, an interview, formal or informal, wasn't really good enough. What was required was a test of some sort, an informal aptitude test. Even better would be a test I could spring on him without letting him know what was going on.

The idea that came to me that night was so good that it wouldn't let me get back to sleep. It kept going round and round in my head, rippling with endless possibilities, all of which I explored in my over-active imagination. By the first light of dawn, and I can well recall what a miserable-looking dawn it was, I had worked it all out, down to the finest detail.

Amelia and Suzanne agreed to it instantly, they both commented that it was an original idea, though remarkably devious. I took that as a compliment, which is how it was meant, I think. Monique loved the idea when I broke it to her, it sounded far more interesting than subjecting Luis to a boring question-and-answer session in the hope that we'd discover what sort of a person he was.

Luis was staying at a hotel near Zurich airport, waiting for Amelia's final decision. Monique and I were booked into the room next door and, just to make sure he was around, he had been instructed to wait for a phone call at the time we were checking in.

The receptionist was a dark-haired young woman, with a ready smile and serious, questioning eyes. I handed her my papers, ignoring her smile, looking away haughtily. In truth, I was terrified that if I smiled then the game would have been given away. As it was, the receptionist was a soul of discretion, if she had any questions then she kept them to herself. My heart skipped a beat when she asked if my husband was going to join us, adding that, if required, my daughter could be given a separate room. Monique looked up at me that instant, looking every inch the eager teenager, as if to say that she too wanted a room on her own.

'No, thank you,' I said coldly. 'My husband is in London, his first wife is taking him to court again. My step-daughter and I will share the room.'

The receptionist did as she was told, she booked us into the room, and if she had any inkling that Monique was not my step-daughter she said nothing about it. We had done our best to look our parts. Monique was naturally very young-looking, her long curly locks and small round glasses made her look like a petite young student from the Sorbonne. I had my hair tied in a scarf, my face was heavily made up, as if I were trying to make myself look younger not older, and my clothes added a decade to my age without making me look unattractive. We didn't exactly look like mother and daughter, but wicked step-mother and innocent step-daughter looked a distinct possibility.

'Why can't I have my own room?' Monique demanded loudly as we waited for the bell boy to fetch our cases. We were still in earshot of the receptionist, I glanced at her but she was looking away, though there was no doubt that she was listening.

'Stop whining, girl!' I snapped. 'Isn't it enough that your slut of a mother is bleeding us dry?'

Once in the safety of our room we laughed ourselves to tears. We had fooled the hotel staff but they weren't our real target. Amelia called moments later to let us know that Luis had been told that he should stay in the hotel so that any important messages could be got to him quickly. She had suggested that he go down for a drink and he had agreed.

'Well, mother?' Monique asked brightly. 'What next? You still haven't explained how this is going to work.'

'That's because I don't really know,' I admitted. 'We need to improvise. The object of the exercise is to get Luis into some tight spot and see how he reacts. Any ideas?'

'How about we get him into our room?' she suggested.

'No, not straight away. Why don't I go down and meet

him first, you stay here and look like a schoolgirl. And whatever you do,' I smiled, 'keep your clothes on. You're an innocent young thing today, do try hard and remember what that was like.'

'You cat!' she laughed, throwing a pillow at me. I kissed her on the mouth then left, not forgetting to remind her to wipe my lipstick from her soft pink lips.

Luis was tall and good-looking with a long straight nose, sharp chin, olive skin and intense black eyes. He was seated at the bar, which was totally deserted, nursing a drink and staring into nothing.

'Do you work here?' I asked, sliding onto the stool beside him and peering round for the barman.

'No,' he said softly. 'He's just gone to get some drinks from the store room.'

'Thank you.' I smiled, sliding round to face him. He kept his eyes on me for a split second then looked away. 'I didn't mean to offend you,' I said. 'I saw you here alone and thought you worked here.'

'I'm sorry,' he countered, his face breaking into a smile. 'I'm not offended. It's just that I've got a lot on my mind.'

'Haven't we all?' I sighed, crossing my legs so that my skirt was tight across the top of my thighs.

'You too,' he sympathised. 'On holiday?'

I shook my head, leaning forward across the bar. 'No, I live here. Though I wish to God that I didn't. Would you like another drink?'

'Yes, thank you,' he agreed.

The barman had returned and I ordered a mineral

water for Luis and a glass of wine for myself. 'Simone Grant,' I said, offering my hand.

'Luis Delgado Lopez,' he responded, squeezing my fingers in his. 'So, what's so bad about Switzerland?'

'After London and Paris? Don't ask,' I said witheringly. 'And what about you, Luis? Is this a holiday? Or do you have some lonely rich widow tucked up your sleeve?'

He laughed. 'No rich widows, though I might be in need of one soon.'

It was my turn to laugh, edging closer to him, knowing that he could breathe my perfume, feel the warmth of my body close. 'I'll have to remember that,' I said. 'What about very rich and very bored wives? Do they rate higher or lower than rich widows?'

He flashed me a smile that was somersaulted into my belly, making my heart beat faster as the desire shot through me. 'It depends on the woman, of course,' he said, his voice low, so that I had to move closer to hear him – no, not to hear him but to feel him. 'For example,' he continued, 'if she were like you, then it would make no difference whether the woman was a widow or married to a Grand Duke.'

I swallowed hard. 'I think you're a very dangerous young man,' I told him softly, connecting directly with the darkness in his eyes.

'I'll take that as a compliment, shall I?' he asked, his face was next to mine, hard, unsmiling and fiercely attractive.

'My husband is away,' I whispered, fearing to move away, as if the atmosphere would snap and disappear forever. 'Come up to my room. This rich young wife wants to spend her husband's money.'

There was no hesitation, he smiled and offered me his arm. We walked out together, my arm in his, and I felt a wicked thrill, as if I really were seducing a young virile lover while my husband was away. We stopped at the reception desk and Luis asked if there were any messages for him. The receptionist shot me a look that was half disgust and half pure jealousy. I smiled back sweetly, thrilled to bits that my deception was proving so successful.

There were no messages and Luis was careful to hide his impatience. He noted the way the receptionist was looking at me so he kissed me on the mouth. His tongue traced the inside of my lips and he held my chin, lifting me slightly so that I had to cling to him. He released me and I turned with a smirk to the receptionist who had pursed her lips disapprovingly, as if it was she that was being betrayed and not my non-existent husband.

The elevator was empty and he took me in his arms once more. We kissed passionately. I could feel his muscular body pressed into my body, powerful arms holding me just the way he wanted. His prick was hard and pressed against my belly, making me feel weak with an aching desire deep in my sex. Amelia was right, he was an excellent lover, he had the poise and confidence of a man who knew how to make love to a woman properly.

'Can you just wait a second?' I asked apologetically when we reached the door to my room.

'My room is next door,' he pointed out.

'It's all right,' I said. 'I'll just be a second.'

I left him waiting at the door and slipped inside quickly. Monique wasn't in the room, and I guessed that she was in the shower. I crossed the room, my mind racing, wondering what to do next.

'Did you find him?' Monique asked, emerging from the bathroom just as I opened the door. She was wearing a thick towelling robe, her hair dripping wet.

'He's outside,' I whispered.

'Shall I disappear?' she suggested, sounding a note of panic.

'He thinks he's about to seduce a bored wife while her husband is away,' I explained. 'He doesn't know about her daughter, yet.'

'I'll disappear,' Monique repeated. It wasn't a bad idea. I wanted Luis desperately, my pussy was wet with wanting, but it didn't fit in with my plans.

'No,' I decided quickly. 'Get back into the bathroom. Stay there for about five minutes then sneak out, but don't be too sneaky about it.'

'I'll catch you at it,' she agreed. She disappeared back into the bathroom and I had a chance to check my face in the mirror. I looked good despite the make-up.

'Sorry about that Luis,' I smiled, pulling him into the room. 'Just a minor problem.'

'Did I hear voices?' he asked, looking around the room suspiciously.

'Don't worry about it,' I reassured him, pulling him across the room to the bed.

'Who's worried?' he asked nonchalantly. We kissed again, our mouths tingling with excitement. My hands were all over him, down his back, over his firm masculine backside, stroking the length of cock trapped in his tight trousers.

'Are you lovely and wet for Luis?' he teased, whispering in my ear as if I were a young girl and not a faithless and adulterous wife about to give herself to an ardent young lover.

'Is this what you do to all your rich widows?' I sighed, letting myself be wrapped in his arms. His prick was pushing against me again, a maddening reminder of what I wanted deep in my pussy.

'Rich widows, amorous wives and exciting senoritas,' he chuckled. He released me and began to strip off, slowly unbuttoning his shirt to reveal his broad hairless chest.

I watched for a second, excited by the way he was undressing, stripping off with an almost feminine delight in his own body. It was rare to see a man with an understanding of the erotic impact of his own nudity. I was transfixed for a moment, unable to take my eyes from him. He was naked and my panties were soaked through, the excitement inside me close to fever pitch.

He kissed me again and his nakedness felt so sensuous against my clothed body. His prick was a hard throbbing rod of flesh, silky skinned yet deliciously hard. I knelt down in front of him, my eyes fixed on his prick, my mouth tingling with anticipation.

'So, this is why you wanted me to stay locked in the

bathroom, is it?' Monique cried, her voice thick with
anger and disgust.

'What the hell do you want?' I demanded, the anger in
my voice more real than feigned.

'Who's she?' Luis demanded, looking down at me
and then at Monique, with an expression of pure horror
etched on his face.

'She,' Monique spat, 'is her daughter. And you,' she
pointed an angry finger at me, 'are an absolute slut!'

'Don't talk to me like that,' I retorted. 'I told you to
stay in there, didn't I? You'll not get a penny now.'

'What's going on?' Luis demanded.

Monique ignored him. 'You won't buy me off this
time,' she warned. 'I'll tell daddy everything and he'll
kick you out and get my real mother back.'

'He'll never take her back,' I stated coldly. 'Now, get
back in there and shut up. When you're older you'll
understand why your real mother left and why I'm doing
what I'm doing.'

'How much did you pay him?' Monique taunted, with
all the malicious glee of a real teenager.

'I'm going,' Luis said quietly, bending down to pick
up his clothes.

'No, don't go,' I cried, clutching at his waist with both
hands. His prick was in my face and I closed my mouth
around it, taking him deep and sucking hard. He tasted
divine and the feel of it in my mouth made me dizzy with
desire. The play-acting was becoming terribly real, the
emotions I was feeling were indistinguishable from the
real thing.

'That's disgusting!' Monique cried, her voice crystallised with pure loathing. I was aware of the slamming of the bathroom door, but I didn't care, all I wanted was Luis to fuck me in the mouth and then in my cunt.

'This is wrong, very wrong,' Luis whispered, his voice strained. He took me by the arms and pulled me to my feet. 'Senora, talk to your daughter,' he said sternly. 'This is wrong, you should not treat her like that. If you are having marital problems then you should not involve her. Please, talk to her.'

I threw myself on him, overwhelmed by an intense feeling of joy, a feeling of joy mixed with a strong dose of animal desire. He had to peel my body from his, to force my lips from his mouth. His eyes were full of pleading, he nodded towards the bathroom door then scooped down to pick up his clothes.

'You're a good man, Luis,' I said quietly, breathing hard, almost gasping for breath.

'Talk. Who knows?' he smiled weakly. 'I may see you later.'

Monique was out of the bathroom as soon as the coast was clear. Her robe was open, her breasts pink, her nipples erect points of flesh. From the look of desire in her eyes and the flushed colour of her cheeks, I knew that she had been fingering her pussy, which must have been as slippery with sticky love-cream as mine was.

'Isn't he lovely?' she beamed excitedly.

'Did you hear all that?' I asked, sitting down heavily on the bed, tired out by the intense emotions that had overtaken me. It was the first time I had ever consciously acted out a part and I had surprised myself by how well I had played it. At the time, of course, I had had no inkling of the significance, all I had cared about was testing Luis.

'I heard every word,' Monique told me, sitting down beside me. She touched me and I realised that I was shaking. 'You poor thing,' she said softly, 'you're trembling like a leaf.'

'It's silly, isn't it?' I said.

'No, you were very good,' she said. She turned to me and kissed me on the lips, taking up where Luis had left off.

'There aren't any doubts, are there?' I asked.

'No, he gets the job,' Monique agreed.

'Good,' I sighed, pulling Monique closer to me. I pulled the cord from her robe and her breasts were in my hands, soft and warm, and tipped with lovely hard nipples.

Monique undressed me quickly, pulling the blouse over my head, too impatient to unbutton it. My knickers were soaked, Monique pulled the silky garment off and brought it to her face, licking it with her tongue and breathing in the cloying scent. 'Let me suck you,' she whispered, kissing me so that the taste of my pussy was transferred from her mouth to mine.

I lay on my belly, lifting my bottom up so that she could slide a pillow under me. She parted my rear cheeks with her fingers and gazed down lovingly at my tightly puckered arsehole and the glistening folds of my pussy. My desire was so strong, Luis had aroused me to such an incredible extent, that I began to cruelly pinch and play with my nipples. The pleasure was intense, driving through me in waves that made me moan softly.

Monique kissed me on the bottom cheeks – big wet kisses that made me squirm. I wanted her inside me. She parted my cheeks and then licked from the dripping mouth of my sex right up over my rear hole. I lifted myself, arching my back. Her tongue was electric. She explored me, taking her time so that my pleasure rose, driven to a peak that had me thrusting myself up to meet her mouth.

I played with my nipples with one hand and slid the other under my parted thighs. I pulled myself open, sighing as my fingers brushed the sensitive inner folds of my pussy lips. Monique's tongue was going into me, slipping deep so that she could suck at the dewy cream pouring forth. I cried out as the climax shook my whole body. But I wanted more. Monique had not finished, her tongue was still lapping at my gushing pussy and my fingers were going into me too.

I cried out, climaxed again, pushed over the edge by Monique's exquisite probing and the feel of my fingers stroking my throbbing cunt-bud. I came in waves, orgasms crashing against the shore with all the primal force of nature. I felt dizzy, spinning through space, driven on by the pure sensations of my body.

A little later, after we recovered, we called Amelia with our duly considered verdict. She was delighted by the news and insisted on hearing every detail of what had transpired. Monique and I obliged, we reported on everything, from the disapproving receptionist to the moment Luis had left our room, a last-minute entreaty on his lips. My plan, which is what the improvised sequence of events had been christened, had given us a chance to see what sort of person lay beneath his seductive exterior.

Both Monique and I had wanted to break the news to him there and then, Monique begging like the teenager she had pretended to be, but Amelia was insistent. I could see what lay behind her thinking. Luis had been tricked, no matter how good our intentions, and even the positive outcome couldn't change that.

We checked out of the hotel that same afternoon. The receptionist eyed me frostily as I paid the bill, perhaps recognising that our hasty departure had something to do with Luis. Monique played up to her, whining constantly like a spoilt child.

'Stop it,' I snapped wearily, putting on my best harried-mother look.

'No,' Monique retorted petulantly.

'Maybe this will stop you,' I said impulsively. I caught her by the arm and pulled her towards me. Our lips met and were joined in a long searching kiss. I closed my eyes and just enjoyed the feel of her mouth on mine.

'Oh, mummy,' Monique sighed ecstatically, breathing hard with excitement. We looked at each other for a second then kissed again, as passionately as the first time, my hands massaging her lovely backside at the same time.

We separated and saw that the business of the hotel lobby had come to a complete standstill. I turned coolly to the open-mouthed receptionist and picked up my credit card. 'Thank you so much,' I said casually.

'Please call again,' the receptionist replied automatically, her conditioned response stronger than the shock on her face. Monique and I breezed out of the hotel, holding hands happily, followed by countless pairs of eyes. The thrill of breaking the taboo, even if only in make-believe, gave the pair of us a fantastic kick. We talked about it incessantly for months afterwards.

I met Luis again a few days later, Monique and I were there to greet him on his arrival at the school. We were in Amelia's office, wondering how he was going to react. Amelia had explained the situation to him and, according to her, he took it in his stride. In his situation I would have seen the funny side of it, I was sure of that, but then not everybody shares my warped sense of humour.

'The lovely senora and senorita,' he said warmly when he came in, giving each of us a friendly peck on the cheek.

'We're sorry about the deception,' I said, speaking for all of us. He looked in fine form, dressed casually in the stylish sort of clothes that cost a minor fortune.

'I understand, it's the people at the hotel that didn't,' he laughed, his dark eyes sparkling with sly good humour.

'The receptionist, you mean?' Monique guessed.

'She was very interested, especially in you, Melissa. She was fascinated by what she had seen. She seemed to be half in love and yet full of loathing for you. She was a strange young woman, she wanted me to give her your phone number. But it wasn't just her, everybody in the hotel was talking about your leaving scene. It made a certain impression,' he said.

'We like to cause a stir,' I said, making a mental note to get the girl's number, she was the sort of intense beauty that is always worth seeking out.

'Half of the people thought you two were sick perverts,' he added, pausing so that I wondered if he himself felt that way, 'and the other half were incredibly turned on. There were endless rumours about what had happened between the three of us.'

'You ought to go on stage,' Amelia suggested to Monique and myself, taking Luis by the arm at the same time, a possessive gesture that was not lost on anyone in the room.

'Well, we are sorry, but it has had a good result,' I finished. 'I'll see you later perhaps,' I added, heading for the door, aware of the grateful smile on my aunt's face.

Monique and I went down for a cup of coffee, each of us strangely subdued. I was thinking about Luis, unable to forget the taste of his prick or the heat he had aroused in me. The way that Amelia had held him suggested that, at least for a while, he was going to be her pampered toy – at her side and ready to serve her, sexually or otherwise, at any moment. I couldn't blame her of course. I was just a bit jealous, especially as I could have made love to him at the hotel had I been less scrupulous about my work.

'What are you thinking about?' Monique asked, sitting down at the kitchen table, a cup of strong black coffee to hand.

'Nothing,' I mumbled, taking a seat opposite her.

'Liar! You're thinking of Luis,' she said confidently.

'Maybe,' I admitted.

'It was a good trick we played, wasn't it?'

'Do you know something,' I said, 'I keep thinking about that last kiss in the lobby. I don't know about you, but I felt really turned on by it.'

Monique laughed. 'I know exactly what you mean, every time I think about it I get excited. As we're making confessions, I may as well admit that I've been fantasising about it constantly and frigging myself at the same time.'

'God, we're terrible,' I said, shaking my head.

'You heard Amelia, we ought to be on stage,' Monique reminded me, her manner suddenly subdued.

'That was a joke,' I said. The feelings that had been inside me while I played the part of the amorous mother had been real, more real than I had imagined possible, but at the time I didn't understand the full significance of it, nor did I understand what Monique was getting at.

'There's many a true word . . .' Monique commented, giving me a sideways glance.

'What are you suggesting?' I asked, frowning.

'Just that there are many possibilities waiting to be explored,' she said subtly.

'Aren't you happy here?' I asked, taken rather by surprise. Monique was sitting with her back to the window, her body framed by the grey view of misty mountains. Was she really dissatisfied with her life at the school?

'Yes, of course I'm happy,' she responded, a little too vehemently for me to believe her completely.

'I don't understand,' I admitted. The grey day, visible

in the large square window, filled me with a melancholy feeling, a feeling of vague nostalgia, for there was nothing to be nostalgic about.

'I don't know, I don't know,' Monique sighed. She stood up, walked to the window. 'Do you ever talk to the girls here? Do you ever listen to what they say?'

'What exactly?'

'They lead such exciting lives, so varied, so interesting. They've travelled half the world, they can speak half a dozen languages, the world is full of endless possibilities for them.'

'But they come to us, even with all those possibilities,' I pointed out, going over to the window too. In a way I blamed the weather for her mood, as if the grey misery spread before us was somehow seeping into our souls. I took her by the shoulders and turned her towards me.

'Yes, they spend a year here, two years at the most. And then?' she asked plaintively.

'And then they move on,' I said softly. 'But so what? We'll have other girls here, eager to learn, willing to love and be loved. We're helping them, giving them something that they'll carry forever.'

'You're still new here,' Monique said flatly, seeking not to explain my words but to excuse hers.

'No, it's not just that I'm new,' I protested. 'This place has a purpose and we're here to help achieve that purpose. It's not just a job, we're not like that. We're here because we want to be. Don't you feel that? There has to be a spark of idealism or it's all meaningless. You're here because you want to be.'

'I know,' she agreed, turning from me to face the window again, looking out across the valley, swept with a fine grey drizzle. 'I'm not unhappy, it's just that sometimes I feel that there's so much out there and that we're missing out.'

I kissed her on the shoulder, very softly, very affectionately. 'Perhaps you need a break,' I suggested. The weather had changed, it was now too cold for her to go to the clearing and lie under the gushing water. Without her time alone, a time that was as much a release from work as anything else, was she going to be able to unwind from the daily stress? It was a thought that had never occurred to me before, but I realised then the importance of her secret place, why she wanted it and the value of a private place cut off from the world.

'No, I'm all right,' she said decisively, forcing a smile. 'It's just Amelia's comment about the stage, it got me thinking about what could be, one day.'

'Is that what you'd like to do?'

'It's just an idle fantasy,' she laughed. 'Being on stage is just one of the things I'd like to do, just one of the ambitions that have been put aside for the moment. Now, how about cheering me up properly?'

'And how might I do that?' I wondered, taking her in my arms and planting a kiss on her pouting lips.

'You could pretend to be mummy again,' she proposed, licking her lips with lustful delight. She smiled and her smile was infectious.

'You *are* a bad girl,' I scolded, finding it remarkably easy to slip into character, even the sound of my voice and the rhythm of my speech changed. 'I want you up in my room, now. And I won't have any arguments, you'll do as you're told, my girl.'

'But, mummy . . .' Monique complained, her eyes already filled with a dark and intense desire. We both knew that we had to finish the game that had been started in the hotel lobby.

12

Amelia kept a tight rein on Luis, probably enjoying him all the more because she knew that every female in the school had the hots for him. I kidded her about it, accusing her of being too possessive. But she just laughed and her eyes shone with a pleasure that took the bite out of my remarks. She looked radiant and that made me happy too, although I couldn't help but be jealous of them both. It was one of those odd situations when I didn't care which of the couple I had, I was desperately lusting after my aunt as well as Luis.

In the end I managed to climb into bed with Luis first. That it happened the way it did was only partly down to me, for the most part it was thanks to Isabella. Her first encounter with Pierre and Alex had been put off time and again, partly because I had been distracted by the encounter with Luis at the hotel and because she still appeared too nervous. When I quizzed her about it she made vague excuses about being too busy. My instincts told me to press ahead but for once I decided to hold back.

Isabella wasn't being completely untruthful in complaining of being busy. Now that the painful shyness had been banished she had plunged headlong into all the activities on offer. She was always going off skiing (she had to be the only girl at the school who hadn't mastered the art yet) and, in particular, she loved Monique's computer classes to distraction. It was a gratifying transformation and I was proud that I was, in large part, responsible for it.

Maria too was very happy. She graced us with a surprise visit and the reunion between mother and daughter was tearful, intense and genuinely moving. We left them alone for an age, just talking, hugging and getting to know each other all over again. Afterwards Maria gave me a long and very arousing kiss on the lips before presenting me with a pair of diamond earrings. I was embarrassed, I tried to explain that I'd only been doing my job but she insisted and I graciously accepted the gift. A little later Isabella gave me a gift of her own, a very sexy top in black latex from the London fashion house of Ectomorph. I was thrilled to bits. It was the most exciting garment I had ever worn and, of course, Isabella insisted that we try it on together.

'Now, Isabella,' I told her sternly one day, a few weeks after Luis had settled into the house, 'we really ought to arrange a date with Pierre and Alex.'

'But Mel . . .' she started to complain. We were in her room, I had stopped by to have a chat with her and found her swotting up on her books.

'No ifs or buts,' I said, 'you can't stay like this for ever.'

'Why not?' she challenged, flicking me a look that was proudly defiant.

'How can you be sure that you only want to love other women without first trying men as well?'

'I can be sure,' she explained with that fervent certainty of the young and inexperienced. 'There's nothing better than having another woman sucking my nips or fingering my pussy. And I like nothing better than to lick out another pussy, can anything compare to that pleasure?'

'Well, yes, actually,' I smiled. 'Let us have this one session, the two of us with two of the boys, and then you can decide for yourself. Is that a deal?'

'What about our last deal?' she reminded me.

I smiled awkwardly. 'Ah, that. A deal is a deal,' I acknowledged. 'You can start getting me into shape as soon as you fulfil your side of the bargain.'

'Good,' she smiled. 'I'll have you running six miles every morning,' she promised with a wicked glint in her eye.

'Oh don't,' I shuddered. 'Can't I just be allowed to cut down on sugar?'

'I'll be lenient on one condition,' she said, looking up from her book with a shy smile on her lips. 'I'll cut it down to two miles a day if it can be Luis and Pierre.'

'I see,' I said noncommittally, even though I wanted to jump up and down with excitement. 'Why the sudden interest in Luis?'

'It's nothing really,' she said, trying to brush aside my natural curiosity.

'Come on,' I persisted, 'what is it? You know I have your interests at heart.'

'Oh, you're so nosey,' she scolded playfully. 'It's nothing much. He saw me on the stairs yesterday. I had dropped a couple of books and was reaching down to pick them up.'

'He saw you? How much did he see?' I guessed that the encounter was a deal less innocent than the elfin young Isabella was suggesting.

'Well . . . I was wearing that short black skirt I borrowed from Monique, you know, the loose flared one. And I guess I was bending down very low. He was at the foot of the stairs. From where he stood he could see right up my skirt.'

To me it sounded as if Isabella's exhibitionist inclinations were coming to the fore. 'How long were you bending over for?' I asked, crossing my arms and giving her a disapproving look.

'I dropped a few books,' she smiled. 'Honestly, it was an accident,' she insisted, returning a sly smile to my stern face. 'Well, it was at the beginning.'

I broke into a smile. 'It sounds to me like you're making up for all the time you've lost.'

'I dropped one of my books, bent down and saw him looking up. He didn't notice me looking back. I hesitated, dropped another book and bent down lower. The look in his eyes was wonderful, he was eating up the view of my long legs and my black knickers pressed tightly between my thighs. I moved back, sort of pressing my legs straight. Then our eyes met.'

'What happened then?'

'I blushed. I couldn't help it, I was so embarrassed.

But he just flashed me a delicious smile and offered to
carry my books for me.'

'Did he say anything else?' I asked, able to understand
the feelings of excitement that must have been going
through him. It was a credit to his self-control that he
hadn't taken Isabella on the stairs, sinking his stiff prick
into her virginal pussy.

'Yes . . . He said that I should bend over more
often . . .'

My laughter triggered hers. I bent down and kissed her
softly on the forehead, brushing my hand through her
luxuriant curls. 'I think that Senor Lopez should have his
wish granted. I'll talk to Amelia and see what can be
arranged.'

'In that case, maybe I'll let you get away with a one-
mile run in the mornings,' she giggled as I left the room.
I had to strike while the iron was hot, so went directly to
my aunt's office.

Amelia was very good, she listened patiently to my
request and laughed when I told her the story about
Isabella bending over. 'You're sure that you've no ulterior
motive for choosing Luis?' she asked.

'Absolutely not,' I lied. She knew that I was lying and
I knew that she knew. It was a game and both of us were
playing to the same unwritten rules.

'You've convinced me, darling,' she said, smiling
generously. 'Make sure you return him to me in the same
state that you find him. I don't want the poor boy too
exhausted.'

'Don't worry,' I assured her, 'he'll be well looked after.'

'Good. Now, darling, we've another new girl that might be starting soon. Another problem girl I'm afraid.'

'Are there any other kind?'

'Well, Melissa, it's only because you're here now that we're even considering girls like Isabella and Fiona. But don't worry, this one is a very different character. Will you talk to her and see if she's right for us?'

'Of course I will. Is she in Zurich?'

Amelia shook her head. 'No, in London. Would you fly there tomorrow or the day after? I'd like it sorted out as quickly as possible.'

I sat down heavily in the seat beside Amelia's desk. 'London?' I asked. It sounded like I was being asked to travel halfway around the world.

'Yes, you can be in and out in a day if you like,' Amelia reminded me, taking note of my obvious reluctance.

'Can't she come over here?' I asked, not at all relishing a return to the grey and unforgiving city that had rejected me.

'No, I think it's better if you fly out. There's one other thing, Charlotte's parents are in London. Charlotte would like to go to see them, would you mind travelling together?'

'Can I think about this?' I asked, suddenly flustered. I didn't want to go to London, I didn't want to meet this new girl, or Charlotte's parents or anything.

'Why not talk to Charlotte? I'm sure she'll persuade you,' Amelia suggested.

'What if my answer is still no?'

'Then I'll send Suzanne in your place,' Amelia said flatly. 'I'm sorry,' she added quickly, 'that wasn't supposed to sound harsh. I'll understand if you don't want to go and nobody here would want to force you to do something you didn't want to. All I'm asking is that you think about it and not reject it out of hand.'

'Thanks, I appreciate that. I do want time to think before I reach a final decision.'

'I understand,' Amelia smiled reassuringly.

'Now, I'd better talk to Luis and Pierre,' I said, turning my attention to something I was going to enjoy.

Isabella was in my arms, her eyes closed so that she could enjoy the pure pleasure that I was giving to her. I had pulled her sweatshirt up, exposing her smooth belly and bare breasts. Her nipples were delightfully erect. She was wearing a short skirt and white panties, my hand smoothing up and down the soft skin on her inner thighs. I looked at her, her eyelids fluttering, her lips puffy from being kissed so violently, a face so sweetly innocent I almost wet myself every time I had her in my arms.

'In heaven,' she whispered lyrically, 'every moment will be like this one.'

I made no reply, I kissed her, pausing so her breath mingled with mine. I was wearing a loose top, the buttons undone to my belly button, my breasts bare under the flimsy material. I lifted her skirt and stared at her long smooth thighs and her snow-white cotton panties. The dark hair of her pussy mound was a shadow against the pure whiteness, a shadow that was soiled, her pussy secreting its juice as I kissed and sucked her breasts and mouth.

She sighed, put her hand inside my blouse, took one breast and squeezed it, massaging the globe, the nipple crushed in her palm. Of all the girls in the school she was the one that knew how best to play with my breasts. She knew how to excite me beyond endurance, how to bring me off just by skilfully mouthing my nipples.

Her eyes were still closed. She was still floating in a sensual dream world, lingering on the edge of orgasm to prolong the ecstatic state for as long as possible. I looked up, the door was open and Luis and Pierre were entering, sneaking in like thieves in the night. The two of them were almost naked, Pierre still wearing a tee-shirt that reached down to his waist and Luis in a pair of tight shorts. Pierre's thick rod was hard and, judging by the bulge in Luis's shorts, so was he. I put my finger to my lips, not wanting to disturb Isabella, who was in for quite a surprise, I hadn't told her that we were to be joined by the men.

'Do you remember how you felt when Luis was looking up your skirt?' I whispered to her, smothering her face with a volley of quick kisses to keep her from opening her eyes.

'Mmm, I felt my pussy getting wet,' Isabella said dreamily, 'and I wondered if Luis could see it.'

'And if he had?'

'It would have been horrible,' she sighed, taking my hand and placing it between her thighs. 'I only want you to know how hot and wet I can become.'

'How would you feel if Luis could set eyes on these lovely titties?' I asked her, biting a nipple. She arched her back, her body tensing as if ready to climax, I released her, wanting to intensify the pleasure.

'I'd get very nervous,' she admitted, 'I think he'd laugh at me. Only other girls understand. They love my breasts, I have to fight them off,' she smiled.

'That's not true,' a strong male voice dissented. Isabella cried out, her eyes opened wide, a look of real fear and shock set hard on her face. She tried to pull her sweatshirt down but I held it in place.

'Luis is correct,' Pierre added, standing beside Luis, a foot from Isabella who was trying to hide herself in my arms.

'Why didn't you tell me?' she whispered, her lips quivering, eyes full of tears.

'We agreed,' I said reasonably, unable to quite understand why she felt betrayed. I lifted her sweatshirt higher and shifted round on the bed, deliberately exposing her breasts to the appreciative eyes of the men. Luis whispered something in Spanish and from the look of adoration in his eyes there was no question of what he felt.

'You are so very beautiful,' Pierre said, stepping closer to her, his eyes glued to her large breasts while her eyes were fastened on his thick cock.

'I think you boys ought to show Isabella how much you admire her body,' I suggested.

Pierre sank to his knees and gently put his mouth to one of her nipples. He kissed the hard bud reverently, a soft chaste kiss. Luis followed suit, reaching across Pierre to kiss Isabella's other breast. In an instant we were a mass of bodies, the two men greedily mouthing Isabella's bosom while I sucked her lips and rubbed the inside of her thighs.

Her misgivings were swept away in that same moment and her sighs filled my mouth. She threw her head back, cupped her breasts and offered them to the men, leaving her neck bare for my lips. My finger was tracing a long slow line from her anal hole to her pussy, pressing firmly over her wet panties. Pierre and Luis were all over me too, stroking, touching, exciting me by their sheer presence and the pure animal sexuality of the way they were eating Isabella's pouting nipples.

Isabella cried out and arched her back as I slipped a finger into the reservoir of pussy cream. She cried out again and again, her voice higher and higher until a last strangled cry signalled her climax. My fingers were wet and I sucked them greedily, swallowing her taste with a thrill of pleasure.

'It's time you took a good look at the boys,' I told her, sounding more like a biology teacher than I had ever imagined possible. The men understood at once and stood up, eager to show off their hard masculine bodies to a young lady enjoying the privilege for the first time. Pierre threw his shirt off and Luis pulled down his shorts. They stood side by side, like two models in a life class at art college, except that models are rarely in so obvious a state of excitement.

Isabella's eyes scanned from one lovely hard cock to

the next. Luis took his in his hand, holding it by the base so that it looked bigger, sticking it out so that she could get a better view. I signalled and Pierre turned round, offering her a view of his tight round posterior, the dark pouch between his thighs clearly visible.

'This dear girl,' I lectured with a smile on my face, 'is a lovely strong specimen of prick. Used properly it can give you the most intense pleasure you can imagine, equal to anything you can get from another woman.'

She sat up on her knees, peering forward to get a better look at the two men displaying themselves for her benefit. I pulled her top off completely and she made not a murmur of protest. I reflected how lucky she was – I wished that I'd been offered such fine young men when I was her age.

'Can I touch?' she whispered, her embarrassment taking a back seat to her natural fascination. Luis edged a little closer, still holding his cock by the base. Very gingerly Isabella reached out and touched him, her finger tips barely caressing the finely veined tool.

'Like this,' I showed her, tapping Pierre's backside to get him to turn round. His prick was as big and as thick as Luis's, but it looked different, the skin a different tone, the glans a little fuller perhaps. I took the organ in my hand and ringed the base with my fingers, squeezing lightly.

Isabella followed suit, squeezing Luis, exploring his prick with a tenderness that was astounding. I could tell that she was scared to break it, as if somehow his cock would fall apart in her little hand. I began to rub my fingers slowly up and down Pierre, enjoying the feel of his silky hardness and making him sigh. 'That feels good,' he whispered.

For a half a minute Isabella watched, not sure whether to look at the action of my hand or the pleasure on Pierre's finely chiselled face. She watched and then copied the movement, running her fingers softly over Luis's prick then pulling back with a firmer action. His murmur of appreciation gave her more confidence and her rhythm was becoming more assured with every stroke.

'Good girl,' I said encouragingly. 'If you carry on like that you'll have a reward of thick sperm spurting all over you.'

'Is it that good?' she asked Luis disbelievingly.

'Yes, Isabella. I imagine that this is what it feels like when another girl fingers your sex,' he said, putting a hand on her shoulder to balance himself as the surges of energy passed through him.

'Pricks aren't just for masturbating like that,' I added, 'they taste good too.' I leaned forward and licked the jewel of pre-come that was balanced on the tip of Pierre's tool. I licked again, my tongue started halfway down his prick and then finishing at the tip. I relished every pore of his cock, his throbbing muscle rippling on my tongue.

Luis's prick was dribbling a thick line of fluid and Isabella had smeared it on the underside with her fingers, making his tool glisten seductively. She looked at it lovingly then put her tongue out and lapped at it. The feel and taste of it had the desired effect. She twisted her head and put her mouth to the glans. Her lips were the same colour as the prick head and, from where I sat, it seemed that his glans had been doubled in size and her lips were part of his cock.

I opened my mouth and began to suck Pierre's rod, using my fingers to rub and caress the thick round base of his manhood. I moved my head up and down, enjoying the rush of oral penetration, his hardness brushing through my lips and into the back of my mouth. I twisted round and saw that Isabella was a natural fellatrice, her mass of dark curls were bobbing up and down on Luis's abdomen while her mouth worked its magic on his lovely cock.

The view of Isabella and Luis added to my own excitement. I sucked and licked with glorious abandon, using my hand and mouth to make Pierre moan deliriously. With my free hand I stroked his tightly packed balls and explored between his buttocks, tickling the tight bud of his rear hole. He began to writhe, jerking his prick further into my mouth, his cock twitching dangerously.

I pulled away quickly and began to wank his spit-soaked cock with both hands. Looking round I saw that Isabella was still mouthing the cock in her mouth, twisting and turning her head, devouring it intently. I pulled her away and pushed her back on her elbows. Luis seemed to understand instinctively what I wanted. He knelt on the edge of the bed with one knee, took his prick in his hands and began to rub himself. Isabella was dazed, she looked a little lost but her eyes were wide with fascination. I positioned Pierre next to Luis, my hand still riding up and down rhythmically on his cock.

Isabella cried out, putting a hand to her mouth. Luis

and Pierre seemed to climax at the same instant, their cocks gushing out thick globules of white spunk. I watched the spurts of cream arcing out and onto Isabella, flicking rivulets of come onto her chest and face. The look of wonderment on her face was a joy to see. The boys stepped away and left the way clear for me.

I touched a finger in one of the pools of come sliding down from her chin. I showed her the spunk on my fingertip, a droplet of whitish cream that had spurted from a raging cock. I put the pearl to my tongue and licked it away. A second drop I offered to her. She hesitated then lapped it up, savouring it in her mouth, letting the taste suffuse for a second, then she swallowed it.

'Good?' I asked, not at all certain that she would like the taste of fresh come as much as I did.

'Good,' she nodded excitedly. I cupped her breasts, caught the tears of come as they flowed jerkily down to her nipples. I hesitated, not sure of my next move, but Isabella had her own idea. She sat up and pressed her breasts against mine. I felt the warm come slide between us, a gooey sticky feeling, then she pulled away. Both our breasts were wet with thick smears of prick cream. I bent and began to suck her breasts clean, enjoying the taste of prick smeared across the soft texture of breast, especially the thick globules that beaded her fine hard nipples.

She climaxed, her breasts seeming to glow as the force of orgasm shook her body. I kissed her on the mouth and I felt her using her tongue to lap up the come still on my tongue. I sat back and then she began to lick my breasts clean, her eager mouth working furiously to lap up every last drop. I climaxed too, for while she sucked at my nipples one of the boys, I guessed it was Pierre, began to massage my rear hole.

Isabella and I kissed lovingly, all her misgivings had been proven to be unfounded. Her body glowed with that freshly fucked radiance that can be instantly recognised. We had both climaxed, but that was only the beginning.

'Now, my darling,' I whispered softly, 'it's time that you had a nice stiff prick inside your sweet pussy.'

'You'll be with me, won't you?' she asked, her grey eyes looking deep into mine for reassurance.

I pushed her flat on the bed and parted her thighs. Behind me both Luis and Pierre were ready again, stiff pricks straining. Her panties were soaked through, as if deluged by the wash of juice from her sex. I pulled the garment down and brushed my fingers through the sticky hair at the mouth of her vagina. I opened her softly. The glistening pink folds of her pussy were warm and inviting. There was no way I could resist the temptation, my tongue was soon lapping at her heat, flicking playfully at her thick bud.

Her sighs, a pure song that I loved to hear, filled the room. It was time. Luis edged forward, fitting his body between her open thighs. I took his throbbing prick and steered him to the gates of heaven. Isabella's eyes were full of apprehension. I kissed her on the mouth, and I knew that she trusted me. Very slowly Luis entered her, his prick only going in an inch or two.

'How does that feel?' he asked anxiously, afraid to hurt her.

'That's nice,' she whispered, but her voice was laboured.

'Close your eyes and imagine that it's my fingers,' I advised her.

She closed her eyes and Luis pressed his hardness in further. When she made no protest he went further still. I checked with my fingers and found that he was halfway in, his thick round cock forcing open the delicate lips of her sex. Suddenly he plunged deep into her and her cry was more of surprise than pain.

'That's so good . . .' she whispered, knowing that she had taken all of his hardness into the velvety warmth of her sex. They didn't move, just looked at each other for a moment, their eyes locked. Then he began to move in and out slowly, his rhythm strong and sure. Her eyes were closed but the measure of her breath changed, as he went in she inhaled, then exhaled as he withdrew.

Pierre was behind me, sitting on the bed. He began to massage my breasts, his mouth on my neck and shoulder. I parted my thighs and put his hand on my pussy, wanting him to caress me for a moment before he speared me with his prick.

'Melissa . . . Melissa . . .' Isabella moaned, turning to me, her face a mask of ecstasy.

'Yes, darling.'

'Kiss me on the mouth while Luis fucks me,' she asked, the passion making her voice sound faint.

I lay on my belly beside her, my breasts pressed against her arm. My backside was thrust out as I curved my spine, offering myself to Pierre. I kissed Isabella, forcing my hot tongue deep into her receptive mouth, and at the same time I felt Pierre's tongue between my thighs. In the strange orgasmic dissonance it felt as if I were tonguing my own sex, every movement of my tongue in Isabella's mouth being echoed by Pierre's tongue inside the red heat of my pussy.

I was hardly aware of Luis, thrusting hard and fast into Isabella's gushing pussy. Her cries and sighs of desire were a music, her breath was hot on my face and I was feasting on her lips and sometimes on her delicious pink nipples.

Pierre swallowed the honey that flowed with my climax, his tongue still deep in my sex as I arched my back for final release. He kissed me gently on the rear hole then moved his body over mine.

'Fuck me, please . . .' I begged. I twisted round and Luis took my mouth in his. Isabella was tweaking my breasts even as she was being driven inexorably to a climax herself. Pierre pierced me with one strong thrust of his hips, his prick plunging into me.

It was ecstatic, four naked bodies, bathed in sweat and come, twisting and turning with one object in mind. I couldn't tell who was touching me, who was fucking me, who was kissing me. And I couldn't tell what I was doing, whose body I was caressing, whose mouth I was kissing. Isabella climaxed several times and each time I felt the tremor echo through me too. I climaxed later and felt Pierre's prick shooting thick hot cream into my pussy.

We fell apart, momentarily sated, still tingling from

the explosion of pleasure that we had all shared.

'Well, Isabella,' I asked lazily, breaking the long silence that we had fallen into, 'do you think you'll always make love to girls now?'

'How silly that must have sounded,' she sighed, kissing me on the shoulder.

'How do you feel?' Luis asked softly, his strong hands rubbing up and down her thigh insistently.

'Like a woman,' Isabella replied.

I felt Pierre stirring. I looked round and saw that his delicious prick was rising once more. He still looked strong and I guessed that Luis too must have recovered. I turned and sucked the hardening rod in my mouth. I tasted myself on Pierre's prick, and tasted the salty come that he had filled me with. Luis came towards me. He gestured to Pierre and the two of them swapped places.

'There's no such thing as too much of a good thing,' Pierre laughed softly, reaching down to plant a long slow kiss on Isabella's breast.

I sat up on hands and knees, hollowing my back down and thrusting my buttocks up. 'Why don't you try it like this?' I said to Isabella. She turned and adopted the same position, on hands and knees, facing me. We kissed passionately, knowing that we would be able to watch each other being fucked.

Luis spread my thighs and began to lick my pussy and my rear hole. It was maddening, his tongue seemed to move like lightning but never stayed in one place long enough for me to enjoy it. He was teasing me, exciting me beyond endurance. 'Suck me . . . Suck me please,' I begged, knowing that he liked to be begged, that the torment I felt was purely erotic.

'Where?' he teased, a thick finger brushing my pussy lips open while his tongue kissed my tight anal hole.

'I want your mouth in my behind,' I begged. He obeyed, his lips planted on my rear hole, his tongue probing tentatively. I looked up and saw that Pierre had already entered Isabella and that he was fucking her slowly while pinching her nipples.

Isabella kissed me on the mouth, her hot breath at one with mine. 'This is so good . . . so good . . .' she was whispering, an incantation that faded to nothing as Pierre began to fuck her harder, his big prick filling her tight wet pussy.

I cried out, Luis had suddenly pulled away and pressed his hard cock into my sex. My backside was still tingling from his tonguing and that became part of the pleasure of his lovemaking. I felt myself falling again, slipping from reality into that dimension where the pleasure seemed to be coming from all over my body. Every pore, every cell screamed in pure blind ecstasy. I climaxed, recovered and climaxed again, and all the time Isabella was kissing me and Luis was plunging his cock deeper and deeper into my red-hot quim.

Sometime, in the delirium of my orgasm, I thought I heard Isabella's angelic voice singing out with joy, crying, 'I love you . . . I love you . . .' as she too reached the peak of pleasure.

13

It didn't take much to persuade me to go back to London for a few days after all. Charlotte was desperate to accompany me and one look from her dark imploring eyes was all it took. The poor girl was devoted to me and though all my attention had been lavished on Isabella she had not made one complaint. She asked me hesitantly and I didn't have the heart to turn her down.

It was the right decision to take, of course. My initial reluctance to leave Switzerland was due more to the way the trip had been sprung on me than anything else. It had been totally unexpected and Amelia had hardly done a good job selling it to me. But the timing was just right. If the trip hadn't come up I would have invented some other reason to get away for a few days. The session with Isabella, Pierre and Luis had been intense, passionate and emotionally draining. It had gone far better than expected and, far from fighting shy of the men, Isabella had been unable to get enough of their attentions. But now it was time for a break, time for me to sit back and take stock of the situation, hers and mine.

Isabella's demands for my attention were growing rather than lessening, a development that was far from what I had intended. For a while she had been making excellent progress on her own, as she herself attested and as many of the other girls were happy to tell me. But this healthy development had stopped and she now seemed to include me in all her plans. While I could understand why she wanted me to be with her when she first gave herself to a man, I could not understand why she wanted me for all her subsequent erotic adventures. But she refused to have anything to do with Pierre or Luis or anyone unless I was at her side, a willing partner in our threesomes and foursomes.

I asked her if she was still pursuing the other girls but she just smiled and shook her head. She told me that she had gone off girls, that all she wanted now was to join me in a series of erotic encounters with the opposite sex. When I tried to reason with her she refused to listen, her sulks and bad humours became a familiar occurrence again.

A trip to London was just the tonic I needed and it left Isabella to her own devices for a couple of days. There was no doubt that a few days alone would change her mind, her appetite for sexual satisfaction was such that a few days abstinence would be unbearable.

My reasons for accepting the trip were kept from everyone else. I told Amelia I was going because my job demanded it and that there was no way I could allow Suzanne to go in my place. I told Charlotte that I would love to join her and that it would be a pleasure to have some time alone with her again. I told Isabella that I had to go because Amelia demanded it, that some time alone would do her some good and that Rudi was dying to spend some time with her. There was truth in all of these statements but none of them was the whole truth.

Monique alone guessed that there was more to it than met the eye. Her melancholy moods, her yearning for something more, had seeped into me. We both tried to pretend that everything was fine and as it should be, but we didn't fool each other. She had awakened something in me, a sense of the limitless, a feeling that the world was endless but that we had closed our eyes to'it. Our lovemaking would sometimes take on a dark edge and we would lose ourselves in bitter sensuality, our blind joy masking out the questions and the doubts.

'I hate paradise,' she whispered to me one morning in the cold darkness before dawn. I made no reply, I felt it too, a kind of suffocation in the midst of plenty. The trip to London, a trip away from paradise, was going to be my time to think, my time to look again at my life and ideas.

I knew very little of Charlotte's background, not much more than that her father was a diplomat from a small island republic in the French Caribbean. I also knew that he was highly thought of, that he was successful and that he doted on his daughter. I imagined her background to be dull and worthy, a trifle unsophisticated perhaps, a little down-at-heel too. I had hardly given a thought to our flight from Zurich, the details had been left to Suzanne to arrange, but I assumed that we would be flying out on one of the scheduled flights to Heathrow. My reaction to the private plane was therefore one of complete and utter astonishment.

We were met at the airport by one of the embassy officials, a serious-looking young man with a permanent worried frown, carrying a sheaf of papers an inch thick. He was very polite, shaking my hand after introducing himself, and very respectful to Charlotte, hardly daring to look at her directly. The formalities were taken care of in an instant, we were waved through with barely a look at our papers and without much of a baggage check either.

We boarded a minibus, the embassy man loading our cases for us.

'Where's our plane?' I asked, searching for the gleaming white airliner that was to take us to London.

'It's the jet on the left,' the young man told me, pointing out the sleekest of half a dozen executive jets to one side of the airport.

'But that's a private plane,' I said rather stupidly.

'Yes, madame, it belongs to Monsieur Dupuy,' the man explained, with hardly a note of condescension in his voice.

'But I thought we were . . .'

'I'm sorry,' Charlotte smiled, 'I thought you knew. My father prefers me to travel this way. I think it makes him feel more secure.'

'Monsieur Dupuy is an admirably cautious man,' the embassy official added. 'This is certainly as safe a way to travel overseas as any.'

'But the expense . . .' I started to say but stopped, I had already made enough of an idiot of myself. We were to be travelling by private plane, so what? I tried to be cool about it, to imagine how incredibly mundane it must be for some people, but all the same my pulse did quicken and I gawked like an idiot as we approached the plane across the wide open space of the airport.

The pilot and co-pilot, two severe-looking crew-cut Americans, were waiting for us by the side of the jet. We stepped out of the bus and I went straight to the plane, admiring the smooth lines, the polished metal, the pure design. A machine is a machine, or so I had always thought, but this was something different, this aeroplane was special and I could understand why some people fall in love with them.

'If you'd care to board, ma'am,' one of the Americans said, looking at me through mirrored glasses, my reflection cast back at me, a look of childish wonder captured on my face.

'Yes, of course. What time are we leaving?'

'Our slot is in fifteen minutes,' he informed me, the hard lines of his face not softening into anything like a smile. It was a pity, he looked quite good in his mirrored shades, short hair and dark uniform.

Charlotte was waiting for me, the serious young man beside her, looking at his watch anxiously. I boarded the plane, ducking my head as I went in. There was less space than I had imagined, there were only six passenger seats, but the whole thing echoed luxury. The seats were of soft grey leather, the carpet was thick and the walls were lined in suede. Everything was immaculately clean and tidy, it was more like the inside of an expensive limousine than a plane.

249

'Sit here,' Charlotte whispered, 'it is better this way.'

I did as suggested and sat in the seat facing the tail end of the plane with my back to the cockpit. Charlotte sat next to me, facing the same direction.

'Comfortable, ladies?' mirror shades asked, leaning over our seats.

'Yes, thank you,' Charlotte answered coldly.

'Oh yeah, compliments of Mister Dupuy,' he drawled, handing a single red rose to me and one to Charlotte, with all the charm of a steward passing out the sick bags. 'The stewardess got kinda sick,' he added by way of explanation, pushing a hamper between our seats. 'There's eats and drinks in here. There's safety instructions by your seats. The oxygen masks will drop out automatically, you know the drill, right? Weather's good, so we'll make good time and it won't be too bumpy. Have yourselves a nice flight, ladies.'

'What a charming man,' I sniffed, smiling to Charlotte.

'He thinks we will all love him because he drives the plane,' she smiled.

'You mean because he pilots the plane,' I smiled.

'It is better if you think of him driving the plane,' she laughed, throwing her head back so that her dark curls were fluid about her shoulders. She was so happy. I hadn't seen her in such a good mood since Isabella's arrival.

The engines roared into life, gathering speed, the sound climbing in pitch until the whole plane hummed. We rolled forward gently, pulling away from the minibus and the stern young man, still standing with his arms at his side, looking as anxious as ever. The pilots were laughing, chatting to the control tower, going over all the last minute checks. I twisted round in my seat to look at them but they were too engrossed in what they were doing to even notice me.

'I must send Celeste a card,' Charlotte said, lying back deep into her seat.

'Who's that?'

'The stewardess. She is a very nice girl, she often flies out with me. This is the first time I have flown without her in two years.'

'Tell me about Saint Marie,' I suggested, looking beyond Charlotte, through the small oval window and onto the runway.

'It is a lovely island,' Charlotte began. 'It is one of the smallest islands in the French Caribbean but also the most beautiful. We have not let it be spoiled. My father says it is better to have few tourists than many and that the few who come to Saint Marie are worth the millions that go to the other islands.'

The plane turned onto the runway. There was a pause, as if it were psyching itself up, marshalling its energies for the big run. The roar of the engines dipped momentarily then rose to a crescendo and the plane surged forward, gathering speed and power. The airport rushed past and suddenly we were off the ground, rising fast into the thick grey cloud.

I kept swallowing, trying to clear the fogginess that blocked my ears. The plane banked, slicing effortlessly through the grey wisps before emerging into clear sky.

On one side of the cockpit a large display showed the air temperature and the altitude. The temperature had fallen well below zero already and the height was clocking up rapidly.

'Would you like to visit Saint Marie?' Charlotte inquired, looking at me hopefully.

'Yes, that would be nice one day,' I agreed, certain that I'd never be able to afford a trip out to the little island paradise.

'It is so nice,' she smiled. 'The sea is very calm and warm and the beaches are so beautiful, golden sands and never crowded. It would be so good if you could visit . . .'

'Are there many natural resources?' I asked, wondering how a tiny island that nobody had ever heard of could afford a private plane for one of its ambassadors.

'Some bauxite, I think, but there is no real mining industry. Some gold too, up in the mountains. The old people tell stories of finding fortunes in the river beds. But that is not how Saint Marie survives, we have no economy based on natural resources.'

'Then . . .'

'Money, madame,' Charlotte explained patiently. 'Like the Swiss we have some tourism, but a lot of the money is made from other money. Offshore banking, service industries, that kind of thing. My father has done much to promote this policy, he has a vision of Saint Marie in the future, a future based on money and high technology.'

I smiled. Charlotte sounded very sure of what she was saying, she was obviously sincere, but to me it rang hollow. Perhaps it was my cynicism but I could no longer bring myself to believe that things could be so wonderful. However, I loved Charlotte enough to keep quiet, if the dear girl had illusions I didn't want to be the heartless one to smash them.

I looked out of the window, the corner now frosted with a fine layer of ice, at the clear sky above and the grey-white cloud below. It was beautifully clear outside, the air crisp and the rolling clouds carved intricately into swirling mountains and valleys. In the distance a silver dart shot across the sky, a vapour trail slicing through the clear blue. I closed my eyes, listened to the dull ache of the engines, tried to get some sleep and failed.

'Lunch?' Charlotte asked, unbuckling the seat belt and leaning over the hamper.

'What is it?' I asked without too much enthusiasm.

'Chicken, some smoked salmon, cheese, fruit . . .'

'No, not for me, thanks. You go ahead, I'll have something when we land,' I said queasily. It wasn't a bumpy flight but the thought of food was distinctly unappetising.

'There is champagne, would you like a drink?' Charlotte asked brightly.

'That sounds much more like it,' I smiled.

'Good. It is nice and cool,' she told me, reaching into the hamper for the ice bucket. She rummaged around for a second then pulled out a half bottle of champagne, the green glass sporting a thousand dew drops of icy water.

'There's not much, is there?' I complained, unwrapping the heavy foil from the top of the bottle.

'It is only a short flight,' she said seriously, taking

another half bottle from the hamper. We looked at each other then burst out laughing, each of us recognising the other's mistake. Of course there was more than half a bottle between us, it was me being silly again.

The champagne popped rather politely, I poured myself a glass and sank comfortably into my seat. 'Not eating?' I asked, noticing that Charlotte had settled back with her drink too.

'I don't feel hungry either,' she shrugged, taking a sip of the sparkling golden champagne.

'Do you think the pilots want any?' I asked, looking back to the cockpit.

'No, they don't want any.'

'How do you know?' I asked, looking back to Charlotte.

'I asked once, a long time ago, and one of them told me that eating is for wimps,' she shrugged, raising her eyes to heaven.

'They're not much fun, are they?' I sighed, my long cherished fantasy of being fucked by a pilot while he was still flying the plane going out of the window.

'You can still have fun, if you want to,' Charlotte whispered cautiously, looking at me slyly.

'Won't they notice if there are two of us in the same seat?' I joked, wondering just what game my darling Charlotte had in mind.

She drank down most of her glass of champagne and poured herself another. 'Have you finished your drink?' she asked, peering at my glass, still full.

I drank down a mouthful of icy champers and refilled my glass. 'Let me guess,' I smiled, 'this game wouldn't involve this, would it?' I asked, tracing a finger up the long tapering neck of the bottle.

Charlotte nodded happily. She drank a tiny bit more and then reached down and emptied her bottle into the champagne bucket. 'It is a wicked waste of good champagne,' she admitted guiltily. I did likewise, pouring the drink into the bucket, filled to the brim with bubbling liquid and floating ice cubes.

I carefully cleaned the top of the bottle, wiping it smoothly with a napkin. Charlotte had already sat back, parted her thighs and lifted her short skirt. From where I sat I had a good view of what she was doing, she was wearing tight red panties, the dark mat of hair almost visible against the thin silky material. Her long thighs were spread and the panties were biting into her rear, parting the buttocks and indented slightly into the mouth of her sex. The bottle was balanced by her thigh while she used her fingers to rouse her sex, rubbing very slowly up and down, pressing down on her panties. In a moment I could spy a patch of darker red spread across the crotch of her panties.

Her fingers were moving very slowly, teasing and playing. She had closed her eyes, she didn't need to see, her fingers knew every inch of her body. The bottle was standing between her thighs, cold, upright, dark green against her smooth brown skin. A finger was slipped under the panties. I watched, fascinated, as she teased herself open.

The panties were pulled aside suddenly as if she could no longer stand the teasing. The dark brown of her pussy lips contrasted with the deep pink of her pussy, the glistening folds of skin clearly visible from where I watched. A finger was pressed into herself, not rubbing, not teasing, just slipped in deep and held there. She didn't move, she was hardly breathing, her finger had disappeared into her open sex, right up to the knuckle. Very slowly she withdrew her finger, steeped in her sweet essence. She opened her eyes, looked at it for a moment, then sucked it into her mouth, her full red lips taking it in just as her pussy lips had done.

I was wet just looking at her. I twisted round, parted my thighs and began to palm my pussy, rubbing the flat of my hand up and down, making my own juices flow. Charlotte pressed her finger back into her quim, not so far this time. She added a second finger, moving in and out without penetrating completely. I could see how wet she was becoming, her fingers glossy with the sheen of her juices. She carefully took the bottle and wiped her fingers around the rim, wetting her fingers in the pool of her pussy juices several times. At last the bottle was ready, the rim lubricated, coated with a glistening layer of pussy juices.

She smiled at me, her eyes wide with excitement, then turned to look down at her pussy. The contrast of colours and textures was striking, the diaphanous red panties stretched tightly to one side, the flawless dark skin and darker black hair, the green glass with the perfectly shaped neck. My eyes were fixed on her, watching the head of the bottle enter her slowly, her pussy lips widening to take in the smooth glass phallus. She pressed it in quite deep then stopped. I realised that she had been holding her breath and now she was breathing again, relaxing, enjoying the heavy glass rod inside her.

It was my turn, she had turned to me and was waiting, the excitement burning a smile on her pretty face. I was excited already, there was no need to play any elaborate games. I lifted myself from my seat for a second and pulled my knickers off and dropped them into the hamper. The bottle I dipped into the ice bucket, wetting it completely in the icy water still bubbling with champagne. I looked at Charlotte and she nodded eagerly, urging me on with her smile.

I put the bottle to my pussy, rested it for a split second, wincing a little at the icy cold. I parted my pussy lips with the fingers of one hand and pushed the bottle in with the other. It went in smoothly, thick and round, ice cold against the warmth of my sex. I closed my eyes, enjoying the sensation as I violated myself, the penetration sending ripples of pleasure spiralling through my sex. I breathed again and felt my pussy filled with the strange ice-glass.

'It is good, yes?' Charlotte asked in an excited whisper.

'Yes . . . in a very strange kind of way,' I sighed.

'Now we enjoy,' she smiled.

I watched for a moment. She held the bottle firmly by the base and began to move it in and out of her sex. It slid in and out, the glass smeared with her cream. Each time she thrust it in her eyes fluttered and her breath rose, then she drew it out and pushed it in again, deeper and faster. Without intending to she was lifting herself to the thrusts of her secret toy.

She was on the verge of orgasm after only a few thrusts and my excitement was impossible to contain. I began to frig myself with the bottle too. It felt oddly exciting, fucking myself with the inanimate object, the shape of it perfectly designed to fill a hot pussy. Every thrust made me moan, the rush of penetration heightened by the cool glass brushing my clitty. Vaguely I heard Charlotte's sighs growing louder, more intense, but then her sound became part of mine: glass, flesh, the roar of the jet engine and the joyful thrill of being fucked. My body was tingling, the wet heat in my pussy crashing against the impervious glass. I saw Charlotte tensing suddenly, her face strained in ecstasy, half the bottle buried deep in her dark wet sex. She climaxed with my name on her breath and then I climaxed too, my body braced against the glass dildo.

We sat back, temporarily sated, our bodies aglow with orgasm. She let the bottle rest against her thigh, a dribble of her come sliding down from the rim. The bottle was still inside me, the rim pressing into my quim. I smiled, I was hot once more, my pussy tingling. I took the bottle from my sex and offered it to her. She smiled and gave me her bottle in return. I sniffed it, breathing in the heady bouquet of Charlotte's sweet sex and the scent of champagne. Without waiting, I pressed it straight into my sex, wanting to merge her juices with my own. Somehow it made me feel more excited, as if we were sharing an essence of our bodies without making physical contact. Charlotte understood, she parted her panties once more and pressed the bottle to her cunt lips, the droplets of my pussy juice mingling with the dappled cream in her pussy hair. I began to fuck myself again, already aching for climax, the lust pulsing like adrenalin in my veins.

We skimmed through the thick grey clouds and out over the dull grey landscape of Kent. I counted down the altitude and counted up the temperature, watching the display behind the cockpit, the numbers shifting steadily towards zero. Charlotte told me that we were to be landing in Biggin Hill in Kent and that a waiting car was to take us to central London.

Charlotte packed the hamper away and then we strapped ourselves in. I looked out of the window at the dull miserable streets, at the mean little houses and the uninspiring monotony of the landscape. There was no way I could return to it, not permanently, that much I was certain of.

There were almost no formalities at Biggin Hill, the elderly customs official seemed more interested in eyeing my long bare legs than anything else. He ticked our names on his clipboard, eyed our passports from a distance and leered at Charlotte and myself. We smiled pleasantly to him and then passed through. I was back in England once more.

A car was indeed waiting for us, a tall uniformed chauffeur at the ready, tipping his hat deferentially and opening the rear door for us. Charlotte got into the car first and I saw the driver getting a good look at her long smooth thighs. I slipped in beside her, my skirt rising far higher than hers, my legs fully displayed. The driver hesitated, I thought he was going to say something, but he changed his mind and just shut the door.

'I haven't got any panties on,' I whispered to Charlotte, unable to remember where I'd left my knickers.

'They must be still on the plane,' she giggled.

'At least the pilots will have something to remember me by,' I laughed.

The journey to Hampstead seemed to take forever, especially when we crossed the river Thames and slowed to a crawl through the streets of the City of London. The weight of traffic would have been infuriating in normal circumstances but now we were at leisure and it didn't really matter. There was a small bar in the car and a glass of chilled white wine helped to soothe our nerves. In fact, Charlotte took a great delight in the journey, she knew little about the history of London and so my running commentary on the places that we were passing was new and interesting for her. Then she took her turn, I sat back and listened while she patiently explained to me the ins and outs of the Stock Exchange and how money can beget money without anything useful actually being produced.

The Ambassador's residence was a grand house just off Hampstead Heath, hidden behind a high ivy-clad wall, with stiff wrought-iron gates that opened onto a long gravel drive. I noted the security cameras panning towards us, a beady lens keeping us under surveillance as the car passed through the gates and crunched up the drive.

'Mamá,' Charlotte told me, as if I needed a clue to the identity of the woman waiting for us at the door. They looked very much alike, mother and daughter; the same full figure, the same oval eyes, hair worn in the same style. Charlotte's skin was a shade lighter, and her lips fuller, but otherwise they were more like sisters.

The car pulled to a graceful stop and Charlotte was out, leaping excitedly into her mother's welcoming arms. There were lots of hugs and kisses – how very different from the frosty relations that had existed between Isabella and Maria. Here, Charlotte and Nathalie were delighted to see each other again, acting as if they had been apart for years rather than a few months.

'Melissa,' Nathalie turned to me with a friendly smile, 'I'm so happy to meet you at last, Charlotte has told me so much about you.'

'And I'm happy to meet you too,' I said, rather woodenly I thought. She was an immensely attractive woman, dressed casually but smartly, with the kind of pure confidence that has an almost aphrodisiac power. She kissed me on the cheek like an old friend and the feel of her lips and the heady scent of perfume were enough to set my imagination going into overdrive.

'A good flight, I hope?' she asked, hooking one arm in mine and the other in Charlotte's.

'Did you hear? Celeste was ill,' Charlotte said.

'Yes, we must send flowers,' Nathalie said sympathetically.

'But it was a good flight all the same,' I added, not daring to share my guilty smile with Charlotte.

We went into the grand house, the heavy black door creaking open to a spacious reception area. The atmosphere was light and airy, despite the miserable weather, and the soothing colours of the walls added a warmth that made the house feel like a home and not an office. A curved staircase, with ornate banisters and a long half landing that looked down on the reception hall, led the way up to our rooms. We ascended the stairs in silence, under the eyes of the great and the good staring haughtily from the portraits lining the walls.

I was shown into my room, both Charlotte and Nathalie fussing around me to see that everything was to my liking. It was, of course. The room was large and comfortable, if not downright luxurious. The en-suite bathroom I almost took for granted, the en-suite office that had been provided for my use was more of a surprise.

'If there is anything you'd like, just call me,' Nathalie instructed quite insistently.

'There is just one thing,' I said, catching her at the door.

'Yes?'

'I have to interview a prospective student, do you think it would be all right to do that here?'

'No, that's not a problem, would you like us to arrange travel for her? Do you have a date?'

'No, no date. But I'd like to get it done as quickly as possible.'

'Please, not tonight Melissa,' Charlotte cried, sounding quite alarmed, her face breaking into a worried frown.

'There is an embassy reception tonight,' Nathalie

explained, 'it would be a shame if you could not attend.'

'A reception? But I've brought nothing to wear,' I exclaimed, having a vision of myself dressed in Cinderella rags while the other guests floated around in the finest haute couture.

'That's not a problem,' Nathalie smiled, 'you can have the pick of my wardrobe. I insist,' she interrupted before I even had a chance to complain.

'Good, we'll all have a lovely time,' Charlotte said brightly, her eyes sparkling with excitement.

I got the work out of the way as quickly as possible. I called the number that Amelia had given me and spoke to a rather fine-sounding lady. Her name was Josephine and it was her daughter, Fiona, that I was to see. Josephine sounded very keen. She was all for coming round at once to meet me but I put her off for a day. The interview duly arranged, I decided a hot shower was the best thing for me.

An embassy reception – it sounded far grander than anything I had ever been to before. On the one hand I kept thinking that it would be attended by boring old men and fat diplomats puffing fat cigars, on the other I couldn't believe that Charlotte would be quite so excited if that was the case.

I emerged from the bathroom still dripping, a loose towel wrapped around me, lost deep in my thoughts. I guess I didn't hear the door knock. I looked up and Nathalie was there.

'Sorry, I didn't mean to startle you,' she said. 'I

knocked but you must have been bathing.'

'That's all right,' I smiled, letting the towel hang a little looser. She looked very much like Charlotte.

'I came to ask you if you wanted to select an outfit for tonight,' she explained, stepping closer to me. 'Here,' she reached for the towel, 'let me dry your back.'

I gave her the towel, aware of her dark eyes devouring my nakedness. My breasts were sparkling with a thousand beads of water that fell from my nipples drop by drop. I turned and offered her my back. 'Will there be many people tonight?' I asked, trying to sound unconcerned as she began to pat my bare back with the towel.

'Not too many,' she said, her breath hot on my shoulder, 'about a hundred or so.'

'What's the occasion?' I asked, my voice not so still, she was working her way down the small of my back, her fingers casually brushing against my bare arse cheeks. I could feel her so close, her body seeming to exude a heat that was impossible to ignore. She had hardly said or done anything yet I was already aroused, my nipples growing redder and harder.

'We have signed a special memorandum of association with a number of film people,' Nathalie explained, her voice deep and husky, less accented than Charlotte's.

'Film people?' I responded, closing my eyes. Her hands were massaging my rear, the towel was hardly being applied.

'You have lovely soft skin,' she whispered, dropping the towel completely. Her hands were around me, squeezing my breasts, her mouth on my throat. I threw my head back and sighed loudly, covering her hands with mine and massaging my breasts, our fingers running up and down my erect nips.

I turned to kiss her and took her face in my hands. I was eating her and she was devouring me. My sex was aching, hot, the honey flowing already. I took her hand and put it on my sex, pushing her fingers into me. I didn't want to wait. I didn't want seduction or poetry, I wanted to be fucked. My feelings for her were raw, exposed, aching. I wanted both mother and daughter. I wanted to love and be loved without inhibition and with nothing but passion.

We were on the bed. I was naked and writhing in her arms. Our mouths were tight, lips pressed so tight together we could hardly breathe. I was dizzy, my body burning, nipples blazing with incandescent pleasure.

'Suck my tits . . . suck me . . .' I cried, arching my back and offering her my breasts. Her full lips were on me, sucking in a nipple and teasing it with lips, teeth and tongue. Her hand was stroking the inside of my thigh, her fingers dark against my pale skin. She was still clothed, her body hidden from my eyes and hands, but it didn't matter.

I arched my back and cried out, climaxing violently as her lips wrapped tightly around a nipple that was throbbing with pleasure. I felt strung out, my body a flame of sensations, but she was loving me still. Her hands were stroking my sex with lingering touches of her fingers, her palm forcing my pussy open so that the wetness seeped out. I felt wanton and I practically forced her fingers into my sex onto the hard pussy-bud.

'So passionate,' Nathalie whispered to herself, pushing her fingers into me, frigging me forcefully while kissing my mouth again. I was thrashing about, writhing, unable to control myself. She turned me on my side, so that I faced her. I parted myself and her fingers were playing my pussy like an instrument, making me moan deliriously. I cried out suddenly, opened my eyes and closed them again, sinking into a delirium of voluptuousness. The fingers of her other hand were going into my anal hole.

'Melissa? Mother?' Charlotte cried, bursting into the room unexpectedly to find me being lovingly fingered in the front and rear by her gorgeous mother. I looked at her, our eyes met and then I melted, lost in the wave of orgasm that shook my whole body.

14

Although I had been flustered by Charlotte's sudden interruption, I had been unable to hold back, climaxing violently and soaking Nathalie's fingers with waves of pussy juice. It took a moment for me to regain my bearings, I looked up but Charlotte was gone.

'Was she upset?' I asked Nathalie, kissing her pussy-scented fingers.

'It would have been better if she had not caught us like this,' she said, a sad smile on her face.

'Shall I go after her?'

'No, let her alone,' she counselled. 'She'll make her own decision on how to handle this.'

'But I feel so . . . so guilty,' I stammered. 'I'd hate to hurt her, she means so much to me.'

'Come on,' Nathalie said, standing up, 'let's choose something for you to wear this evening.'

I dressed quickly, putting on any old thing, while Nathalie explained that she and Philippe, her husband, were only staying in London for a few days. They lived in Switzerland but spent a good deal of time shuttling between Europe's capital cities. However, her wardrobe travelled with her and she had brought a fine selection of party dresses and ball gowns to London specifically for the function at the embassy.

The costumes were wrapped in cellophane, each complete with matching accessories. Nathalie insisted I choose first and the choice was not an easy one to make. Even the most fashionable shops in Zurich would have been hard pressed to match Nathalie's collection. After dallying for ages, I finally settled on a beautiful satin black dress, over the shoulder, with gold studs around the plunging neckline and cut outs just below the chest. Nathalie then chose long black gloves and a pair of leather and suede court shoes.

Nathalie then selected for herself a tight red lace dress with a high neck and a short skirt which was almost transparent in places. It was a daring choice, a perfect little dress for a quiet evening out with a lover, but I wasn't convinced that it was the right thing to wear to a formal function.

'This one is one of Philippe's favourites,' she told me, perhaps sensing my doubt as to its suitability. 'He likes me to look beautiful and sexy. He enjoys the admiring looks I get from the other guests.'

'Well, it's the sort of dress that is bound to get you noticed,' I laughed.

'Have you made your business arrangements?' she asked, changing the subject to something more mundane.

'I'll be seeing the girl tomorrow, if that's all right.'

'Yes, tomorrow will be fine. And then?'

'I'm not sure yet. Does Charlotte have any plans?'

She shook her head, a sweet smile on her full red lips.

'I don't know, I would think that it depends very much on what you decide to do. She is very fond of you. I have no doubt that if you returned to Switzerland the day after tomorrow she would join you at once.'

'Do you think it's healthy? A girl being so fond of one of her teachers?' I asked nervously, wondering if Nathalic was aware of what went on between me and her daughter.

'I see no wrong in it,' she said, smiling. 'I think you are a little in love with her also, aren't you?'

My face flushed red, suddenly embarrassed by the directness of the question and the frank look in Nathalie's dark eyes. 'Yes, I think I'm in love with her too. But I'm older, it doesn't have the same meaning for me,' I said. 'I hope you don't mind me speaking so plainly,' I added after a pause.

'I understand,' she said quietly. 'I am happy that you love Charlotte as you do and I am happy that she is in love with you. I think that love is the most important thing in the world, it adds to our identity, it takes us out of ourselves.'

'So you understand why Charlotte was upset when she caught us earlier?' I asked, looking away from her for a moment, my heart going out to Charlotte. I didn't want to hurt her, not in the least.

'She'll understand,' Nathalie repeated, 'I'm sure she will.'

'I hope you're right,' I sighed, hoping that Nathalie's confidence was well placed. Charlotte hadn't raised a whisper of complaint while I was making love with Isabella, but making love with her mother was a different thing altogether. It was a strange triangle of forces, each of us pulling in a different direction, each pairing leaving one person isolated.

'Don't worry,' Nathalie whispered, pulling me close and giving a friendly hug, 'everything will be just right, you'll see.'

I kissed her on the mouth, a loving kiss just to thank her for being so understanding, but my pulse quickened and the desire shot through me like a thunderbolt. She returned my kiss and I knew that we were going to make love again.

A limousine picked us up later that evening, all three of us dazzlingly dressed, our hair expertly styled, our faces beautifully made up. But, despite our smiles and the excitement that we shared, there was something in the air, an unspoken tension that none of us could quite dispel. Several times I caught Charlotte looking at me strangely, her dark eyes accusing, her lips pouting sulkily. It made me afraid to talk to Nathalie, as if Charlotte would take that as further evidence of betrayal.

The embassy was in the heart of London, in one of the tightly packed streets not far from Park Lane. We arrived a little before ten and by then the party was already in full swing. As we emerged from the limousine there was a rush of bodies and the flashing bulbs of the cameras. The crush was disconcerting but Nathalie and Charlotte were totally blasé, ignoring the calls of the press photographers, looking stylish and smart, while I gawked like a country bumpkin. The three of us walked into the embassy arm in arm, the photographers following us right to the doorway.

'How tiresome,' was all that Nathalie could think of saying, in a voice so full of boredom it left me speechless. I realised just how different our two worlds really were.

I had barely enough time to reflect on this before we were being introduced to the host and hostess for the evening, the Ambassador and his wife. If I had been alone I'm sure I would have curtsied, but Nathalie simply kissed them both and then introduced me. He was rather short, full bellied, a dignified-looking black man with a deep stentorian voice. Madame L'Ambassador was younger, a fine-looking woman with her hair wrapped in a colourful ethnic headband.

We passed through to the main hall, thronging with people. There was a cheerful murmur of conversation and sweet rhythmic music in the background. The boring old generals that I had been expecting were few and far between. Most of the guests were smart young things, good-looking and successful, and I could see why the press photographers had gathered outside.

'Where's your father?' I asked Charlotte, taking a glass of champers from a passing waitress.

'Probably in a room somewhere talking business,' Charlotte said, raising her voice above the background of clinking glasses and joyful laughter. 'He said that he'll see us later,' she added.

Nathalie tapped my elbow, I turned and she pointed to a small group gathered in one corner. 'Recognise him?' she asked. I looked carefully and noticed at once the very tall blonde standing beside a shorter older man.

'Is that Guy Chappel?' I whispered, recognising the shaven head, bristling with short spiky hair, the black leather jacket and the raucous laugh that could be heard above the din.

'Yes, the one and only,' Nathalie laughed. 'The blonde is his latest protégée. They'll be making a film together in Saint Marie some time next year, assuming he hasn't grown bored with her by then.'

'Have you met him?' I whispered, turning my attention to the tall, busty blonde, her severe face notable only for the glossiest, sexiest lips I had ever seen.

'Guy? Yes, he and Philippe cooked up the film scheme last time we saw him in Switzerland.'

'Would you like to meet him?' Charlotte asked, smiling properly for the first time all evening.

'What would I say?' I cried, laughing. What could I possibly have to talk about with the *enfant terrible* of European cinema?

'Nathalie! Charly!' his voice boomed, catching sight of us across the crowded room.

'Come on, you'll like him,' Charlotte promised, taking my hand and pulling me across the room, her voice full of enthusiasm and her eyes ablaze with joyous excitement once more.

The tall blonde looked to the heavens when she saw us approaching. She said something to Guy and I saw his face darken. He said something under his breath, something hard and forceful because she immediately fell silent, turning away from us.

'Charly, darling,' he cried, rushing up to Charlotte

and planting a big wet kiss on her lips, 'they didn't tell me you were going to be here! And Nathalie, you look divine, absolutely divine.'

'Does that mean I get a part in the film?' Nathalie laughed.

'Darling, the part is there if you want it,' he said seriously, 'you've only to say so.'

'Guy,' Charlotte interrupted, 'this is my friend Melissa.'

'Pleased to meet you, Mr Chappel,' I said, offering my hand.

'Don't ever let me hear you call me that again,' he warned fiercely. 'If you're going to be my friend too, you simply have to call me Guy. Now, let me hear you say it.'

'Sorry, Guy it will be from now on,' I smiled. He took my hand and pulled me closer to him, planting a big soft kiss on my lips too.

'Now then,' he laughed, 'what are the three most delicious-looking women in London up to this evening?'

'What do you mean!' the blonde snapped, her shrill voice bringing silence to the surrounding faces. 'What about me? What am I then?'

'Don't be a pain,' he warned, keeping his back to her.

'Don't be a pain,' she mimicked. 'This is a dump, let's get out, let's go to a club.'

'You go to a club,' he hissed, turning to face her angrily. 'You want out, you get out.'

'I will! You're boring! You're all boring!' she cried petulantly, her voice cutting through the sudden silence. She saw that everyone in the room was looking at her then stamped off, her heels snapping like gunshots as she stormed out. We watched her go, followed by every pair of eyes, a photographer at her heels snapping her in all her infantile fury.

'Well,' Nathalie said, breaking the silence, 'I'm sorry about that, Guy.'

'Sorry?' he laughed loudly, the pure delight expressed in his broad smile and grey eyes. 'What's there to be sorry about?'

Charlotte laughed too. 'You've been playing a trick on us, haven't you?'

The din of the party rose with the clink of glasses, the murmur of a hundred whispered conversations and the whirring of the cameras. 'That, my dears,' Guy told us conspiratorially, 'was the most skilful piece of acting that young lady has ever performed. She didn't know she was acting, of course, but my improvised performance was all that it took.'

'But why?' I asked, not making sense of it.

'Because I was bored with her, she's not much fun. Now that she sees herself as an actress she's lost the one thing going for her and that was her naivety. But I'm an old softy, I couldn't just dump her now that she's made a name for herself. This was my solution. She'll be in all the papers tomorrow and on TV in a few days. No doubt someone else will want her for a film soon. I shall get my name in the papers too, free myself of her for the next film and have myself a little laugh. What could be nicer?'

'You manipulative old cynic,' Nathalie said in admiration. 'What about us? We'll be in the gossip columns tomorrow too, accused of causing the split between the two of you.'

'You're not serious?' I asked, dumbfounded, realising that she was absolutely right. Guy Chappel was notorious for his tangled sex life, I could well imagine what the gossip columnists would make of a trio of sexy women turning up at a party and causing his current girlfriend to storm out.

'Serious?' he looked at me oddly, a question on his face. 'Melissa darling, the problem with life is that everything is serious. If we all decided that nothing was serious, then life would be a damn sight better.'

'What about the Saint Marie film?' Charlotte broke in, looking at him with doubt in her eyes.

'That's still on,' he assured her. 'I'll just need to find someone to replace dear Samantha.'

'I'm sure that will be no trouble,' Nathalie told him, a knowing look in her eye.

'I've got an excellent idea!' he laughed suddenly. 'Which of you three lovelies wants to make it in films? Nathalie? Charly? Melissa?'

'Come on, Guy,' I said, 'you're not being serious.'

'Why not?' he asked, growing more excited. I could see him working it all out in his mind as the idea took hold.

'I'm afraid I'm going to have to turn you down again,' Nathalie apologised. 'I already have a bad enough reputation back home. Making a film with Guy Chappel would only make it worse.'

'So? Who cares what they think?' Guy roared. He was

almost pacing up and down. He gave the impression of a caged animal, of raw animal power.

'It's not that simple, Guy,' Nathalie said and I couldn't ignore the note of wistful sadness in her voice.

'Charly? Melissa?'

'What about it?' Charlotte asked, turning to me eagerly. She took my hands and held them tightly, her dark eyes gazing into mine.

'I'm not so sure . . . Perhaps . . .'

'You'll be great!' Guy cried triumphantly. 'You'll love it, just don't turn actressy on me . . . Don't take acting lessons . . . Just be yourself, it couldn't be easier.'

'There is just one condition,' I added, knowing that I had to strike while the iron was hot.

'Anything, darling,' Guy declared intensely.

'I want one of my friends to be included, she can take Nathalie's place.'

'Who?' Charlotte and Guy asked together.

'Monique, one of our friends from Switzerland. She's very good, you'll like her.'

'Well?' Guy asked, turning to Charlotte.

She nodded happily. 'Melissa is right, you will like her. She'll love it, I'm sure.'

'In that case, it's a deal!' Guy laughed triumphantly. 'There's no script, no title, and no crew. It'll be brilliant.'

'Great!' Charlotte gave him a hug and a big long kiss, the photographers swooping like birds of prey, getting it on film for the morning newspapers.

'Perhaps we ought to tell your father,' Nathalie suggested, pulling Charlotte from Guy's eager grasp.

'He'll be fine,' Guy told us confidently. 'Now remember, this deal's for real. There's no turning back now. I'll be in touch . . .'

'It's been nice meeting you, Guy,' I said as Nathalie and Charlotte waited for me. 'Can I call you when I've spoken to Monique?'

'Of course, darling.' He fished in his pocket and found a tattered business card. He turned it over and scribbled a number on it. We kissed quickly, his powerful arms holding me for a second while his soft lips caressed my own.

'Will Philippe mind?' I asked, catching up with Charlotte and Nathalie, my lips still tingling.

'I should think not,' Nathalie declared easily, 'but I think he'd like to know about it before Guy announces it to the whole world.'

The Ambassador himself directed us to one of the offices on the first floor, up a wide flight of stairs, past the guard barring the way at the ground floor.

'It's so hard to believe,' I whispered, slowly aware of what I had agreed to. Could it really be so simple and so sudden? And what would Monique say? She wanted to act but that was precisely what Guy Chappel wanted to avoid.

The moment I set eyes on Philippe I felt the attraction between us. He was tall, good-looking, with grey-green eyes and a detached expression. His features betrayed a mixture of origins: light brown skin, a sharp nose, a strong chin, rather long face. His ancestry was African, French, Spanish – the history of Saint Marie

277

expressed in flesh and blood.

Father and daughter greeted each other effusively, with much hugging and kissing, the same scene that I had witnessed earlier with mother and daughter. Again I was struck by how unforced it all was, how genuine the affection between them.

And then he turned to me. 'Melissa, I'm happy to meet you at long last,' he said, shaking my hand firmly, his eyes looking directly into mine. I was silent for a moment, I felt as if his eyes could see the desire welling up inside me, ready to burst.

'I'm happy to meet you too, Monsieur Dupuy,' I managed to say.

'Please, please, no formalities. I hope you had a pleasant flight and have enjoyed our hospitality,' he continued, sitting back comfortably into his seat behind a broad mahogany desk that dominated the office.

'Yes, everything's been fine,' I said, feeling my face beginning to redden. What was it about the Dupuy family that I found each of them so totally desirable?

'I do apologise, I have been too busy to come down to see you,' he added graciously. His eyes were still on me, still sucking out the meaning from the look on my face.

'That's why we had to come to seek you out,' Charlotte admonished, wagging a finger at him. 'Papa, we have some wonderful news!'

'You have persuaded Melissa to visit Saint Marie this summer?' he guessed.

'Sort of,' Charlotte agreed, the fire taken from her excitement.

'They have agreed to appear in Guy Chappel's film,' Nathalie told him, her wry smile hinting at the amusement she felt.

'Is that okay?' Charlotte asked, looking at him hopefully.

'You too, Melissa?' he asked.

I nodded. 'Charlotte, myself and our friend Monique, another teacher from the finishing school.'

'I don't want anything too wild, young lady,' he cautioned Charlotte, his smile at odds with his words.

'Oh, papa, I knew you wouldn't mind! Thank you, thank you,' she cried, smothering her father with grateful kisses.

'Will you be home tonight?' Nathalie asked, looking meaningfully at Philippe and then at me. I blushed, the way I was looking at Philippe was so obvious, the hunger in my pussy reflected in the look in my eyes.

'Perhaps, I have many things to arrange,' he sighed. 'You must excuse me, Melissa, I wouldn't wish you to think I am being rude in any way. Unfortunately I still have so much to do.'

'Think nothing of it,' I said, wishing that we could leave before I did something stupid. My nipples had become hard, pressing tightly against my satin dress.

'Why don't you two go back down?' Nathalie suggested. 'Philippe and I have a few things to discuss.'

My throat was dry. There was no doubt what the discussion was going to be about. Philippe's eyes had been all over me and I had been staring at him like a love-struck teenager from the moment I walked into the room.

Charlotte may not have noticed anything unusual but Nathalie had seen it from the start.

'It's been nice meeting you,' I said, after Charlotte had said her goodbye. We went straight back down to the party, Charlotte immensely excited by the prospect of appearing in the film, while I couldn't help but be apprehensive about Nathalie and Philippe.

I spent the night alone, sometimes hoping that either Charlotte or Nathalie would join me, sometimes hoping that they wouldn't. The party had been a lot of fun and I had met lots of new and interesting people, many of them in the film business. Nathalie joined us a little later, and from the glowing skin and the sparkle in her eyes it was clear what she and Philippe had been up to. I felt relieved, for a moment I had been certain that Nathalie was going to be upset because of the way Philippe and I had been looking at each other.

We left the embassy a couple of hours after midnight. We were by no means the last to leave but, apart from a brief glimpse, I did not set eyes on Philippe again. In the car I sat between mother and daughter and flirted secretly with each of them. We arrived home and I kissed them both goodnight, then went to bed, wondering which of them was going to knock on my door. I was hot and restless, perhaps I'd had a little too much champagne. I pulled my clothes off wildly. I couldn't wait, I sat before a mirror and frigged myself deftly using the handle of a black hairbrush, making myself come repeatedly as I watched.

When the knock on the door never came I slipped into bed, too tired, and too sated, to want to work out the implications. I slept soundly and woke very late the next morning to an unexpectedly sunny day. A maid brought me breakfast in bed and with it a note from Charlotte to say that she and her mother had gone shopping and would be back later in the afternoon.

I had a lazy soak in the bath, letting aromatic bath oils seep deep into my skin, soothing away any troubles that were in the back of my mind. Perfectly relaxed, I dressed, went for a walk in the grounds and then returned to the house just as Josephine and Fiona arrived.

'We hope we haven't put you to too much trouble,' Josephine apologised as I showed them to the office that had been put aside for our interview.

'Not at all,' I replied, taking a seat behind the antique writing desk in front of the single latticed window. Josephine sat opposite me and Fiona took a seat to one side, giving me a sideways glance, measuring me up with a practised eye that I recognised at once.

'We're very grateful, aren't we, Fiona?' Josephine continued, trying to smile at me and glare at her daughter at the same time. She was in her late forties and dressed like a woman ten years older. In her youth she may have been pretty but the thick make-up she applied to her skin obscured whatever natural beauty she possessed.

'Yes, we're very grateful,' Fiona agreed without enthusiasm. She bore a slight resemblance to her mother, there was the same hardness around the eyes and mouth.

'Well, Fiona,' I said, smiling brightly, 'suppose you

tell me why you were dismissed from your last college.'

'I wasn't dismissed,' Fiona countered defensively, 'I left because I didn't like it there.'

'And why was that?' I asked, ignoring the pained look in Josephine's eyes. I was being polite, Josephine had already told me that her daughter had been expelled.

'They all hated me there,' she said sullenly. 'And I hated them back. Just because I wouldn't do as they say, because I wouldn't conform to their standards.'

'So you left because you rebelled against their standards?'

Fiona nodded. 'That's right. I hate people telling me how to behave. I'm not a child, I'm a woman and expect to be treated like one,' she said, clearly stating it as a challenge.

'Why was she expelled?' I asked, turning to Josephine.

'It wasn't expulsion as such . . .' she squirmed, her face turning a nasty shade of red.

'Because I used to sneak boys into my dorm,' Fiona said casually, ignoring her mother's obvious distress and utterly indifferent to the fact that she had been caught lying. She looked bored, eyes staring up at the ceiling, sitting back in her chair with her legs stretched out.

'Is that all?'

'Yes, yes, that's all it was,' Josephine sprang to her daughter's defence, she was leaning across the desk and looking at me pleadingly.

'Then why the lies?' I asked, looking to Fiona directly.

She shrugged. 'Because I didn't want you thinking the wrong things about me.'

'You said boys,' I noted. 'How many exactly?'

'Not many,' Josephine stressed vehemently, then regretted it. She looked down at the ground, unable to face me or her daughter.

'A few,' Fiona smiled.

'Be precise. Was it three, four, ten?'

'Is it really so important?' Josephine asked quietly, trying to divert my attention but my eyes were fixed on Fiona.

'Nearer ten than four,' she replied proudly. 'Probably more than ten. I sort of lost count.'

'How many at one go?' I asked, keeping my manner cool and direct, purposely avoiding judgement.

'A few,' she teased, licking her lips.

'Oh God . . .' Josephine muttered, sinking further into red-faced embarrassment.

'You were a busy girl,' I said, a faint trace of a smile on my lips. 'Several boys at once, so that's why you were expelled. Were you caught by a member of staff?'

'Yes . . . no . . . Someone snitched on me. I was caught with two lads, knickers around my ankles and my mouth full, if you see what I mean.'

I nodded. She was certainly proud of herself, I had to give her that. But still the story did not ring true. Yes, I could see that she would be expelled from some colleges, but there had to be more to it than that. 'Who were the lads?'

'Locals, young men from the village.'

'Were they good?'

'Good? Good?' the mother spluttered disgustedly.

'Yes, they were good,' Fiona smiled. 'Two of them were better than one. Though not as good as three.'

'Why did someone snitch on you?'

Fiona hesitated, I saw her turn away from her mother's imploring look. 'Jealousy, what else could it be?'

'That's a good question. Josephine,' I turned to her, 'what else could it be?'

'Jealousy, as Fiona says,' Josephine mumbled, lying transparently.

'You're both liars,' I stated boldly. 'I don't think we've got anything else to talk about.' I stood up, showing them the way to the door. I was furious, not because of what Fiona had done but because she was treating me like an idiot.

'Please . . . please . . .' Josephine begged, a look of purest supplication in her eyes.

'I want the truth, no lies, no excuses,' I said coldly, still standing.

'You tell her,' Fiona said dismissively, her face twisted into an ugly sneer.

'Fiona used to bring young men into the dorms and then sell their favours to the other girls. She and the young lads used to split the money. It was only a harmless bit of fun, high spirits and nothing more. Some of the girls grew quite attached to the boys, but when they had no money Fiona wouldn't let them play. The girls became very angry and informed the Principal. She was indeed caught with two young men but there was another girl involved. She had just handed over her money and wanted the boys and Fiona to have sex with her. I know it sounds terribly wicked but that's not how it was, I can assure you of that.' Josephine had told the story in a low monotone, her voice the sound of defeat. 'All girls want to have a bit of fun, don't they?' she asked, looking to me for support.

'All girls want some fun, but how many of them charge other girls for the same pleasure?'

'It's no big deal,' Fiona broke in, having listened to the story in brooding silence. 'I started by selling myself, I was good at sex, the other girls liked paying me to have sex with them. It was a game. They used to boast to their friends that they'd paid me to lick them out. When I screwed a lad from the village the word got around, then they were begging to pay for that too.'

'Then why did they tell on you?' I challenged, disturbed by Fiona's contemptuous attitude.

'Because they wanted it for free and I wasn't having that,' she declared flatly. 'The bitch that told the Principal wanted to suck prick night after night and not pay for it. She loved having a couple of guys creaming into her mouth, she loved the feel of a hard cock spurting onto her tongue and she loved the taste of thick warm spunk. I'm not unreasonable, but she wouldn't pay her debts. I stopped the supply of cock and she went mad. All she had to do was pay me and she could have had all the cocks she could eat.'

'If you had told me that at the beginning of the interview,' I told her unequivocally, 'then things would have been different.' I turned to the mother. 'I'm sorry, Josephine, but I can't recommend Fiona for acceptance at our school,' I said, my tone less harsh than it had been to Fiona.

'Please, we can pay . . .' Josephine whispered, digging in her handbag for a purse.

'It's nothing to do with money, it's all to do with attitude.'

'I told you,' Fiona sneered, 'I knew they wouldn't have me. Come on, let's get out of here.'

'Fiona's attitude can change,' Josephine persisted, refusing to accept defeat. 'She can be ever so friendly, can't you? Why don't you show Melissa just how friendly you can be?'

'Her?' Fiona sounded disgusted. 'She could never afford me. Let's go, this is boring.'

I waited until they were both gone before I slumped back into my seat. My hands were shaking, and I felt the anger suddenly wash over me, like a rush of adrenalin that set the heart pumping and the blood racing. I tensed violently, held it for a moment then exhaled heavily. I felt drained, tired beyond words.

I heard the sound of a car starting. I looked from the window and saw Josephine's car pull up, a heavy black Mercedes. Josephine and Fiona were standing by the drive, arguing furiously. Josephine was red in the face while Fiona pretended to ignore her. They got into the car still arguing, the recriminations set to last the journey home.

It had been clear to me from the start that Fiona was not right for us. Her amoral attitude, her deceit and her sneering contempt were clear to see and all wholly unacceptable. There was nothing wrong in her healthy sexual attitude, far from it, in fact it had been her only endearing feature. What was wrong was her willingness to exploit her friends, no matter how she tried to gloss over it.

I called Amelia at once and told her the news. She listened silently while I related the circumstances of Fiona's expulsion and then her lies to me. There was no doubt that I had made the right decision. Amelia even apologised for having sent me on a fruitless journey in spite of my own misgivings. I also told her that I wanted to return at once, that I was simply too tired to stay and enjoy London any more.

15

Nathalie had insisted in coming to the airport to see us off, even though she had done her best to dissuade us from leaving. In other circumstances I think I would have accepted her invitation to stay for a few more days, but I felt I had to return. There had been questions and doubts in my mind and now I felt that resolution was close to hand and so had to get back.

Nathalie accepted our decision gracefully, for Charlotte would not hear of me returning to Switzerland alone. I had done my best to persuade her to stay, but she wouldn't hear of it, as far as she was concerned her place was beside me. Secretly I was flattered by her devotion. A thrill of delight ran through me every time I saw the adoration in her dark soulful eyes. Nathalie too seemed happy with her daughter's devotion to me, though dutifully she had to try to persuade Charlotte to stay on a bit longer too.

We left the Ambassador's residence just after lunch, carried away in the big black limousine that seemed to glide on a carpet of air. I hadn't set eyes on Philippe since the Embassy reception and I remember feeling disappointed by his non-appearance. I had wanted to see him once more, just to check that the fire he had kindled in the pit of my belly was still smouldering. Would he undress me with his seductive eyes? Would I feel excited by him once more? The questions were left unanswered and at that time perhaps it was better left that way.

The driver took a different route to Biggin Hill airport, we were skirting London rather than driving through the centre. It made the journey less interesting. The motorway, like all motorways, was monotonous but it served to divert attention inwards. I was seated between Nathalie on one side and Charlotte on the next, aware of the proximity of their bodies, aware of the scent they were wearing, of the rhythm of their breath. There was still something in the air between us, a left-over of the tension caused by Charlotte's discovery of her mother and myself making love.

I had spent the previous night alone again, wondering which of the lovely Dupuy ladies was going to come to my bed. But neither came, as if each had decided to leave me for the other, or perhaps each was afraid of being caught. At breakfast the conversation had been light and inconsequential, and the eye contact had been nervous and fleeting, even though there were no guilty secrets to betray.

It was not how I wanted things to end and, sitting there in the car on the way to the airport, I decided it was time to clear the air once and for all. Nathalie was on my left, sitting sideways in the seat, her skirt tight over her long thighs, her shirt a little open so that I could glimpse the slope of her breasts. To my right Charlotte had crossed her knee, her short dress riding up so that I could glimpse an inviting expanse of lithe flesh. I wanted both of them with equal fervour, for they gave me equal pleasure. I didn't want to choose between them and had no intention of being forced to do so.

'Nathalie,' I began, turning to face her, 'I'd like to thank you very much for the hospitality you've shown me. I've enjoyed my visit very much, thank you.' I leaned forward, twisted my head slightly, put my lips to hers and kissed her long and slow. She hesitated then opened her mouth, accepting my tongue in the coolness of her mouth, her hands finding mine.

I drew back from Nathalie, saw the desire flame in the darkness of her eyes, expressed not with words but with a look, by the parting of her sweet lips and the quickening of her breath. Then I turned to Charlotte, looking at us with pain in her eyes, with a sadness that was real and alive.

'And you, Charlotte,' I said softly, 'I want to thank you too. For inviting me to London with you and for loving me so. I want you to know, I love you too.'

Our kiss was hot and feverish. Our lips mashed together and I pulled her closer, sucking the breath from her mouth as if I needed it to live. My head swam, dizzy with love and desire – a pulsating, palpable desire that roared through my body like a fire that flashes through the forest. I released Charlotte and sat back in the seat, hands shaking a little, short of breath.

Nathalie and Charlotte were on the edge of their seats, waiting expectantly, eyes only on me. I shifted round slightly, my face turned towards Nathalie, looking up at her. She hesitated, trying to read me, to decipher what it was that I wanted from her and her daughter. I waited and she leaned forward and put her lips to mine again, brushing my face with her fingers, her eyes half closed. She sat back and I turned to Charlotte, who was waiting, ready to press her face against mine.

We kissed and touched in silence, Nathalie and I, Charlotte and I, turning from mother to daughter and then back again. My pussy was soaked, my panties wet through, and my nipples were bulging against the tightness of my dress. I took Charlotte's hand and pressed it against my thigh, let her rub me up and down as we kissed. Nathalie took my other thigh, her palm sliding against the smooth firm flesh as her daughter kissed me with a feverish intensity. I parted my thighs, enjoying the sensation of being caressed by two women at the same time.

'I hope I haven't made things difficult between you,' I gasped between kisses, looking at them both guiltily.

'No, why should things be difficult?' Charlotte replied, breathing hard, her eyes barely glancing towards Nathalie.

She moved in close to kiss me again just as Nathalie did so too. I moved back a little and their faces were so close, they could feel each other's breath, look into each other's eyes. Perhaps it was the moment, perhaps the flames of desire were as strong and as uncontrolled as they were in me. Mother and daughter kissed, a long deep kiss, lips pressed tightly, tongues exploring. I climaxed, filled my panties with love juice, aroused beyond endurance by the sight of Charlotte and Nathalie kissing so passionately.

They separated, looked at each other strangely, emerging from a momentary delirium that neither of them had ever imagined. I kissed Charlotte and then Nathalie and then watched the two of them kiss each other again. I shifted, pulled my panties down a little way, eager to have the two women pleasure me with their fingers and mouths.

I moaned, lifted my leg high and opened my sex to the exquisite explorations of a woman's hand. I didn't know who it was and I didn't care. We were a mass of bodies, holding each other, exchanging kisses and whispers, sighs and caresses. I unbuttoned Nathalie's blouse to expose her full and generous breasts – soft brown skin tipped with large dark points of flesh. I held her, flicked my thumbs over her nipples and saw the pleasure pass through her eyes.

And then a second hand was on Nathalie's breasts, touching, stroking, playing with the hard-pointed nipples. Nathalie leaned across and kissed Charlotte full on the mouth again. I watched through half-closed eyes, the pleasure pulsing in my sex as Nathalie used her expert fingers to bring me off. Nathalie moved back and Charlotte bent down and began to suck her mother's breasts, her hot greedy little mouth playing delightfully with the large brown nipples. I passed my free hand up Charlotte's skirt and began to stroke her sex over damp tight knickers.

The car was moving sedately down the motorway, we were hardly aware of the gentle movement, everything was focused on the tight closeness of our bodies. Suddenly Nathalie cried out and arched her back, cradling Charlotte's head, who was still sucking hard. Moments later it was Charlotte's turn to climax, her body shuddering as my fingers slipped under her wet panties and stroked her throbbing pussy bud.

We sat back, side by side, our bodies in various degrees of undress, bathed in sweat and pussy cream. The moment was perfect, and none of us spoke or moved or broke the spell that bound us so closely.

At the airport mother and daughter kissed goodbye, ignoring the shocked look on the eyes of the pilots. Nathalie then turned to me, looking radiantly happy, her hair swept clear of her face, her dark eyes regarding me with a mixture of gratitude and renewed desire.

'I'm so glad to have met you,' she said, taking my hands in hers. 'Charlotte is lucky to have found you as a friend.'

'Believe me,' I smiled, 'the pleasure is all mine. When you return to Switzerland we must meet again, all three of us.'

We kissed and then I passed through the customs, past the disapproving eye of the old man behind the counter. Charlotte was waiting for me by the steps to the plane, looking across the tarmac at the grey world that was England.

'Are you sorry to have to go back so soon?' I asked her, feeling guilty that I was cutting short her visit.

'No, I'm happy that it ended the way it did. I was beautiful, wasn't it?' she asked, looking to mc for approval, looking for me to tell her that what had passed between her and her mother was indeed beautiful.

'That was more than beautiful,' I said, 'that was precious.'

My answer delighted her, she skipped up the steps into the plane joyfully.

I was leaving England for Switzerland for the second time, but how things had changed in those few months. That first time I was fleeing a world that had collapsed around me, fleeing to an unknown future, carrying with me all the fears and doubts that I had allowed to cloud my mind. Now I had changed. I had more confidence, a greater understanding of other people and of myself. I was no longer the naive young woman who had allowed herself to be smooth-talked by a handsome stranger. Now I was in control, a woman made strong and powerful by her own experience.

And now I was flying home, not into an unknown future, but to the place that I had come to know and love, and which I now regarded as my home in every sense of the word. The future had looked dark for a while. I understood what Monique was saying, and in many ways her darkness had become mine, but that was over. I was returning home with news that was certain to make her change her mind, I was bringing her the dream that she had always longed for.

We touched down at Zurich airport as the sun sank behind the horizon. The air was touched by ice but I didn't let that spoil my excitement. Rudi was there to greet us, his strong arms cuddling both Charlotte and myself as we kissed him joyfully. We rode back in the car, Charlotte in my arms all the way, just kissing and cuddling, like young lovers. We spoke without saying anything, the murmur of our voices low and soft.

The sky went from dark blue to purest pitch as the car made its way through the mountains, passing through sedate Alpine villages populated by fat jolly farmers and their ruddy-faced wives. The moon was full, a clear white disc that spilt its silvery sheen over the mountain sides, where it turned the ice blue and white. I should have been used to the view but the timeless landscape had lost none of its splendour in my eyes.

'How's Isabella?' I asked Rudi, catching his deep blue eyes in the rear-view mirror.

'Very happy, I think,' he said over his shoulder.

'Do you think she's missed me?'

He laughed. 'Yes, we have been keeping her occupied but I still think she is waiting for you. She wanted to be at the airport today but Amelia refused her permission.'

'That means Bella is going to be in your bed tonight,' Charlotte said softly, her voice without jealousy or sadness.

'We can all share my bed tonight,' I promised, kissing her fingers lovingly.

I knew that Amelia would be waiting for me, her welcoming smile set to ease away any worries that I might have, but as soon as we arrived I realised I had to see someone else first. We got out of the car, our breath misting in the crisp night air. 'Tell Amelia I won't be long,' I barked to Charlotte and Rudi and then set off to find Monique.

I was afraid that Monique had already made up her mind about the future, that she had resolved to leave the school for good. She had been torn by contradictory emotions, a turbulent swell of ideas and intuitions pulling her this way and that. The school was no longer enough for her, she had glimpsed other possibilities, even if only from a distance. She was right too, in my heart I could not find it in myself to fault her, the world was limitless and so why impose limits ourselves? She was right, but wrong too, and as I ran to her chalet I was seized by a terrible fear that she had made some irrevocable decision and that I was too late.

The chalet was noisy, the sound of laughter and the squeals of the girls filling the air. It was a happy sound, and I knew that I still had time. Monique's room was quiet, I listened at the door, trying to block out the other sounds around me.

'Who is it?' I heard her ask after knocking softly on the door.

I went in unannounced. For a moment our eyes met and then she leapt across the room into my arms. We kissed a hundred times, her hands on my face while I held her by the waist.

'How are you feeling now? Still dreaming of the world out there?' I asked, making my concern quite clear.

'I'm always dreaming of the world out there,' she laughed gaily. 'That doesn't mean I'm unhappy.'

'It makes you unhappy sometimes though, doesn't it?'

'Let's not talk about this,' Monique said quietly, moving out of my arms. It made her unhappy even to speak about it and her eyes took on a darkness that contained all her hopes and desires.

'Remember you talked about being on stage?'

'Oh, that . . .' she said without enthusiasm. She sat on the edge of her bed, her glasses perched on the end of her petite little nose, her tight curls bursting untidily from her head.

'While I was in London I met Guy Chappel . . .'

'The film director?' she asked, looking up as if a ray of sunshine had pierced the night.

'Yes, the film director,' I smiled, surprised at how relaxed I was. 'A very nice man, very smart too. He's going to be working on a new film this summer, on the island of Saint Marie.'

'Where Charlotte comes from . . .' Monique said to herself, staring open-mouthed and obviously about to make a guess at what was coming next.

'Yes. You know his views on improvisation and on the employment of natural actors and actresses. Well, this summer, you, Charlotte and I will be flying to the Caribbean to star in the film. How do you like that?' I asked triumphantly.

For the second time in a matter of a few minutes Monique leapt across the room and into my arms. Her joy was expressed as an endless kiss, her scorching lips sucking at my open mouth.

'You're happy then?' I laughed, pulling her away from me.

298

'You clever thing!' she giggled. 'Now we can work all winter and then spend the summer being film stars. It's perfect, too perfect for words. Let me kiss you again.'

'Slow down, slow down. We've got all winter to make plans. I just wanted to tell you now. I couldn't stand to see you so unhappy, it made me unhappy too.'

'I'm sorry,' she said sheepishly. 'I could see you becoming unhappy too, but I couldn't stop myself. You were the only one I could talk to, the only one who could understand. You're special, Melissa, very special, do you realise that?'

'Don't be silly,' I said, finding the idea of my being special quite strange. How could silly old Melissa, the stupid girl caught in a compromising position by an old hag, the silly girl who unwittingly smuggled things into Switzerland, how could she be special? It was laughable but Monique believed it all the same and it made me happy that she did.

'You are,' Monique said softly. She was gazing into my eyes, looking at me in the same adoring way that Charlotte did.

'I'd better go now,' I said softly, knowing that if I stayed a moment longer I was going to end up in bed with Monique, our bodies locked together in an orgy of wild sex.

'Come back tomorrow, please,' Monique whispered, kissing my fingers as I pulled away from her. I nodded, breathed deeply and turned to leave. A pulse was beating in my sex, hot, wet, throbbing lustfully.

As I made my way back to the main building my step

was lighter, more confident. Monique's words were still echoing inside my head. I had changed, the old Melissa was gone, and with her had gone the old fears and neuroses. I strode into the house feeling ten feet tall and ready to take on the whole world. Now that Monique's problem had been resolved there was only one more thing I needed to attend to.

'You look positively radiant,' were Amelia's first words to me when I strode into her office and it was an exact description of how I felt.

'Thank you, auntie,' I smiled, walking across to take the glass of chilled white wine that she had poured for me.

'I had a very nice phone call from Monsieur Dupuy this afternoon,' she remarked casually.

My heart skipped a beat at the very sound of his name. 'Oh, Philippe?' I asked, trying to sound casual. Amelia pursed her lips into a sly smile, as always it was impossible to keep anything from her.

'He wanted to say how very much he and his wife appreciated your visit, and that I should be congratulated for having the foresight to employ such an able and attractive young woman.'

I blushed like a silly adolescent. 'That was very nice of him to say that,' I stammered.

'I have no doubt that you made an excellent impression,' she smiled, quizzing me with her blue-grey eyes.

'Did Josephine ring?' I asked, avoiding her eyes and skipping to an altogether easier topic.

'Yes, she did,' Amelia said dismissively. 'She was quite nasty, though not as abusive as her daughter.'

'To be honest, I felt sorry for the mother,' I admitted, walking across the room to the window. The moon was shining luminously in the sky over the jagged mountain landscape.

'You did very well there,' Amelia said, joining me by the window. 'She sounded so suitable. When she first approached me I was all set to take Fiona. There was never an inkling that she'd turn out so badly.'

'Why didn't you take her?' I asked, turning to face her.

'Because Josephine made her daughter sound too perfect and perfection always makes me suspicious.'

'Well, at least that's over with. Now,' I smiled, 'I've got some other news, something much better.'

'And what might that be?'

'I'm going to be making a film in the summer,' I told her, laughing gaily, hardly able to believe it myself.

'A film?' she repeated. 'Where? With whom?'

'In Saint Marie, with Guy Chappel. He wants me, Charlotte and Monique to be in his next production.'

'That's lovely, darling,' she smiled, but her eyes gave her away, her smile was forced and suddenly she seemed cold and distant.

'Auntie, what is it?' I asked, putting my drink down and going over to her.

'Nothing, nothing,' she said, avoiding my eyes, 'I'm just being silly.'

'What is it? I wanted you to be happy for me,' I said

softly, my hands on her shoulders. 'Please tell me what's wrong.'

'I'm just being silly,' she repeated, managing a faint smile. 'It suddenly occurred to me that if you enjoy making the film, you'd never want to come back here.'

'What ever gave you that idea?' I said.

'I told you it was silly.' She was blushing. 'But it hit me so suddenly, the awful idea that I could lose you. I don't want that to happen . . .'

'Come here,' I said softly, pulling Amelia close. 'It'll just be for the summer, then I'll be back here, where I belong.'

We cuddled up, hugging each other tightly. I felt myself enveloped in her scent, my body attracted to her warmth. Everything had been resolved, there was only one thing left and I had to face it there and then. Amelia's cheek was pressed against my own, I turned slightly and pressed my lips against hers. We kissed suddenly, powerfully, the same spark of passion igniting both our bodies.

'I'm so happy that you feel that way,' Amelia said breathlessly, pulling her mouth from mine. 'I want you to think of this as home, you belong here, and you make a difference. A big difference.'

I kissed her again, pressing myself forward, my body tingling all over with excitement. My aunt was responding, I could feel her heart pounding, see the desire dilating in her eyes. We kissed again, my hands moving down her back, sliding down towards her lovely round backside.

Suddenly she was pushing me, pulling her lips from mine.

'Let's get something to eat . . .' she whispered, turning from my eyes and stepping away from my arms.

'Why, auntie? Why won't you make love with me?' I asked bluntly, pained by her rejection, a lump forming in my throat and tears filling my eyes. Why did it always have to end this way? I wanted to love her, and I knew that she felt the same incestuous desires that I did, so why stop?

'We can't . . . Not now . . .' she said weakly.

'No!' I cried tearfully. 'Make love with me! Fuck me, auntie, the way you did that first time.'

'That was so long ago . . . It can't be the same, not after all these years. It's been a lovely memory, I've thought of it often, too often perhaps . . . Why spoil it now?'

'It won't be spoilt, it can't be,' I pleaded. 'It was beautiful then, and it'll be beautiful now. Let's make love, not for memory's sake but for now.'

I took Amelia by the hand and walked her to the door, it was a now-or-never situation and I was determined it was going to be now. I had to literally drag her out of the room. She was struck dumb by my determination.

'Your room or mine?' I demanded at the foot of the stairs. Rudi caught sight of us but he must have guessed that something odd was going on because he turned away. I didn't care if he saw us or not but evidently Amelia was sensitive to the impression she gave.

'My room,' she relented, taking her hand back and

straightening her skirt primly.

I went first, tense and nervous when I really wanted to be joyful and relaxed. Amelia was behind me, silent and brooding, her very silence serving to unnerve me further.

'Perhaps you're right,' I said, going into her room first, 'maybe this isn't such a good idea.'

I tried to turn but found myself in her arms. 'Don't be so hasty,' she said, kissing me suddenly. I sank into her arms, let her draw her breath from my mouth. My body was aflame, her touch was electric on my skin, on my lips, in my mouth. She released me, but I clung to her, my arms around her shoulders. I kissed her this time, and she responded again, holding me tighter still. It was a game and we lost track of time. All we did was stand in the centre of the room and swap kisses like a couple of lovesick teenagers.

'I love you,' Amelia whispered hotly, 'and I want to make love to you.'

'You don't know how happy that makes me,' I sighed, taking her hands and putting them on my breasts. My heart was pounding with excitement and I was sure she could feel it too.

I slipped out of my clothes quickly and let them fall to the floor in an untidy bundle so that I was naked apart from a pair of black stockings. Amelia's eyes were all over me and I had the strange feeling that she was looking at me as if for the first time. She pulled me close and kissed me on the neck and throat, sliding her hands down my smooth flawless back.

I sat on the bed and watched her undress herself, keen

to see her lovely nipples, to gaze in adoration at her long bare thighs and the pinkness of her sex. She joined me on the bed and we were in each other's arms, ravishing each other with fingers and lips. I felt a whirlwind of sensations, all of them pleasurable. My nipples were being eagerly mouthed, my pussy gently stroked, my thighs parted. I, in turn, was massaging my aunt's lovely breasts, playing with her nipples so that they stood proud and hard under my fingers.

Amelia pushed me back. I lay down and spread my legs so that she was between them. 'Suck me, darling,' I begged her, pressing a finger into the wet heat of my sex. I stroked myself, then showed her my fingers, glistening with my juices. She knelt down and began to lick and suck, pressing her tongue deep into me then lapping it up to the very tip, playfully rubbing my throbbing clitty so that I cried out with pleasure. She sucked hard and I could feel myself flooding her tongue with waves of pussy juice. I climaxed quickly, marvelling at her skill in sucking pussy.

I had come but now I was eager to taste her sex too. 'Ask nicely,' she teased, pinching my nipples playfully.

'Let me suck you too, please auntie,' I begged, aroused by the very act of having to beg. She straddled me, a knee on either side of my head and my eyes stared directly at the slightly parted brown lips of her cunt. I pressed my mouth to her pussy and forced my tongue into her without playing games, I was greedy for her come, hungry for the sweet nectar of her sex.

She fell forward and began to suck me again, mirroring

every lap of my tongue. I played with her bud and she did the same to me. I pressed the walls of her sex and so did she. In the hothouse of pleasure it all became the same thing, her tongue was my tongue, her pussy was my pussy. I peaked, arched my back and tensed my body. My pussy was wet with nectar that I seemed to be sucking from Amelia.

We rolled over, our faces wet and sticky, our bodies bathed in sweat and sex cream. I was breathing hard, my body still tingling with the aftershocks of orgasm. It was as intense and exciting as I had hoped it would be. The pleasure was pure and sensual, and in giving myself to my aunt I felt an added thrill of wickedness.

'Tired so soon?' Amelia laughed, her hand snaking down between my thighs.

'I told you there'd be nothing to worry about,' I said, kissing her on the shoulder. 'Isn't this lovely?'

'Absolutely divine,' she agreed, kissing me on the lips, her mouth still scented with my sex.

I pulled her closer, rolled her over so that she was flat on her tummy. I sat on her back, pressing my pussy against the firm flesh of her backside. 'There's so much for us to learn about each other,' I enthused, leaning forward so that my nipples brushed the soft flesh of her back. I crossed my hands under her chest and squeezed her nipples, forcing the sensitive little buds together. My sex was wet and sticky, brushing hard against her backside, a thrill of pleasure pulsing through me. It felt good so I pressed harder, really rubbing my slit against her rear.

She began to push herself up against me, lifting her

round arse cheeks so that I was rubbing myself right against her bottom. Each time I stroked forward I felt a thrill of pleasure. My pussy lips were parted and wet, my cunt bud pressed tight against her skin which was slippery with sex juices. I moved faster and faster, moaning softly, as the pleasure grew in intensity. I shuddered as the climax came powerfully, making my arms buckle so that I fell forward onto Amelia's back.

It took a moment before I was aware that Amelia was no longer beside me. Lazily I looked round, expecting to see her at my side, her languid figure stretched out, her firm breasts jutting out. 'Amelia?' I called, turning round.

'Just a second,' she replied from the bathroom.

'Okay.' I turned onto my belly, my body still suffused with that odd emotion we call happiness. Everything had been resolved, now there was nothing at all for me to worry about. I had summer to look forward to and I was sure that the distant sunshine was going to light even the darkest Alpine night. Monique was happy, too, and Charlotte was to be at my side far longer than she had ever dreamed of. For the first time in my life I felt content, things were going perfectly and it was down to me and not to chance.

Vaguely I heard Amelia padding back from the bathroom but I was too lost in my thoughts to pay much attention. I knew that she was going to cuddle up close to me, that her arms were going to hold me lovingly, that our bodies would be joined once more in making love. Her shadow fell over me, I felt her straddle me, and I remember thinking that she was going to make herself come by rubbing herself against my rear. I lifted my buttocks and readied myself, waited to feel the heat of her sex wetting my skin. Instead I felt her parting my bottom cheeks.

'Tongue me,' I murmured lazily, closing my eyes dreamily. I sighed, her hot breath touched my rear hole and then her wet tongue traced the tight circle of my anal hole. I lifted myself and her tongue pierced my behind, slipping into my hole which closed around her tongue. It felt good and I sighed loudly, the pleasure in my bottom connecting with the burning heat of my sex. Amelia tongued me deeper, working her tongue in and out of my arsehole, wetting me, flicking indescribable sensations through my body.

'Don't stop,' I complained when she withdrew her mouth from between my rear cheeks.

'I'm not stopping, darling,' Amelia sighed.

I tensed suddenly. Something cold and hard had brushed against my thigh. I had hardly time to look round when I felt my arse cheeks being forced apart. I cried out, more from the shock than anything else. Amelia was astride me, forcing something into the opening that she had just lubricated with her tongue. It entered hard and deep, filling my virginal rear hole completely.

'What are you doing?' I managed to say, my voice barely a whisper, too afraid to move.

'I'm fucking you in your behind, darling,' Amelia whispered, her voice strained too. 'Relax, Melissa darling, just relax and enjoy it.'

I twisted round and saw that she was wearing some

kind of leather harness. A shiny black phallus was jutting from her sex into my rear. I turned back and pressed my face to the bed, aroused beyond measure by the feel of the thing inside me and by the idea that my aunt was going to arse-fuck me.

Amelia began to move back and forth slowly, drawing the phallus out a little then pressing it back into me. Each stroke seemed to go deeper and the deeper she moved the greater was the pleasure. I relaxed, let the pleasure take over, and soon she was moving rhythmically, going faster and faster. My sighs were real, involuntary, an audible signal of the pleasure of being penetrated so expertly in the arse.

'Fuck me . . . fuck me . . .' I moaned deliriously, lifting my rear up to meet the downward thrust of the phallus. Amelia was fucking me, making me move with her rhythm, to her pleasure. My sex was awash with honey, and I began to frig my clit, keeping to the same stroke as Amelia. The pleasure was too much. I felt myself on the edge and then I plunged down and down. My body exploded. I felt the fires of orgasm once, twice, many times. I was mindless, pure sensation, pleasure in my sex, in my arsehole, on the tips of my nipples. I *was* pleasure and, in a single lucid moment, I wished that it would never ever end.

More Erotic Fiction from Headline Delta

Cremorne Gardens

Anonymous

An erotic romp from the libidinous age of the Victorians

UPSTAIRS, DOWNSTAIRS . . .
IN MY LADY'S CHAMBER

Cast into confusion by the wholesale defection of their domestic staff, the nubile daughters of Sir Paul Arkley are forced to throw themselves on the mercy of the handsome young gardener Bob Goggin. And Bob, in turn, is only too happy to throw himself on the luscious and oh-so-grateful form of the delicious Penny.

Meanwhile, in the Mayfair mansion of Count Gewirtz of Galicia, the former Arkley employees prepare a feast intended to further the Count's erotic education of the voluptuous singer Važelina Volpe – and destined to degenerate into the kind of wild and secret orgy for which the denizens of Cremorne Gardens are justly famous . . .

Here are forbidden extracts drawn from the notorious chronicles of the Cremorne – a society of hedonists and debauchees, united in their common aim to glorify the pleasures of the flesh!

FICTION / EROTICA 0 7472 3433 7

EMPIRE OF LUST

VAMPIRE LUST IN THE CORRIDORS OF POWER!

Valentina Cilescu

Elected to lust!

The malevolent sex vampire, the Master, and his insatiable entourage are extending the boundaries of his hideous but seductive power. While the spirit of journalist Andreas Hunt lies imprisoned in a crystal tomb, his body is inhabited by the Master and used as a tool to forge a seemingly respectable career as a Member of Parliament.

White witch Mara Fleming must also bend to the Master's evil plan. Trapped in the curvaceous frame of flame-haired acolyte Anastasia Dubois, Mara is forced to play the part of a vampire sex-slut. Meanwhile the Master's Queen, the evil dominatrix Sedet, inhabits Mara's luscious body, subjecting it to a series of intoxicating depravities.

As his creatures subvert politicians and media moguls, the Master plans his final assault on government. Is there no power on earth that can prevent him bringing the British Establishment crashing to the ground like a house of cards?

FICTION / EROTICA 0 7472 4191 0

Lust and Lady Saxon

LESLEY ASQUITH

Pretty Diana Saxon is devoted to her student husband, Harry, and she'd do anything to make their impoverished life in Oxford a little easier. Her sumptuously curved figure and shameless nature make her an ideal nude model for the local camera club – where she soon learns there's more than one way to make a bit on the side . . .

Elegant Lady Saxon is the most sought-after diplomat's wife in Rome and Bangkok. Success has followed Harry since his student days – not least because of the very special support lent by his wife. And now the glamorous Diana is a prized guest at the wealthiest tables – and in the most bedrooms afterwards . . .

From poverty to nobility, sex siren Diana Saxon never fails to make the most of her abundant talent for sensual pleasure!

FICTION / EROTICA 0 7472 4762 5

Confessions

Maria Caprio

Tales of seduction

Zena and Jean-Paul are a
sophisticated couple and they have a
sophisticated way of keeping the fire
of passion burning in their marriage.
They play a game called Confessions.
They tell each other true tales of
seduction from their past – and also,
if all goes to plan, from their future.

They agree to part for ten days. To
roam Europe separately in search of
sexual adventures, the more exotic,
the more bizarre the better. To
gather confessions. And then to meet
up to share the fruits of their
experiences. To confess . . .

FICTION / EROTICA 0 7472 4687 4

Now you can buy any of these other
Delta books from your bookshop or
direct from the publisher.

FREE P&P AND UK DELIVERY
(Overseas and Ireland £3.50 per book)

Passion Beach	Carol Anderson	£5.99
Cremorne Gardens	Anonymous	£5.99
Amorous Appetites	Anonymous	£5.99
Saucy Habits	Anonymous	£5.99
Room Service	Felice Ash	£5.99
The Wife-Watcher Letters	Lesley Asquith	£5.99
The Delta Sex-Life Letters	Lesley Asquith	£5.99
More Sex-Life Letters	Lesley Asquith	£5.99
Sin and Mrs Saxon	Lesley Asquith	£5.99
Naked Ambition	Becky Bell	£5.99
Empire of Lust	Valentina Cilescu	£5.99
Playing the Field	Elizabeth Coldwell	£5.99
Dangerous Desires	JJ Duke	£5.99
The Depravities of Marisa Bond	Kitt Gerrard	£5.99

TO ORDER SIMPLY CALL THIS NUMBER

01235 400 414

or e-mail <u>orders@bookpoint.co.uk</u>

Prices and availability subject to change without notice.